W/D

E

1E

T

THUNDER BAY

*The latest thrilling title
in the bestselling Mariners series*

English couple Richard and Robin Mariner are soon to launch the revolutionary
SuperCats, their fast ferry service from
Thunder Bay across the Great Lakes of
Canada. But when the naked body of a
young woman is discovered on the lake,
the ensuing murder investigation takes
precedence over their test-runs.

THUNDER BAY

Peter Tonkin

Severn House Large Print
London & New York

This first large print edition published in Great Britain 2001 by
SEVERN HOUSE LARGE PRINT BOOKS LTD of
9-15, High Street, Sutton, Surrey, SM1 1DF.
First world regular print edition published 2001 by
Severn House Publishers, London and New York.
This first large print edition published in the USA 2001 by
SEVERN HOUSE PUBLISHERS INC., of
595 Madison Avenue, New York, NY 10022

British Library Cataloguing in Publication Data

Tonkin, Peter, 1950 –
    Thunder Bay. - Large print ed. - (Mariners series)
    1. Mariner, Richard (Fictitious character) - Fiction
    2. Great Lakes - Fiction
    3. Suspense fiction
    4. Large type books
    I. Title
    823.9'14 [F]

    ISBN 0-7278-7111-0

Printed and bound in Great Britain by
MPG Books Ltd, Bodmin, Cornwall.

For Cham, Guy and Mark

One

The man ceremonially named Thunder Voice at an ancient Native American encampment on the lake shore at dawn that morning glanced away left across the big-sea water and frowned. He dug his paddle deeper into the restless heave of an incoming wave, knowing that those behind him in the canoe would see and copy his action. At the silent command of the man they had adopted into the Ojibwa tribe of the Native American Nations at the moment of sunrise over the eastern waters, the other braves lining the sides of the huge thirty-six-foot ocean going canoe began to work their lean, tanned bodies. Paddling as one, two dozen of them sent their massive birch-bark vessel skimming through the out-wash where the great waters they knew as *Gichee Gumee* hurled themselves increasingly powerfully against the blue-grey feet of Thunder Cape, beneath the rock formation so aptly called the Sleeping Giant.

Away south-west across the restless water, tall storm clouds were frothing upwards with threatening speed, casting a slate-grey shadow on the great lake's surface below. Already Thunder Voice's sea-wise eyes could distinguish the chalk-white line scraping roughly over the dark slate, signifying a squall. And the squall was rushing rapidly this way, seeking to crush the majestic sea canoe against the timeless cliff. The tall, lean, whip-thewed, newly adopted Native American stirred, easing the aching joint of his left knee in its pad of sphagnum moss. Then, seemingly impossibly, he redoubled his efforts, feeling the head-wind of their swift passage falter and flutter round onto the sensitive skin of his left shoulder and cheek. The eleven others kneeling behind him along the port gunwale of the vessel answered his call and the aspen and birch-branch frame groaned under the relentless power of their paddling.

Amidships, on a rough deck bound to the twisting frame with ropes of deerskin, there lay piled a sizeable hillock of furs – mainly beaver pelts. Like the lattice decking, these were secured in place by deer-hide ropes. They formed the bulk of the great vessel's cargo – for most of the men aboard, the most valuable part. They represented one full season's trapping up in the great forests. Down in the trade area of Grand Portage, furs like these could be expected to fetch enough goods to keep the largely self-sufficient Ojibwa people content until next fall. A few muskets, perhaps; and a good supply of powder and shot. But they would only do so if the canoe rounded the head of the Sleeping Giant at Thunder Cape into the safety of Thunder Bay before the squall rushed upon them like the wrath of their great manitou Missipeshu, god of the winds and the waves, and destroyed them all.

A stronger side-wind, out-runner of the squall, combed through the black beaver pelts, whitening their soft fur in tiny ripples. These little reflections of the huge waves rushing shorewards carried on across the bowed head of that part of the cargo that the brave Thunder Voice thought more valuable than all the pelts in the whole North Woods. Golden ringlets danced beneath their cool caress until the head they adorned was shaken with thoughtless irritation. The woman sitting aft of the soft cargo was forbidden to take an oar, but she was still far too busy to stare around her at the timeless scene. It was enough for her that Thunder Voice had seen the danger and was leading the wild dash for safety.

The big vessel slid silently through the thunderous surf, dangerously close to the grey-blue cliffs, and its white-bark length surged forwards like a living thing, as powerful as the great silver-sided sturgeon native to the bays she was running so rapidly towards. Only the faith of the crew in the wisdom of Thunder Voice allowed them to work with him, following his powerful dictates. Along the furrows between the gathering waves the vessel sped, seemingly saved from disaster only by the unerring ability of the tall lead paddler to read and react to the water. As each wave tumbled inwards, so he pulled the tall curve of the bow upward against the downhill slope and suck towards the shoreward side. As each watery cliff shattered on the flank of its blue basalt cousin, billowing back in clouds of sparkling, icy spray, he allowed the backwash to slide them easily out into the lake, into position to meet the next in the gathering series.

Thunder Voice read more than the water. The next breath of wind arrived, big brother to the zephyr that had stirred the beaver fur. It slapped his weather-wise cheek like an enemy declaring war. His lean nostrils flared and the long, lean hatchet of his face glanced downwind once again, narrow-eyed. The white wall of the squall was rushing down on them like an avalanche in the high country south or west. He glanced right, past the labouring profile of his co-leader, whose job it was to watch for hazards as Thunder Voice watched the weather. There, blessedly, he saw the very point of the cape beginning to fall back like a tall grey tomahawk blade chopping eastwards past them, revealing a distant heave of darkly wooded shore, as black in places as the pelts of the beavers themselves, across the gape of the Bay.

Almost tearing his arms from their sockets, Thunder Voice pulled the head of the big canoe hard right. As though reading his mind, his opposite number back-paddled for an instant, whirling the canoe through ninety degrees of heading within its own protesting length. Immediately above the labouring braves, like the storm taken living form, a dozen huge herons thundered screaming out of the misty whiteness and battered across the heaving water towards their nests on the stunted shoreline trees. The noise of the herons' wings was lost in the advancing howl of the squall, rushing up behind them now. There was no time to rest – or even to hesitate. By main force, Thunder Voice and the men behind him hurled the canoe right round ninety degrees more – while the inland team did not slacken pace at all this time. The thick wet wind swept in over them, as low as the herons had been – and a thousand times louder. The wash of the storm waves behind the squall wind destroying themselves at the feet of the Sleeping Giant lifted the canoe's high, silver stern and the laden vessel surfed in towards the safety of the first cobble-floored beach in the wide maw of Thunder Bay itself.

Only now did the relentless power of the paddlers' efforts ease and the upwelling of simple timeless joy begin, for they had taken on the fury of the greatest inland water on the surface of the earth, and had beaten it, hand to hand. The tall brave on the right-hand side of the prow reached across to slap Thunder Voice on the shoulder in a gesture of awed and thankful camaraderie, far beyond mere words.

But then the blonde woman midships spoke, looking up from what she was doing and revealing at once a laptop computer on her knees and a pair of tiny headphones beneath the tumble of her wind-tossed ringlets. "Hey, Hiawatha," she called to her weary husband in the prow, "chuck back the Global Positioning handset, will you? The pilot in our guide chopper saw something in the water just before he cut and ran with those herons when the squall hit. He says it looks like there's a body dead ahead. All the other shipping nearby seems to have run for shelter. Should we go take a look?"

12

Two

Richard Mariner sat back in the prow of the pitching canoe, silent for just the blink of an eye it took him to jump back out of the character of Thunder Voice, the Iroquois warrior.

"That's not my decision, Robin," he said, sounding very English, for all he looked lean and dark and tanned enough to be an Iroquois for real – except that his eyes burned a breathtaking, Anglo-Saxon blue. "This isn't my vessel. Ben? What do you say?"

Richard turned to Ben Black Bear, the only full-blooded Indian aboard, an Ojibwa, curator of the little Native American museum on the outskirts of the bustling Thunder Bay international port and trading city.

"Hell, Richard, I don't know. This canoe and these furs represent almost all the collateral the museum owns." He looked out across the cauldron of the squall-shrouded bay. White water foamed inwards off Superior as though the whole great icy lake was boiling fiercely in great, gasping heaves.

"But there might be someone drowning out there!" said Robin, her urgent tones every bit as cut-glass English as her husband's.

"*Just* out there," emphasised Richard.

"Yeah, well, I'm game," said Ben. "What about you guys?"

The rest of the local historical society nodded to a man. They spent a good deal of spare time recreating the adventures of the original inhabitants of the place – and the *Voyageurs* with whom they came, in time, to trade. A real adventure was an unlooked-for treat for most of them. They would have set off there and then, but Richard was an old, old hand at waterborne rescue and he knew that things would get worse before they got better. Five minutes' forethought and preparation now would save an incalculable amount of grief later on.

"We've done the *absolutely authentic* bit for today," he decided. "Robin, darling, break out the wetsuits and the life preservers, please. And everyone, once you have your top and your life jacket on I want you to check your safety lines and your paddle retainers. You'll be no use to us frozen, overboard or using your hands as paddles!"

The equipment Richard was talking about was all stowed in the bilge beneath the fur-laden lattice deck. In less than five minutes they were all incongruously well prepared. If

14

they looked out of place in their birch-bark vessel, the canoe itself was perfectly adapted for the job in hand. And this was a fact they would be grateful for, also, in time.

As one man they were in action, following Richard's lead, slowed only by the thickness of the black neoprene and the life preservers round their necks. And by the stiffness of fatigued shoulders, though none of them would admit it. The moment they swung away from the shore, the rain arrived. Combined with the spray, it deluged them all in an instant like the coldest of showers so that all of them were immediately grateful to Richard for getting them half-dressed at least. Vision shrank to little more than the spheres of their heads at first, but soon even the least experienced of them realised that the raw wind was tearing the whiteness to tatters with sufficient force and regularity for Richard at least to see where they were heading.

In the last steady instants before the heaving maelstrom took hold of them, Robin scrambled up and wedged herself in the bow where the upward curve of the forepeak offered a little support and protection. It was too much to expect that the laptop would function – or even survive – in these extremes, but she had the GPS handset and a clear idea of where the chopper pilot had reported the figure to be floating. "Richard," she bellowed in a voice only a little softer than the huge forepeak loud hail that had earned him his honorary Indian name that morning, "bear right. She should only be a hundred yards or so."

"She?" Richard's voice carried even over the hurly-burly all around.

"That was the pilot's impression."

"Anything else?"

"No. He was low but in a hurry."

"Fair enough. If she was out in this channel beyond where we turned in, then she'll be washing in to shore pretty quickly."

"Not for a while, though. The back of the bay must be ten miles in from here. We've plenty of time to catch her. And we'll go in just as fast with this lot on our left quarter."

Another hill of freezing foam heaved in, given height by the upward shelving of the shallow bay floor – but thankfully not enough height to gain a crest. The canoe slid up the leading face, almost as firmly at home as if in a dead calm. The weight of the beaver furs midships steadied her, as did the water collecting in the bilge.

"Even so, we'll be lucky to find her in this."

"We've been lucky so far today. Come right a little more..."

It was certainly luck that took them to the floating woman. What sort of luck, Richard

16

was never able to work out. On the whole, he soon became convinced, it was very bad luck indeed.

They found her just at that moment when Richard became convinced that the water in the bilge was no longer steadying them. It was swamping them. The waves hurling in from Superior were no longer slipping under the canoe's lively keel and vanishing shorewards to thunder into surf beneath the tall grain-stores among the massive ships that filled and emptied them. They were beginning to crest and break in over the gunwales and the weary paddlers along them. The protection of the wetsuits was becoming ineffective against the unrelenting chill of the icy water. Even Richard's almost limitless stamina was running low and thoughts of giving up were beginning to loom. Then, for the most fleeting of instants, in a tattered rift of clarity torn between sheets of driving water, a wave crest heaved into view dead ahead and there, beckoning from the white-foaming cap of it, there waved an arm.

Ben saw it too and the two men were galvanised by the shock. In that one electrifying instant, all thoughts of failure were banished and the wallowing bulk of the canoe was torn forward again by main force and the sheer effort of indomitable will.

17

"Coming alongside her!" bellowed Richard, tearing his throat. "We'll come down on her from upwind and up-water, though we've nothing much of a lee!"

Robin squirmed over and joined Ben at the lee-side pick-up point. It was lucky she did, for Ben was not well practised in waterborne rescue and was fooled alike by the speed with which things happened, by the intractability of the floating woman, by her leaden dead weight – and, most disturbingly of all, by the simple horror she presented.

It was obvious to Robin from the outset that the woman they were trying to rescue was dead. The beckoning wave from the tumble of surf had simply been the body rolling over, stiff-armed onto its front. As Richard brought the canoe down the front of the next wave, across the weather, Robin's eyes fastened on the mottled blue-white of the woman's back. She floated, like a birch log, stiff and white and still in the foaming, freezing crystal of the water. Inconsequentially, Robin was struck by the glass-pure clarity of the deep-lake water as it swung the pallid nakedness of the body up against the side of the canoe with a dead thump. Long black hair swept over slim white shoulders and reaching arm-tops, then away into an eddy like skeins of silky ink. Once the hair was gone, the slim, swollen corpse was utterly stark. Robin reached down, aware that Ben was doing the same at her left side. On her right, one of Ben's inshore team was reaching outwards a couple of paddles further back, but he hesitated, finding himself with a too-intimate choice of handhold – either mottled buttock or marbled thigh-top. Robin had seen some corpses in her time, but none like this. None preserved in icy water, dead white and near-frozen. The mottling of the skin from shoulder to heel gave her the immediate impression that the girl must have been brutalised and beaten to death before she was dumped into the water.

With these thoughts and impressions tumbling almost instantaneously into her mind, Robin reached down. Her hands plunged into water so cold it seemed that only its wild motion kept it liquid. At once, every joint from elbow to knuckle seemed to swell and ache – and the rest of her twinged in sympathy. A wave of numbness reached magically up from the lake and just at its very extremity she felt her fingertips brush a solid slickness, like the flank of a frozen eel. She grabbed again and held hard.

That instant she was hurled sideways against the canoe's sharp gunwale by an incredible force. As though the very spirit of Lake Superior, living just below the surface like the Greek God Poseidon, wished to keep the dead girl to itself, the power unleashed by Robin's simple attempt to hold her was awesome. The dead girl herself seemed to spring into a wild, fighting life and for an instant Robin wondered whether she had in fact awoken. She realised that her eyes were tight closed and was just about to open them when she felt Ben throw himself outward at her side and a little of the weight came off her shoulders for an instant. But the easing somehow let her knees lose purchase a little, so that when Ben shouted with horrified surprise and let go again, only the sure anchor of her safety line stopped her going over the side herself – for the moment, at least.

The eel-like arm was slipping inexorably out of Robin's grasp – especially as the new priority of staying aboard had entered the equation. She opened her eyes and looked steadfastly at the curled fingers that seemed to be trying to grasp the gunwale mere inches above the rushing spindrift of the water. They were so pale that Robin wondered if the girl was in fact wearing some clothing after all – a pair of white gloves. But them she saw the fingernails, like little pools of ice at the finger-ends. Square cut, short and practical – unnervingly identical to her own. The ready surge of sympathetic identification made her look up at last into the face of the woman whose hand she held.

There were no eyes. Pink pits with bone-white rims stared blindly back at her, terrifyingly huge and expressionless. The nose also was gone, leaving a dark-floored shadow seeming to reach into the deepest recesses of the woman's ravaged head. Water washed out of the three gaping hollows – colder than tears; thinner than blood. The lips were gone too, the flesh eaten away to reveal pale gums and neat white teeth. From between the pale rows of incisors the tail of a little fish protruded, wiggling wildly, re-placing in the horror of the face the tongue it was so clearly eating.

Had Richard not appeared then, Robin would have lost the girl and gone overboard herself. And, in all likelihood, her departure would have tipped the rest of them into the stormy water too. But the sound of Ben's reaction – and his startled movement away from his station – called the canoe's acting chief to the side of his intrepid wife. And not a moment too soon – for his strength and rock-like steadiness were all that kept things together and afloat.

"Hold tight!" he ordered, grasping the belt of her safety line and pulling her back firmly while putting his own weight onto the upwind side of the tilting vessel. Robin obeyed his request as well as she could, feeling the lively vessel settling more surely beneath her while the way in which the next wave slid out from under it lifted the woman's body into a more controllable position.

"Ben!" shouted Richard, and that one word seemed to hold sufficient strength, explanation and direction to motivate the man it named. Ben came back to Robin's side and together they slid the white length of the dead girl over the heaving gunwale between them and onto the cold dark bed of beaver furs. The added weight of the corpse seemed to pull the whole vessel down, as though she was supernaturally heavy. Both men turned at once to the business to getting the canoe herself back to safety now that her desperate mission was complete.

Robin herself pulled the beaver pelts free and covered the woman with simple respect and reverence, preserving her modesty and the last pale shreds of her dignity. And hiding from their sickened gaze the horror her face had become. So it was Robin, and Robin alone at that time, who got the first strong indication of exactly how the woman had been killed.

There, on the left side of her chest, precisely over her heart and encroaching onto the flaccid half-moon of her breast, there were ten neat wounds. They were bloodless now and weeping nothing thicker or warmer than water. Short of a post-mortem examination there was no way to be sure of their depth or of the damage they had done. But there was no doubt in Robin's mind as soon as she saw them that, no matter what else had been done to her, this was how the poor girl had been murdered. For someone had driven the broad blade of a big knife repeatedly into her. Driven it into her ten times, to be exact – and he had been exact. Forming with perfectly medical precision a wound the size of Robin's palm, from which the skin had been stripped away. A wound in the shape of a five-pointed blood-red star.

Three

The drab, rain-swept modernity of the dock at the north end of Thunder Bay's great harbour seemed to Richard that evening to be about as far as it was possible to get from the timeless beauty of that historic Ojibwa encampment in the misty mauve promise of the dawn. The contrast was almost painful.

On the one hand, the cobbled beach at the back of a hidden, unfrequented bay. There the spruces swept murmurously to the shore, fragrant with the smell of balsam pine, the blue-green shadows beneath them sparkling with the occasional flash of feathered or petalled brightness; long vines of purple beach peas sprawled almost to the water's edge. The cry of a loon echoed over the silken infinity of the barely stirring waters. The ageless pinnacle of rock at the little bay's heart was where Ben had written *Thunder Voice* in Ojibwa pictogram as Richard became a tribal warrior just at the golden moment of dawn.

On the other hand, the rough concrete of the slipway ran with oily drizzle down to the sinister hump of the half-beached canoe. Here the foggy gloom of evening rang with the moaning of the fog warning giving all that wilderness of brick, metal and prefab a voice, as the bad-egg stench from the pulp mills gave the clinging mist its own perfume. Even the light, a dull security beam, seemed weary and faintly rotten. It was exactly the colour of a bad egg's yolk.

Somewhere out above and away from all this drizzling gloom, the sun was settling magnificently westward, lighting the watery pathways of the Iroquois and the *Voyageurs*. Not here, thought Richard. This was what mankind had made of the world, after all.

"Penny for your thoughts, love," said Robin quietly.

"You wouldn't want to buy them," he answered with a weary stab at an old joke.

Ben came back with the detective then. The local police officer was not in uniform and fitted perfectly with the downbeat, unromantic present rather than with the legendary magnificence of the past. At least he was brisk and efficient. Ten minutes taking preliminary details and he dismissed them all to get warm and dry on the promise that they would give full statements at Headquarters in the morning. The last thing Richard saw, glancing back as he followed Robin off the slipway, was the detective standing in a strange pool of darkness. The darkness was half of shadow and half of scattered beaver pelts, but it made a sinister backdrop to the tall man looming over the starkly uncovered corpse of the dead girl, speaking urgently into a tiny cellphone as he called, no doubt, for back-up.

The water of the shower was near scalding. It could hardly have presented a stronger contrast to the icy drizzle outside. Even so, Robin still needed Richard to massage some life and heat back into the frozen flesh of her shoulders. The shower stall en suite to the master bedroom of the house they were renting on the outskirts of town was big, but the frames of the man and woman wedged in it were on the large side too. Richard's hard flat belly was wedged tightly against

25

the slippery curves of her back and bottom as he worked. He was using soap instead of massage oil and the foam beneath his powerful fingers escaped to run with the thundering water down the valley of her spine into the deeper valley below. The back of the shower stall, beneath the roaring head, was tiled with mirror tiles and as he worked life and warmth into her shoulders and upper back, Richard's eyes strayed lazily to the clouded pink and gold image which the mirrors revealed. Like him, she had retained a youthful slimness and vigour to her body. Neither of them worked out. Their personal trainers were the exigencies of an active, strongly physical professional life combined with the imperious demands of ten-year-old twins. Even when, as now, the children were away at boarding school, Richard and Robin seemed incapable of rest. Fat and idleness had never been a problem to the Mariners – and were never likely to be.

Richard's hands slid forward off the big muscles of Robin's shoulders and lingered for an instant on the delicate ridges of her collarbones before slipping down onto the soapy fullnesses of her breasts. She leaned back sensuously under his caress, then, with a tensing of her buttocks and a flick of her hips she turned, sliding her tummy tightly against his. They slid into a lingering embrace as the hot water pounded down upon them, and then he lifted her out of the shower stall and laid her on the huge, soft bath mat. Drying each other with massive, cloud-soft, toast-warm bath towels became a kind of foreplay. They had turned the central heating up full blast as soon as they came in and so there was very little chill on the still air of their bedroom to hurry their sensual transition from washing to love-making and the huge duvet was soon pushed aside as the temperature of their passion got hotter and hotter on the big old extra-king-sized double bed.

After the last, lovingly satisfied kiss, Richard rolled back and stretched, as he always did at such moments, then he rolled off the bed and padded back into the shower-room for a quick wash. Robin remained, apparently sleepily, lying on the bed. As Richard came back into the bedroom, however, he saw that Robin was not asleep. Her left arm was crooked under the golden tumble of her hair and the nail on her right index finger was tracing a pattern on the curve of her chest and the upswell of her breast. Lingering lines of white, darkening to pink, traced the outline of a five-pointed star a little larger than her palm.

Richard padded to her side and sat, covering her hand with his and bringing its motion to a stop. At once her wide eyes opened, as still and grey as the deepest Superior pool, but warm where the lake was icy.

"You have to stop thinking about her," he said.

"Maybe I will, in time," she answered. "But not until we've done everything we can to help catch the man who did this to her. She must have died a terrible death and I want him to pay."

"Fair enough. You're right. But we have other priorities here too."

"I know we do, darling." She fell silent.

Richard left her then; he slipped on a bathrobe and went to lock up, switch off for the night and perform his final nightly duty. This was always to check on his voice mail and e-mail and consult the Heritage Mariner Web site. He did all of these things on the powerful little laptop, which accompanied him almost everywhere these days. He had providentially not allowed Robin to take this one with them this morning. The dead machine trapped, like the pile of furs, in the canoe that was all the Canadian authorities had by way of a scene of crime, had been lent to her by the hapless Ben. The GPS handset had come from the chopper pilot who had flown them out and then guided them back through the day.

When Richard returned an hour later, up to date and on top of things, every inch the corporate giant at rest, she was still tracing that pattern, her face folded into a frown. He stopped in the doorway and watched her silently. She was a single-minded, fiercely intelligent person. He knew at once that there was something about the condition of the dead girl's body that was nagging at her mind. Something beyond the terrible state of it. A clue, perhaps, to what was going on.

"So, Captain Mariner, tell me what you're doing in Thunder Bay." The detective glanced down at Richard and Robin's passports lying on the desk in front of him. His voice was light, his gaze intelligent and keen. His manner this morning was more courteous. He had met them at the main door of what Richard could not help thinking of as 'the police station', all spruce and chipper in a blue uniform. Richard had noted the badges on his sleeves and shoulders denoting him as a sergeant in 'O' Division. And the name on his ID tag was Sgt S. McKenzie.

Sergeant McKenzie had shown them past the booking desk and welcome facilities – both a-bustle – into the quiet sanctum of his little office, clearly concerned to put the English couple at ease. They had after all performed a service requiring a great deal of bravery. They were not under investigation here. His eyes rested on Richard, though in fact both he and Robin held the rank of captain. They had each commanded every type of vessel in the big Heritage Mariner fleet – except for the new SuperCat passenger catamarans which they ran so successfully across the Channel and which they were hoping to introduce to the Great Lakes too.

"Have you seen the Heritage Mariner SuperCat?" asked Richard as a prelude to his reply.

"That big ultra-modern-looking vessel fitting out and crewing up down in the passenger dock? Yeah. Looks like quite a piece of work."

"It is. It's state of the art; ultra-new. It's been designed to transport several hundred people, vehicles and freight at the better part of one hundred miles an hour. My company, Heritage Mariner, is looking at the feasibility of running a fleet of Super-Cats out of Thunder Bay into ports all around Superior from Duluth to Sault Ste Marie, north shore and south."

"Canada and the States," mused the detective, all too well aware that United States jurisdiction started at the border crossing the great lake only a few miles south of here. "You looking for a back door into the USA?"

"Yes, I am," admitted Richard with no hesitation. "I spent most of last year running around everywhere from Las Vegas, of all places, to Washington trying to get clearance for a SuperCat service running out of several ports in US waters but it was all getting bogged down in red tape. This seemed a better approach. Your people in Ottawa have been quicker with the initial clearance, and the State Department in Washington seem happier with the idea of having the SuperCats running in and out of their seaports if they are actually based outside the US itself. That's the way it looks at the moment, anyway."

"Fine. That all hangs together – and matches the visa stamps in your passports. Next, then, how did you manage to get yourself adopted into the Iroquois nation?"

"That was Ben Black Bear and the boys. They adopted me but I really think it was Robin they were after..."

The bright, enquiring gaze swung to the silent woman. The raised eyebrows were interrogation enough.

"They heard about some work I did with the US Army Corps of Engineers while Richard was in Vegas," she said. "I rafted down the Colorado from the Hoover Dam to the Sea of Cortez in a big inflatable. The US and Mexican authorities had cooperated to restore the flow south of Tucson and we were publicising the fact..."

"So that was you? I heard about that. But

31

if it was you they wanted why adopt your husband here?"

"When it got right down to it, there was no authentic ceremony to adopt a woman into the tribe. Short of conquest, kidnap or rape, I guess."

"It's always been a man's country." The detective laughed, thoughtlessly patronisingly. His amusement seemingly dismissed the whole twentieth century and the women's movement which characterised so much of it.

"I noticed," answered Robin, beginning to fire up.

"But it was well meant," said Richard placatingly. "And it ensures Heritage Mariner will always have a stake in the community. Corporate sponsorship of the museum..."

This time the detective's bark of laughter was at one more genuine and somehow darker; almost a sneer. "I might have known there'd be a financial angle," he said. "Ben Black Bear's always up to some scam or other to raise a few dollars. They're all the same."

The officer did not make it clear whether the generalisation was to do with Ben's profession or his ethnic background but even Robin, still slighted by his dismissal of her entire sex, thought it better to let things lie.

If Heritage Mariner was going to become a part of the burgeoning, bustling business community of Thunder Bay, swallowing a little pride to stay on the right side of the law was a wiser move than alienating people at the outset. And besides, Robin already felt a deep-seated need to help – in however slight a way – to solve this case. From the look of things, this detective sergeant was not going to welcome the thought of involvement of a well-meaning foreign female amateur sleuth in the first place, so giving him a good excuse to dismiss her would be cutting off her nose to spite her face.

But then the clichéd little phrase brought the dead girl's face back into her mind again. A face with no lips. No eyes. No nose.

An icy little silence fell.

"Even so," continued McKenzie, more placatingly, after an instant, "it was a good job. You all did well and we're grateful. Now," he leaned forward, "with the background out of the way, let's get onto the actual discovery of the murdered girl. You are by all accounts the people who can give me the most detail all round on that. And I need all the detail I can get..."

By the time they had given their evidence, the frosty atmosphere had thawed again. They knew that the detective's name was Sam McKenzie. They knew a good deal about his personal life and his professional plans. He knew he was dealing with two steady, intelligent and above all observant witnesses. Any new-world prejudice about patronising Britishers he might have harboured was gone; any hackles unconsciously raised by their accents, which sounded almost pompously upper-class to the Canadian, were soothed by the warm urbanity of their manner. And the thought arose in Sam's civic mind that they were, after all, hoping to bring money and employment to his city as well as doing everything in their power to further his investigation and thereby to enhance his career prospects. That was when he offered them a cup of coffee and started to get a little less formal with them.

So mellow was Sam feeling towards Richard and Robin by the end of the interview, that he was happy to answer some of their questions, giving away more information about the investigation than he would otherwise have done.

In fact, the interview might have extended itself into a second cup of corporate coffee, but the expansive detective was interrupted by his desk phone. He answered it, then glanced up at the clock that hung on his wall beside a picture of Sir John Macdonald, Canada's first Prime Minister and Minister of Justice, founder of the Northwest Mounted Police. He gave a stifled expression of surprise. "Almost missed the time," he said.

"Come on. We have to go."

"Where?" asked Robin, piqued that her probing of the investigating officer had been so rudely interrupted.

"Press call. We have a thousand baying hacks awaiting us, all a-thirst for blood and information."

Four

It was inevitable that the story should get out pretty quickly – into the local media at least. Too many people had been involved for any hope of keeping the news hounds at bay. And the story of a bunch of men – and one lovely woman – dressed as Iroquois braves battling one of Superior's notorious storms in an open canoe to pull a naked girl from the water was a gift to almost every section of every local newspaper, magazine and programme. And when it was discovered that the naked girl had been brutally slain and strangely disfigured, interest became even wider.

A story like that could go national, maybe even federal – the victim could have been killed in American waters, after all, and drifted north over the border. There were more careers than Sergeant Sam McKenzie's to be made here.

Not surprisingly, then, the press room was packed and heaving with excitement. Richard and Robin really only became involved because they were with Sam himself. None of the other witnesses were there and the English couple would have been quite content to see it all on TV like the rest of the canoe's heroic crew. But fate had other plans for them.

Because they entered with Sam, they would have been able to follow the pathway that opened for him along the length of the room and up to the dais at the end below a big framed picture of the mayor. They would have been able to – for the path through the crowd remained open after he passed as the press surveyed the newcomers. But Richard was content to stay at the back of the room and Robin was happy to stand at his side.

Now that they were here, it never occurred to either of them to leave the room and go home. Even had Richard wanted to – for he usually avoided the limelight if he could – Robin would have remained here alone, already caught up in the need to bring the murderer to justice. He knew that and would never leave her here alone. And so they stayed. And allowed Fate to weave her web a little tighter still.

On the dais there was a plain wooden table forested with microphones and equipment, behind which a thin, bespectacled figure waited. Above this man, incongruously, on the wall beside the crest, left over from a previous briefing was a poster advertising the famous Mounties' Musical Ride. From the look of things it was happening somewhere in the city right now – a shocking contrast to the proceedings in this busy little room.

Sam paused only an instant when he realised Richard and Robin were not going to follow him. "We'll finish up later," he said *sotto voce*. "In the meantime I'd appreciate if you talked to no one but me..." Then he was off. He ran up onto the low stage and swung in behind the table with assured confidence, radiating trustworthiness and competence from every pore.

"Thanks for coming, folks. What I propose to do is this. I'll fill you in on the discovery of our Jane Doe, then hand you over to Dr La Paix, the pathologist from the Forensic Laboratory service. He'll give you his initial findings. Very initial. Then it's question time. OK?" Without pausing for a reply, even as the grey man on his right was still nodding to those who recognised him as the local pathologist, the busy officer plunged straight into a detailed and perfectly

37

accurate summation of everything Richard and Robin had told him about yesterday's adventure.

"The body was removed from the slipway to the municipal morgue in the basement of this building at twenty-three thirty local time last night. Dr La Paix took over at midnight and he will present you with his findings now."

"Thank you, Sergeant McKenzie," said the slight grey man, rising to his stooping height and surveying the crowd over the tops of his spectacles. His tone was scholarly and gentle. His accent was as French as his name. He made the horrors he was describing sound almost seductive. "At midnight today I was presented with the corpse of a young female. Her height is one point seven metres precisely. Her weight is one hundred and ten pounds, allowing a little for the weight of the missing body parts. She was aged at the time of her death between twenty-five and thirty years. I cannot be more accurate at this stage without performing some much more detailed work than I have done so far. Likewise it is not possible at this moment to estimate the time of her death as she has been immersed in near-freezing water for some length of time.

"Primary estimates as to racial origin were hampered by the damage to the face but basic measurements of the skull, taken with the shape and configuration of her body as well as the hair type and colour, allow me to guess that she is of mixed race. Caucasoid, perhaps, but more strongly oriental in type. The missing eyes would have had a distinct slant to them and would have been coloured brown. You will readily recognise that such a racial mix is by no means uncommon here. She could be of Native American or Inuit origin. Or she could have been from one of the lively subcultures in any of our larger cities – anything from Chinese or Japanese to Slavic or Ukrainian, in fact. I have of course sent samples to the Violent Crime Linkage Analysis System, ViCLAS, run by the RCMP-GRC in Ottawa, and indeed to the FBI's Violent Criminal Apprehension Program. I have also sent her fingerprints and a DNA sample, which have also of course gone to our own Immigration and Federal branch in Ottawa. We will know much more about her racial and personal origins soon, I am certain. This is particularly true as our Immigration people have such close links with the Federal Service in the United States. If she has any kind of ID either down there or up here, we'll know all about it in a matter of hours."

Dr La Paix broke off here and began to fuss with some of the equipment on the table, snapping up a tall video screen with practised ease. Then he took a fastidious sip of water and proceeded.

"It has been almost as impossible to fix her time of death so far. The same is true of the method of her death. As I say, she has been in the water for at least one day. The body is in a state of some disfigurement. The eyes, nose, lips and tongue are all missing, as is a star-shaped section of skin immediately over the heart. Such wounds, inflicted on a living person, would, individually and collectively, cause death quite quickly. Much of the facial disfigurement, however, could well have been caused post-mortem by seabirds and fish. Some of it certainly was. But I have no way of being certain at this stage whether she had eyes, nose and lips when she went into the water or not. The missing section of skin was certainly removed prior to immersion but once again possibly post-mortem."

The doctor touched a button on a box on the table and the screen behind him lit up. On it appeared a lurid picture of the dead woman's chest. The nipple of her left breast was up in the top right-hand corner of the square screen. The gathering fullness of the breast itself flattened by the forensic light. The brightness of the red-floored star of muscle and matter beneath where the skin had been was disturbingly enhanced. It was possible to see that the ten straight-sided stab wounds which formed the edges of the

40

strange pattern had some considerable depth. There was a collective gasp from the room.

If the doctor registered the sound he did not show it. "These ten wounds all entered the thoracic cavity," he continued. "Although the removal of the skin would have caused severe bleeding, it would not in itself have been fatal, save through shock to a weak heart. The stab wounds would have been, however, for several of them lacerated her left lung and the two which join to form the topmost point of the star itself punctured both the victim's heart and the blood vessels surrounding it. The superior vena cava and the pulmonary artery were both severed and the aorta was nicked. The right ventricle was pierced with a wound fully three centimetres long. Naturally, had these wounds been inflicted while the victim was still alive she would have died at once. She would have bled copiously. As you can see from this photograph, she has been completely exsanguinated, again, probably largely while she was in the water. There is almost no blood left in her body at all, so if it had been drained away on land it would have made an inordinate amount of mess. Eight pints of blood; lymphatic fluid, urine and such. Certainly there is little or none left in her as she is.

"There is a good deal of secondary

damage not attributable to her time in the water. She shows evidence of physical abuse. She has been beaten both with fists and objects. There is some evidence that she has been restrained. She has certainly been tied up and had struggled with her bonds. There is sufficient bruising of her breasts, pelvic regions and genitalia to make me certain that she has been sexually abused. Probably raped. Her time in the water, however, has done a very good job of removing forensic evidence. I have taken a sample from her vagina that looks to be a sperm sample. It is hard to say at this stage if there is enough matter there to be of forensic use and it is to my mind doubtful as to whether it will ever amount to enough to convict the last man who slept with her – even if he was her murderer."

Dr La Paix stood back, sipped and sat. He left the picture up on the screen. There was a short silence. Sam McKenzie got up. "That's all we have for you at the moment," he said soberly. "Any questions?"

Pandemonium ensued, with Sam trying not very successfully to get some order to the Babel of shouted questions.

"So she was tied up, beaten, raped, tortured, disfigured, stabbed, skinned, sucked dry of all her blood and then slung in the water? Is that what you're saying?" demanded the loudest voice.

Dr La Paix rose. Stillness settled as he waited for a chance to answer. "Possibly," he said. "On the other hand, as I have tried to emphasise, the damage to the body could have been inflicted over time and by different agencies. She has certainly been restrained. She has been beaten and, perhaps, raped. At some time during this horrific process she has died. That is clearly the case. But what I cannot be certain about is the precise sequence. She may well already have been dead when she was stabbed and this wound inflicted." He gestured up to the stark picture on the screen. "And there is enough evidence to make me think that she lost her eyes and nose, perhaps, and her lips and tongue more probably, to seabirds and fish. And her blood to Lake Superior. Not to some crazed cross between Jack the Ripper and Dracula at all."

At the mention of Jack the Ripper, Sam McKenzie's eyes closed. Like Richard, who had seen press conferences explode out of all control in his time, the detective was beginning to realise that the good doctor had made a terrible error of judgement.

"Jack the Ripper?" bellowed that same loud reporter's voice. "You mean there's a *Jack the Ripper* on the loose out there..."

La Paix raised his hands as though to ward off the outrageous suggestion. Sam

McKenzie leaped to his feet once more, but even he could not make himself heard.

"Time to leave," said Richard to Robin, stooping to put his lips to her ear. She nodded and he reached for the door handle at his back. Luckily the door opened outwards so they were able to step silently back out of the bedlam and into a quiet hallway. Behind and on their right, the door to Sam McKenzie's office stood ajar. On the left, the hallway widened into the reception area where the duty sergeant guarded a desk and the opening to another corridor – this one leading, no doubt, to the cells. Beyond the airy reception overlooked by the desk sergeant stood an imposing pair of swing doors leading, they knew, to the steps going down to the street.

Richard took Robin's arm and they turned towards the swing doors and the sane, safe street when all of a sudden a broad-shouldered, deep-chested, executive-suited body was thrust in front of them. A wing of hair, the colour of a golden eagle's wing, sat above intense, intelligent moss-green eyes. "The name's Marie Antoine, local TV news," she said. "You're the guys who found the girl. Can I have a moment of your time?"

No sooner had the question been asked than Marie's team was in behind her like a rugby scrum, the cameraman, lighting girl and sound engineer making an impenetrable wall.

"This is for the noon broadcast," persisted Marie without taking breath. "We'll be able to edit everything, so don't panic. I'll do an intro then I'll chuck a few questions at you if that's all right." Without even pausing for a reply she swung round to focus the intensity of her gaze on the camera. "Three ... Two ... One. This is Marie Antoine at the headquarters of the Thunder Bay division of the Ontario police. I have beside me the husband and wife team who discovered the Lady in the Lake, as she has become known, and brought her back last night. Now, folks, I understand you're not from round here, is that right?"

It was in Richard's mind to explain that they had been forbidden to talk to anyone before their interview with Sergeant McKenzie had been completed. He tensed himself to speak, searching for some formula which would make the refusal less obstructive and offensive.

But he needn't have worried, for as he drew breath to speak, a Mountie flew in backwards through the swing doors across the hall. This Mountie was in full dress uniform, red top and all. He would have made an arresting sight standing squarely on his feet. Flying through the air, he was simply breathtaking. He all but destroyed

45

the doors with his shoulders, did a kind of butterfly-backstroke in midair, throwing what looked like a beaver away to one side. Then he hit the floor in the middle of the space in front of the sergeant's desk. As this was made of polished marble tiling, he came skidding across it like a ball in a bowling alley. For an instant, Richard had a vision of Robin, himself and Marie's crew all going down like ninepins, but the RCMP officer managed to roll over, stop his slide and begin to pick himself up. He slipped on the beaver-like object he had thrown aside and kicked it out of the way, up the hallway towards his stunned audience.

Such was the noise of the detective's spectacular arrival that the back few rows of reporters came out of Sam McKenzie's briefing, agog. The new arrivals were just in time to see the doors fly open again, only this time they did not close. Torn from their hinges, they exploded inwards almost as spectacularly as the Mountie had done. The Mountie was now diving under the air-borne panels going for the tackle like a rugby full-back. The man he was going to tackle staggered in through the wreck he had made of the door then, wearing two more Mounties round his neck like a long, muscular, multicoloured and active scarf.

Marie and her team surged down the hall towards such an obvious televisual scoop

46

and the Mariners went with them – perforce, as the rest of Sam's briefing audience were boiling out behind them to see what the commotion was all about.

The man wearing the Mounties was the biggest Richard had ever seen in his life. He looked to be more than seven feet tall. His chest must have measured fifty inches and more. He had a bull-neck the better part of a yard in circumference and a face that seemed to have been cast of molten bronze. He was bellowing with rage and shaking his head from side to side, trying to clear the blood out of his cavernous eye-sockets. He did so just in time to see his third opponent's rugby tackle. Taking firm grasp of each of the other two in fists bigger than their heads, he steadied himself and lashed out with a leg like a redwood tree trunk. It connected with a sound like falling timber. The Mountie skidded backwards, his rugby days clearly over for the time being. The sergeant leaped into life then, reaching under the desk for a gun.

Perhaps it was coincidental – Richard would never know – but as the desk sergeant straightened, the giant's fist succeeded in tearing the right-hand Mountie free of his neck – and the whole Sam Browne with its holster and side arm free of the detective. Before the sergeant could call a threat or a warning, the giant had torn the pistol free and swung it wildly around, moving so that the body of the last Mountie clinging round his neck came between him and the sergeant, straight into the line of fire.

Richard felt a movement by his side. It was Sam McKenzie, pushing through the dumbstruck crowd of reporters. One glance was enough to tell Richard he was armed and ready to open fire. Automatically, Richard began to push Robin sideways, looking for a safe place to put the pair of them if this got any nastier.

"Put the gun down," bellowed Sam, with a good deal more voice than he had used in the briefing. He raised his pistol and aimed squarely at the giant's head. The giant looked back at him and raised his own enormous fist. The gun within it looked much, much smaller than Sam's. Like a toy gun. Hardly dangerous at all. Sam, suddenly alone in the corridor apart from Richard and Robin, did not flinch. "I'll give you a count of three," said the police officer steadily. "And then I'll drop you where you stand."

"*Menya zovut* Vasily Bikal," slurred the giant. "Jou annerstan? Sailor. Me. Russian ship *Aral*. I come out Petersburg. Yes?"

"A count of three," grated Sam. "One..."

"He's Russian!" said Robin urgently. "He's drunk. He's probably got no idea..."

"*TWO!*" shouted Sam, using the bellow to

cover the releasing of his pistol's safety.

"Sergeant," called Robin, as loudly as she dared.

The huge Russian's eyes caught the light like rubies as they switched to her. The gun, also, swung her way. All Richard could think to do was to step in front of her, protecting her body with his.

"THREE!" bellowed Sam at the top of his lungs as a crisp report rang out. Richard flinched, for the sound had come from the Russian's end of the hall and Sam had not fired at all. He stepped back, looking down automatically. But there was nothing to see and no feeling of having been hit.

He looked up again. The Russian was sinking to his knees almost in slow motion. He looked across at Sam. Sam was standing with his weapon, unfired, pointing at the ceiling above his head. There was a massive, slumping crash. He looked down the hall again and there, behind the fallen Russian, there stood a tall woman outlined against the light with a piece of timber from the shattered door in her right hand. It looked about the size of a baseball bat and had clearly made a very effective truncheon. In her left hand the woman held a bright official-looking ID. She held it high in the air so that everyone there could see it, though Richard could not see it well enough to work out exactly what it was.

"The name's Jeanne La Motte," said the newcomer. "Inspector, Royal Canadian Mounted Police, ViCLAS seconded. Who's in charge here, please?"

Richard suddenly found himself back in very welcome obscurity as the press pack followed Sam McKenzie down the hallway to talk to the stunning newcomer. He turned to Robin, lips parted to suggest they find a back way out, only to find that she had retrieved the furry object thrown aside by the flying Mountie. It was a hat. The hat was so big it could only have belonged to the giant. It was a dirty, oil-spiked thing made of what looked on closer inspection like dead cat. It smelt rancid. It was of standard cold-weather design with ear-flaps and a turned-back square peak which must have sat on the outward thrust of Vasily Bikal's simian eyebrow ridge. The square peak was held up by a badge pinned roughly through two layers of the repulsive fur and it was this badge which was holding Robin's attention with almost supernatural force.

Like its owner, the hat was timelessly Russian, a throwback to Stalin's days.

And so was the badge. It was a blood-red five-pointed star.

Five

"I'm sure the star means something!" insisted Robin angrily. "It has to be significant."

"OK," snapped Richard. "Then take it to Sam McKenzie or that Mountie Inspector La Motte. If it is any kind of evidence you shouldn't still have it anyway. And the damned hat it's pinned to is stinking up my ship!"

Part of Richard's irritation arose from the fact that they had been having the same circular argument for nearly two hours now. Robin believed the red star on the Russian's hat was somehow significantly tied to the red star carved on the breast of the corpse in the water. The Lady in the Lake. Richard believed the exact opposite and neither of them was willing to move.

Most of the irritation, however, could be put down to simple tension. The canoe ride had been supposed to be a holiday from their real work here. Yesterday had been planned as total relaxation. Today the pair of them were supposed to be overseeing the crucially important sea trials of the big SuperCat with an untried crew of relative

51

strangers across waters totally new to them.
And here was this dead cat with a badge
pinned to it coming between them when
they needed to be at their closest. It sym-
bolised the way in which the whole situation
here suddenly seemed to be sliding out of
control, and Richard for one did not like it.
"At least get it off my chart table," he said
more quietly, as Captain Steerforth and
First Officer Pugh looked across at them.
"We have to get the course properly logged
in to the system. We have the conference
with the Harbour Master and the pilot in
fifteen minutes and we're nowhere near
ready."

"And we're wasting time talking about a
dead cat with a star stuck on its ass," completed Robin, putting what he was thinking
into her own mouth, word for word. "Yes, I
see that, but if the star is relevant to the
murder investigation, we can't just let it go!"

"Fine!" capitulated Richard. "We need
you here but we can get by without you. Go.
Go find your Inspector Whatever-her-name-
is and explain what you've found to her,
then for crying out loud leave her to do the
investigating. You get back here and focus
on the task in hand."

Robin ran down the gangplank onto the
main dock. The passenger service end was
far away from the slipway where they had

beached the canoe thirty-six hours ago. That was down at the pleasure-boating section. In between stood the huge commercial dock section where the massive ocean-going ships came and went through the St Lawrence Seaway to and from ports all over the world. A cursory glance at their livery showed big freighters from China, South America, South Africa, Britain, Germany and Greece. There had been no great surprise to find a Russian matelot out of bounds. That he should have chosen the Mountie Ride as the venue for his drunken exploits was something only Dostoyevsky could explain. Robin suspected wryly that there was a section in *The Idiot* that would cover seaman Vasily Bikal's actions pretty well. With a grim smile on her lips and the dead-cat hat in her hand, she ran across to the passenger terminal where the taxis congregated.

Robin took her evidence back to the Provincial Police headquarters because she had no idea where else to go. Thunder Bay was a large city, sprawling and bustling, ringed with suburbs as well as golf courses and a range of other civic amenities. It was quite possible that it would have its own Mountie station. Perhaps even its own centre for this ViCLAS organisation that Inspector La Motte was associated with. But Sam McKenzie would be able to help her with that if she could get to him and his office was in the Police HQ. So was the dead girl, come to that, unless the Inspector was a very fast worker indeed. From Dr La Paix's report there was still an awful lot of post-mortem work to do on her. With a large number of experts to be consulted all over the place.

By the time she had reached the cab rank, Robin was frowning fiercely, her mind caught up with the continuing public humiliations being heaped onto the frail, abused figure as the massive, impersonal machinery of the full investigation really got under way. No secret fold of body, character, lifestyle or relationships would be left unexposed. What would happen to her next was almost as obscene as what had happened to her so far, thought Robin, her mood darkening to the colour of the black fur which made up the Russian sailor's mock-beaver hat.

But if Robin's mood was dark, she soon discovered that this was nothing compared with Sam McKenzie's. She ran up through the makeshift doors and across the hall to the sergeant's desk. She would have stayed there, but for the fact that the sergeant was unaccountably missing and, even out here, she could hear Sam's voice raised in angry conversation.

" ...hand over the whole investigation to

some Mountie office girl from ViCLAS! Inspector my ass! About the only thing she's inspected'll probably be a computer keyboard. And maybe some Chief Superintendent's personal equipment. And don't think I don't know who she is. Jeanne Two-Feathers before she married and buried poor Ed La Motte all within six months. I got friends in the RCMP; I got her number all right. A shoe-in from the Aboriginal Cadet Development Program! Troop Seventeen have a lot to answer for too, letting in women in the first place. It's all political and now she's being given my investigation..."

Robin tiptoed across the hallway while this tirade was going on, drawn inexorably by its bitter fluency. But then, abruptly, from behind her came the sound of the desk sergeant returning and she realised that her fascination had placed her in the extremely embarrassing position of an eavesdropper. Like a schoolgirl about some mischief she panicked and dashed across the hall into the room where the press conference had taken place. She swung the door open and stepped in, leaving it as she had found it, slightly ajar. Automatically she looked up towards the table on the dais where Dr La Paix had given his lecture. Looked up and froze. For an instant she even had the ridiculous impression that her whole body had turned to ice.

Sitting behind the table, with her hands held up as though she was praying and her face as pale and blank as the face of a plaster saint, sat Jeanne Two-Feathers La Motte. Sam McKenzie's voice continued to boom across the hall and ring on the air in the silent room, every word as clear as if it was being broadcast.

The eyes of the two women met. No words were exchanged. Robin pulled the door shut until the decided *click!* of the lock cut Sam's tirade to a distant rumble.

"My name is Robin Mariner," Robin began.

"I know," said Jeanne quietly, lowering her hands onto a pile of case notes spread before her. "You found the body. Brought her back in."

"I've found more than that," said Robin, striding purposefully down the room. "I found this."

She reached up and put the sailor's hat on the table, to one side of the neat, clean notes. Inspector La Motte picked it up, wrinkling her long nose ever so slightly. She examined it with almond eyes so dark that they were almost black. The arrow point of a tongue caressed the up-curving junction of perfect cupid-bow lips as she thought about it. Long, slim fingers with almond-shaped nails cut short and square turned the rancid mess of oil and fur until the star was uppermost. Her breath hissed in with a shock of revelation.

Jeanne put the hat down and looked at Robin. The black holes of her eyes seemed to suck Robin inwards with the intensity of the intelligence at work behind them.

"Is it important?" asked Robin. Suddenly she cracked a smile. "I had to put my marriage on the line to bring it in to you."

Then she remembered what Sam McKenzie had said about Jeanne's husband – married and buried within six months. Perhaps it was a bad joke after all.

But the inspector, surprisingly, allowed her eyes to wrinkle in the slightest hint of a grin. "It was worth it," she said. She reached into the case notes and pulled out a photograph. She held it so that Robin could see it. The bright image showed a woman's chest, left nipple in the top corner. Ten deep stab wounds carved a star in the stark white flesh. The floor of the star was skinless and poppy-red.

"I know," said Robin a little dully. Perhaps the inspector was not so quick after all. "I've seen it."

"Not this one," said the inspector from the Violent Crime Linkage section of the Royal Canadian Mounted Police quietly. "This is a different woman altogether. And that's why I'm here."

Six

"Who was she?" asked Robin, stunned.

"We don't know. A non-person. The invisible woman."

"But she must be *someone*!"

"She is. Somewhere. But that's my point. Not here."

"Not in Thunder Bay?"

"No. She's definitely not from Thunder Bay. She was taken out of the water at Point Noir..."

"That's on the Seaway."

"The St Lawrence. Yes. But she's not from there either. She's not, as far as we can ascertain, from Canada at all."

"But how can you be sure?"

"ID – this one had a face. Fingerprints. DNA. Dental records. The whole shooting match. We don't know who she was but we know she's not been reported missing anywhere in Canada or..."

"Reported missing. Maybe no one knows she's gone yet."

"Ten days ago. Time for us to check every database on the continent. Nobody matching her details is missing in the States either.

She's a ghost. She simply doesn't exist."

"She's a ghost with a family now."

"That's right. And I have a dying investigation suddenly up and running again." She paused, then added with something strangely akin to self-loathing, "Once we got past a certain point, this was always our best bet in the end anyway."

"What do you mean?"

Jeanne gave a strangely French moue of her full Native American lips that combined with a shrug to dismiss herself and her colleagues as hopelessly inadequate. "When the last dead end closed off, we knew the only hope we had was to wait for some other poor woman to turn up with a red star over her heart. Hope he made a few mistakes this time that he didn't make the last time."

"That must have been terrible. Waiting like that. Knowing he was out there somewhere and waiting. I don't think I could have slept."

"I don't sleep much at the best of times," shrugged Jeanne.

Into the almost sisterly silence that ensued, Sam McKenzie burst through the door brandishing his gun.

"Oh," he said, freezing, with the weapon cocked and pointed straight at Robin, "it's you again." He snapped the side arm up until it was pointing at the ceiling and carefully released the mechanism. The snap as the safety went back on echoed across the room. "The desk sergeant thought he saw someone sneaking in and we checked the security tapes."

"Can't be too careful," said Robin equably. "Not after yesterday. You had the door fixed pretty quickly, though. How are the Mounties?"

"Back in the saddle again, so I'm told," said Sam grudgingly. He holstered his side arm. "We never finished our chat."

"No need to now, is there?" It was Jeanne who spoke. "Captain Mariner can talk things over with me."

"Yeah. I guess." The spleen Sam had vented to whoever was on the far end of his phone connection seemed to have calmed him. Almost mollified him. "You want to use my office?" he offered.

"We're fine here. Thanks for the cooperation, though."

"Yeah, well ... Hey!" his eye had fallen on the pile of fur beside Jeanne's left hand. "You found it!"

"What?" Not even Jeanne could follow that leap of association.

"The big guy's hat. Vasily Bikal's hat. Jesus, was he ever ticked off at losing that. Even worse than the charges, the fines and rollicking from his captain back on the old *Aral* this morning. Hey, you want to make a friend for life, why not take it back to him?"

60

The women looked at each other with speaking eyes. Who in their right mind would ever want to make a lifelong friend of a drunken giant whose only interesting feature was the number of Mounties he could swat with one hand?

But Sam McKenzie had his reasons. "I mean you might not get much social chit-chat, if you know what I mean, but I believe he would deliver the goods."

Just at that moment another officer pushed into the room. This time it was the desk sergeant. "Fax for the inspector," he said shortly and strode forward to drop it on the desk. Jeanne picked it up and began to read it.

"Old Luke will bear me out on this," said McKenzie as the desk sergeant came back towards the door. "A wild woman's dream, old Comrade Seaman Vasily Bikal. Built to scale and a good bit more. And we've seen him in the shower, so we know!"

Jeanne looked up from the fax, her eyes blank and her mind clearly travelling at light-speed somewhere far, far away. "Thank you, Sergeant," she said into the deflated silence. "That was an excellent suggestion. Please tell me what berth the *Aral* is in and I will return the seaman's property at once."

She folded the fax and slipped it into the pocket of her chic non-uniform blazer. She rose and picked up the stinking pile of cat fur as though it was almost sacred. She stepped elegantly down into the body of the room. As she passed the dumbstruck men, she pulled Robin ever so gently by the sleeve. Robin followed her out, but so did the other two, so the women remained silent as they walked down to the sergeant's desk. Here they waited the instant it took him to look up Seaman Vasily Bikal's address – his ship and berth number – and then they were off.

"Cab," said Jeanne almost to herself as they ran side by side down the steps outside the rudely repaired door. "Squad car would be too official. And I should be calling this in. But someone like Sam McKenzie'll only think of a good reason to stop me doing it."

"Doing what? Going aboard?"

"Going aboard, scouting around, going back tonight before she sails. It's a long shot but you've got to start somewhere."

"What are you talking about?" asked Robin, beginning to feel as though she were wading through treacle here. "What did the fax say to make so much difference?"

"It gave me a name," said the inspector as the cab drew in beside them. "It put me back in business." She opened the door. "Coming?"

How could Robin resist? She slid into the

back of the taxi and slammed the door as Jeanne gave the berth of the *Aral* as their destination.

"Whose name?" she demanded as the car slid silently into motion.

"Victim number one," answered Jeanne. "The invisible woman's. Not so invisible after all. She gave a complete set of samples as part of a well-paid drug-test programme while she was at university. They've got a hundred per cent positive ID from that."

"Drug test?"

"Some hormone thing. Part of the 'morning after' pill. It was all the rage with the researchers at the time."

"They test drugs on university students?" Robin was horrified. Sidetracked.

"Not here they don't. Nor in the US. Thailand, mostly. Or, in this case, Bashkortostan."

"Where?"

"Russia. South of the Urals. Our first red-star woman was Anna Rakhmov, graduated University of Orsk. Trained as a nuclear scientist, last recorded working as a secretary and part-time prostitute in the charmingly named town of Luck, in the Ukraine."

"Luck," said Robin dully.

"Luck," repeated Jeanne. "What she ran out of all too early in life, by the look of things. Figuratively, then literally. Out of Luck and onto Pointe Noir, with a red star

63

carved on her heart."

There was a little silence, then Jeanne said, with brittle brightness, "You want to come and give big Vasily Bikal his hat back?"

Seven

The Russian freighter *Aral* was a frantic bustle of activity. The only place aboard of relative peace and quiet was Captain Alex Zhukov's dayroom, and even that was piled with paperwork.

Aral had come out of St Petersburg, her home port, six weeks earlier, fully laden. The bulk of her cargo consisted of a combination of Chinese rice, trans-shipped from the paddy fields of Guandong province via Shanghai, and Russian sheet iron from the blast furnaces of Beloretsk. The paperwork generated for the freighter's long-suffering captain by the juggling of two such widely different cargoes, tracked literally across the length and breadth of Asia into the St Petersburg docks, was enormous – especially as half of it was in Cantonese and an almost impenetrable Russian translation.

After a slow, stormy North Atlantic passage, *Aral* had come into the St Lawrence battered and late, only to get caught up in a jam in the Soo Canal which had put her badly behind schedule at Thunder Bay. She had unloaded the rice and then been forced to join a queue for a part-cargo of wheat which she would take with the iron down to Duluth. The wheat was an extra investment – an attempt by the desperate Captain Zhukov to get back into profitability and ensure there would be a chance of some pay for her officers and men at the still-distant conclusion of the voyage.

While the further delay irritated Captain Zhukov, it at least gave him the opportunity to arrange a little sightseeing for those of his crew most dangerously in the grip of cabin fever. It also gave him the chance to get the Chinese paperwork in close enough synch with the Russian paperwork and the actual, demonstrable cargo on his lading officer's manifest to satisfy the Canadian customs service.

First among the fevered escapees, of course, had been Vasily Bikal, so the plan had backfired somewhat. Captain Zhukov, never a particularly cheerful person, was even more irritated than ever. Everyone aboard leaped to their duties with more than usual alacrity – except for Bikal himself, who was secured below under punitive restraint until the captain could think of a punishment sufficiently horrific to fit his crime. The crime in question had nothing to do with getting mad-drunk, frightening several highly trained horses, destroying a section of stadium and part of a station house and hospitalising three Mounties. It had to do with creating yet another mountain of paperwork. This would, like the Chinese paperwork, have to be completed satisfactorily, in triplicate, before *Aral* would be allowed to leave port.

And even then she would only be steaming, dangerously behind schedule, running out of fuel, food and funds, through a rapidly worsening weather forecast towards two further sets of paperwork for the American Customs in Duluth; one in Canadian English with sections of French which the Russian, frankly, understood more clearly, and the other in what passed for Russian in the wilds of Bashkorostan.

The last thing on God's green earth Alex Zhukov, captain of the *Aral*, had the time or the inclination to do was to entertain two distractingly officious women. Women who seemed to be aboard his command for no better reason than to return this disgusting hat to the captain's least favourite crewman.

It was all the first officer's fault, thought Zhukov, eyeing the two Western interlopers with undisguised loathing. That arrogant little shit Ivanov should have stopped them at the head of the gangplank, no matter how official their warrant cards. Simply letting them onto the walkways athwart the gaping hatches of the main deck was an invitation to disaster. To conduct them personally to the bridge, past the swinging cranes with their massive loads, beneath the cascades of wheat like waterfalls, between the wildly rushing teams of sailors, all without checking for permission or even issuing them with hard hats simply beggared belief. Perhaps First Officer Sergei Ivanov should have gone ashore with the other head-cases yesterday. But no. God alone knew what disasters and what paperwork that would have generated.

Captain Alex Zhukov was not alone in wondering about First Officer Sergei Ivanov. Ivanov was occupying Robin's thoughts as well. Jeanne and the captain fell into a halting conversation carefully designed on her part to cover up the fact that both Robin and she spoke a little Russian – a secret likely to prove useful if their spying mission came to anything. Robin fell into a brown study. A full ship's captain for a decade or two, her experience of ships and their officers was practically limitless. She had recognised it in the wry arrogance of the first officer, in the casual manner he had brought them aboard with only the briefest

67

glance at Jeanne's ID and no request for her own at all. She had seen it in the secret, twisted smile with which he had conducted them here, through the occasionally extremely dangerous work on the deck without due warning or adequate protection. She was personally convinced that only her own experience and her ability to guide Jeanne away from some of the unexplained, unexpected dangers of the journey had got them up here unscathed. Only an extremely forceful hand on the Mountie's shoulder, for instance, had made her hesitate – and thus saved her from being knocked headlong from a catwalk into a grain-hold by a wildly swinging crane hook. Ivanov hadn't even glanced over his shoulder to check on the near-disaster.

The strongly negative impression was compounded by the fact that Ivanov was no longer smiling when he rapped on the captain's door and ushered them in without waiting for the captain to reply. He was scowling with what looked like disappointment that the women were still alive behind him. It was more than enough to trigger a train of very disturbing speculation in the English captain's mind.

Robin sat silently, looking across the untidy jumble of paperwork at the puffy face of a weak, defeated old man, all too well aware of who really ran the ship. And of the manner in which he probably did it. And, therefore, of what sort of a ship it might easily turn out to be.

Robin realised with a shock of surprise that, although her eyes were wiser than most and had been extremely busy since they had stepped aboard, she had only seen crewmen at work here. And on a modern Russian freighter that too was highly unusual. None of the officers or crew, it seemed, above deck or below, was female. That was when she decided who would return the hat to the giant Bikal and who would get lost in the corridors to do a little secret exploring below. The only thing she couldn't make a clear decision about just now was which of them would stand in most urgent need of the solid little automatic Jeanne was carrying in her bag.

By the time Robin had come out of her brown study, Inspector La Motte had explained to Captain Zhukov that the returning of the hat would give her a chance to complete one or two formalities with Seaman Bikal. Intelligent and intuitive, she added that a word or two between Bikal and herself would obviate the need for the majority of the paperwork in the case and allow the captain to return to far more important matters. Like loading up and getting out before the weather closed down again.

The little squall just after *Aral*'s arrival forty-eight hours ago was the playful spitting of a kitten compared with the raging Siberian tiger of a storm the weathermen were promising in a day or so. Safe haven in Duluth was the captain's fervent dream. He leaped at the offered chance to realise it without any further thought. He moved a small Alp of paperwork to uncover an old-fashioned wooden box with a series of switches on it. He pressed one of these and a voice squawked in Russian too garbled for Robin to follow. A moment later a crewman appeared. He was ill-kempt and ill-shaven. He eyed the women with lazy speculation. "These nosy bitches are from the Mounted Police," said the captain, blissfully unaware that both women understood every word. "They need to talk to that stupid bastard Vasily Bikal. Take them down."

"Yes, Captain."

He led the two of them to the door and held it open. As they stepped over the threshold, Captain Zhukov abruptly looked back up from his paperwork, as though struck by a sudden thought. "And, hey!"

"Yes, Captain?"

"Bring them up again."

Robin's Russian was basic but she could follow the gist of a conversation. The captain's words echoed in her mind. She glanced across at Jeanne and the inspector was also frowning. The captain had not said "Bring them up *here* again," or "Bring them up *to me.*" He had just said, *"Bring them up again."* And it hadn't sounded as though he had meant it as a joke, either. Score one to multilinguicity, she thought, trying to quell the crawling sensation deep in her stomach.

The slovenly crewman showed them to a roomy elevator and stood beside them as the car descended. He smelt of Russian tobacco, sweat and perfume, at least two of which should have been hard to come by after a long voyage, even for the captain's steward. "Have you seen much of the city?" Jeanne asked brightly in English.

The crewman gazed at her, frowning slightly. "Thunder Bay is quite a tourist centre," babbled Jeanne. "There's golf, ski-ing, rock-climbing and spelunking all right at hand. And the watersports..." She rolled her eyes. "Tried any?"

The crewman frowned.

"They had a nice indoor stadium too," supplied Robin brightly. "Until Vasily Bikal got his hands on it."

The seaman's face cleared. "Vasily Bikal," he said. He beamed and nodded.

"Think he understands?" said Jeanne in the same bright tone, smiling and nodding.

"Not a syllable," said Robin, nodding and smiling.

71

"Let's hope we're right. What's the plan?"

"You talk to the giant. I'll nose around."

"Why not me? I've got good eyes."

"Been on many ships? Know your way around a boat?"

"Point taken. I'd get lost in five minutes flat. I may pick up some unguarded Russian in the giant's quarters, though."

"And I'll report in detail anything I see. It's your investigation."

"Damn right it is."

"Right. Let's get this farce on the road, then," said Robin.

The lift hissed to a stop. The doors opened. The three of them stepped out. They found themselves in a short lateral corridor each end of which turned through 90 degrees into two more short corridors. On the blank wall straight ahead there stood a picture Robin recognised as St Petersburg. It was more than six feet high, and was remarkable for focusing on one of the few really unphotogenic areas of the city – the commercial docks.

"I need the toilet," said Robin to their guide. "Toilet? Head?"

She gave a vivid little pantomime of urgent need and he pointed down one corridor without apparent thought or suspicion while leading Jeanne down another.

It was only when she was alone in the smelly, rumbling gloom of the dingy corridor, looking about her and wondering where to begin her Jane Bond Junior impersonation, that she remembered the gun in Jeanne's handbag. She had really wanted the relative security of that powerful little side arm out here in Indian Country alone.

"It's too late to worry now," she said to herself, bracingly. But she wasn't really convinced. That slimy little shiver in the pit of her tummy told her the all too brutal truth.

It was *definitely* too late.

It was definitely *not* too late to worry.

Eight

The first thing to do, Robin thought, was to find out where the toilet was actually located – as a kind of fallback position. Then she could branch out from there in a series of increasingly adventurous sorties, and check with Jeanne in Bikal's cabin in due course, depending on how things went.

Like if the pair of them survived, for example.

She looked down at the face of her digital watch and decided to give herself ten minutes. She set the timer with trembling fingers and looked up again, like Joan of Arc at the stake.

Robin was not being unduly melodramatic in her fears. This ship had a strange atmosphere. It might be something to do with its nationality, its time at sea, the cabin fever among its crew and the fact that they were all men. It probably had a lot to do with Robin's very negative first impressions of the three *Aral* shipmates she had met so far. It was certainly based on her observation of the state of this battered, rusty, uncared-for hulk, which obviously stood in need of so much love and attention, above deck and below.

But there was more to it than that. She had the feeling that this was a bad ship, somehow. That there were bad things going on aboard, as well as bad men commanding and crewing her. It was a sensation amounting to a psychic certainty – and Robin was the least sensitive person she knew. Even Richard picked up on atmospheres more swiftly than she did. Still, the worst thing to do in almost any situation, she reckoned, was to stand around worrying.

The corridor was dim because most of the lights had failed – the ship's supply officer was clearly running low on bulbs. The shadows were enhanced by the rust-streaked, nicotine-darkened drabness of the walls. There were the remains of an old-fashioned handrail along them but that had been reduced to a series of empty supports now, the rail itself long gone. Above the supports the wall had long ago been painted cream. Below, brown. On the deck lay the Russian equivalent of linoleum, dangerously perished. It rose in bilious blisters; most of them burst open to reveal a kind of coir matting beneath. The whole place smelt like a combination sweatshop, vomitarium and latrine.

The doors along the passageway had been painted to match the cream and then further darkened with wear, scuffs, scrapes and dirty fingerprints around their handles and edges. Some had writing on them but it was in Cyrillic script and indecipherable.

The first door Robin tried was unmarked. It opened to reveal a dingy cabin that smelt like a pigsty and was clearly home to two crewmen. She sorted through it swiftly and discovered little more than the colour of their underwear, the fact that the ship's laundry was in a parlous state, and their taste in pornography. It was not just the laundry that wasn't working all that well, either. The ship's basic maintenance system wasn't up to much by the look of things. Wardrobe doors hung off their hinges. The fronts of drawers pulled away in her hands and had to be replaced with the utmost care. Such springing as the bunks might have had had been replaced by boards – boards which sagged dangerously. Beneath the lower bunk where the sag was half-hidden by a little doorless cupboard, a collection of books and magazines presented a range of women all alike in their state of undress and the range of partners, positions, predilections, torments, tastes and life-forms that they accepted or assumed. In the deserts of depravity, it seemed to Robin, no stone had been left unturned.

The second door hid an identical chamber that was, on the physical, moral and maintenance level, almost equally disgusting. The third door was one of those that had been marked. It opened into the latrine, but the state of the place – and the stench of it – were so terrible that Robin recoiled in disgust. Had her need for relief been real, she would rather have shoved her bottom out through a porthole than used this place. Nevertheless, she was here on a mission. A cursory inspection was the least she expected of herself. It would last exactly as long as she could hold her breath. She entered on tiptoe, hoping to minimise not the sound she was making but her physical contact with the place. It was a latrine designed for male use but there were several stalls, all unoccupied. She pushed the door of each one open with her knee and glanced in, feeling the filth of the place settling onto her skin like leprosy. They were filthy, stained, and marked with graffiti, which she glanced at in the spirit of enquiry. There were no toilet seats – merely a slightly thickened steel rim. Steel which had originally been designed to be 'stainless'. At the bottom of each steel bowl slopped a little pool of effluent which, like the pornography and the graffiti, only received the most cursory glance. Or the first three did. In the fourth, floating in the sludge, almost indistinguishable from the bodily wastes around it, there floated a tampon.

Robin gasped. Breathed in. Left swiftly, choking.

Out in the corridor, she paused to catch her breath, looking round, listening as well as looking, with fierce concentration. There were women aboard, or had been, recently. Who? Where? Could her wise, experienced eyes have overlooked a feminine form among the crew on deck? She thought not. They had all been working stripped to the waist in the hot day. Only one of them, a slight but wiry figure, was wearing a vest – a miraculously white one, she now recalled. But he had been dark, with a mat of chest-hair exploding to his throat. The careless crane operator? Someone among the junior officers? There must be stewards, cooks and other helpers aboard. Perhaps there were women on these teams. It was all possible. Except that she could not imagine the fastidious stewards, galley-staff or any of the officers having to use the latrine on the crew deck.

The most likely explanation was that someone had smuggled a prostitute aboard. She'd need to be pretty desperate to come to a place like this, though. Desperate enough to keep working, in spite of the time of the month. Yes. That made most sense. But somehow it still didn't satisfy Robin. She pushed on down the corridor, working more swiftly now, aware of the passage of time, looking for more evidence of a female presence aboard.

Five minutes later, she thought she had found it. She opened the door into a cabin that was an island of cleanliness and order in the sea of untidy filth. Clothes were pressed and neatly hung in a carefully maintained wardrobe. Personal effects and underwear all resided, carefully folded, in a chest of drawers that worked properly. Not only a civilised person but also a DIY enthusiast. But, most likely, a man after all: a photograph, wedged in the corner of a mirror, showed a wife and family waving with the sad smiles of farewell. Another, close-up of a face in a typical ID portrait mode. The name Sholokov was written across the throat. This was probably the name of the cabin's owner. In the cupboard beneath the lower bunk, which did not sag and was clearly unused, the carefully stored books had pictures nowhere but on the covers – and precious few even there. Some were in Cyrillic and some in Western print. Of the latter she recognised some words – mostly names. SOLZHENITSIN, BULGHAKOV, MICHAEL SHOLOKOV. She paused, struck, looking up at the photo on the mirror. The man had the same name as one of his favourite authors. Was that coincidence or what? She wondered.

Behind the neatly arranged piles of literature there lay other things, half concealed. Because Robin instinctively felt she liked and trusted this man Sholokov who maintained such decency in the face of so much barbarism, she felt she must not take anything here on face value. Trust was a weakness aboard *Aral*, she suspected. She pushed herself half under the bunk to see what it was that lay behind the books.

And that was when Robin heard it. The sound of a woman crying. It was so distant as to exist only at the edge of her imagination. She held her breath and tried to still the thumping of her heart. I'm not making it up! she told herself, but even the voice within her head seemed to have more volume than the sound.

But no. There it was again. As desolate as the wind in wires or the midnight call of a westbound train. The saddest noise in the entire world. It went on and on and on, just at the limit of Robin's hearing. Requiring so much concentration simply to keep it in her ears while she tried to work out where in God's name it was coming from.

So that when the alarm on her watch went off, it made her jump like a startled hare. She smashed her head on the solid bottom of the lower bunk and bit her tongue. She saw stars and tasted blood. And the sound of weeping stopped. With a torrent of mental invective, she scrambled backwards, pausing only to restore the piles of Russian literature and close the polished doors of the under-bunk cupboard. She cast one last look around the pristine cabin and stepped out into the corridor.

Straight into the arms of the hairy man with the pristine vest, who was just about to enter. She looked up. His was also the face on the ID photo.

Of course, she thought, *who else?* Her stomach gave a back flip, nevertheless, and the stars continued to dance before her eyes – with shock now, not concussion.

"What are you doing in my cabin?" he asked. His voice was deep, suspicious, abrupt.

Robin gasped as though he had slapped

her – but he had only spoken in English. He smelt sharply of sweat and soap. "Thank goodness I've found someone," she gabbled. "I've been wandering around these corridors for ten minutes. Lost. I haven't seen a soul. The other two went to talk to Vasily Bikal but I had to go to the toilet and when I came out, I don't know how, I somehow lost myself."

She gazed earnestly into his eyes. They were dark, guarded, quizzical, unconvinced. He did not believe a word of this, she could see all too clearly. Abruptly one of the pornographic pictures from the collection in the first foul cabin sprang into her mind: a girl tied naked on a bed watching the red point of a lighted cigar approach the tender curve of her breast. It had struck her particularly because it was a scene she remembered from a James Bond book. And now it struck her as a distinct possibility for her own future. Followed in due course by a long deep swim in water she would no longer register as icy-cold. With or without a red star carved on her heart. She realised with another gasp of shock that she hadn't even told Richard where she was going. Her throat went dry. Her mouth seemed to shrivel. Silence fell like the blade of a guillotine.

Then, after an instant, "Bikal," said the man in the white vest. "But his cabin is in

81

corridor number three. This is number four. You are badly lost, madam. I must guide you there at once." He bowed slightly and smiled tightly. His teeth were as white as his vest. His eyes remained guarded and dark. The smile did not extend to them at all. He marched off decisively and Robin followed. There was nothing else she could do. But she still had an overwhelming suspicion that he could as easily have been leading her to slaughter as guiding her to safety.

Nine

The two women sat at a small table at the back of the bustling cafeteria. Two cups of cold coffee lay untouched between them. Outside, the afternoon was beginning to darken towards evening over the passenger facilities of the Thunder Bay docks. If Robin had risen and pushed her way through the tea-time throng to the windows, she would have been able to see the gleaming, twin-hulled outline of the SuperCat *Swiftsure*, where Richard was lengthening a busy day into some expensive overtime with the captain and crew, preparing for tomorrow's trial run. Like *Aral*'s captain, Richard was concerned about the threatened storm. He wanted to ensure his shakedown cruise was over before it struck.

It had occurred to Robin that she should at least go aboard to tell her beloved husband that she had survived her adventures aboard *Aral*, but that had only been the champagne dizziness of relief affecting her thoughts. Richard would probably throw a fit if he knew that she had even ventured aboard, so she would never get to tell him how she had got safely off. So the good offices of the strange man in the white vest, the man called Sholokov, would remain for ever secret. She shivered with dangerous, illicit pleasure – the secret Sholokov. It was a little like having a lover.

"I've got to get back aboard," said Jeanne, recalling Robin's wandering mind. "It's all very well seeing her papers and getting the authorities here to hand over her manifests and crew lists."

Both of which things Jeanne had done since leaving the ship, after hearing Robin's report of what she had found. She had also checked on the phone with the local divisional headquarters of 'O' Division RCMP-GRC and with the Violent Crime Linkage office. She had even visited the local provincial police headquarters only to find Sam McKenzie was out investigating another murder. It had been a busy but ultimately fruitless time. They had then gone on to Customs and Immigration and finally to the Harbour Master's office before finally coming to rest here.

"They simply won't hold *Aral* here on your word, Robin. And I know they're not about to go back aboard. It'll take more than a tampon and a whisper to start the ball rolling on this one. But your first impression was right. There are no records of any women passengers or crew. So, unless your first guess was also right and they've been smuggling whores aboard, then they must have a girl stashed aboard in secret somewhere. An unhappy girl. A kidnapped girl. And that is against the law, so I've got to put a stop to it."

"You should let it lie," said Robin. "Pass the word down to the FBI or whoever and let them go aboard in Duluth."

"Too risky. The moment they get even a breath, they'll have her over the side and there'll be one more dead woman polluting Superior."

"With or without the star."

"I can't let that happen."

"Who can you go to? Your superiors in this ViCLAS thing you belong to? Didn't you say they even had an office here in town? Yes of course, you called them on the phone earlier..."

84

"According to them I should be at the moment filling in a two hundred and fifty-question booklet about the progress of the case. New procedure. But they won't act quickly enough. Not on a tampon, like I said."

"Immigration?"

"They're geared up for this sort of thing on each of the major seaboards – especially the west coast. People smuggling is big business there. But the local Immigration people seem to be more laid back. They've given *Aral* a clean bill of health. The moment she completes loading and the paperwork gets finished, she'll be gone."

"She'll be fully laden before midnight. And she doesn't have to wait for much in the way of a tide."

"She'll be gone by dawn, I'm sure. I can check with the Harbour Master's office once again to make sure but you're right; they're almost laden and I've cut the captain's paperwork in half. I'll have to go on board tonight."

"Security looks pretty lax at any rate," said Robin.

Security was tight enough at the dock gates a couple of hours later. Even as the guard logged them in on the strength of their various IDs and clearances while their cab roared away into the balmy night, so he

85

demanded to know which ship they were going aboard. Caught a little unprepared, Jeanne opened her mouth to tell the truth but Robin was quick to speak for both. "The Heritage Mariner SuperCat *Swiftsure*, same as usual," she said. "My husband and some of the crew are likely to be aboard all night."

Jeanne picked up on the good sense of covering her tracks even at this early stage. "We're what you might call R and R," she said.

The guard looked up. "I'd never call a Mountie anything of the sort, Inspector," he drawled, deadpan.

They felt his eyes on them as they crossed towards the distant SuperCat. It was only in the darkest shadows between the sodium-yellow beams of the security lighting, therefore, that they slid sideways and began to run along the dockside towards the commercial end where *Aral* still sat under the lights and bustle of the final stages of loading.

They stopped in the last shadow before the pool of golden brightness at whose heart *Aral* was tethered. Here they lingered, side by side, all but invisible in the shadows as they watched. Soon, beneath their quick gazes, the apparently patternless activity became less like the movement of a disturbed ants' nest. Teams of men were carrying equipment on and off, much of it packed away in cases and grips like the one Jeanne had brought with her. The crew of *Aral* herself seemed to be working aboard for the most part and the men coming and going up and down the gangplanks looked to be labourers and longshoremen, engineers and fitters. Nobody was bothering to check anyone for IDs or authorities. No one seemed to be bothering with any sort of security at all, in fact. Possibly because only a couple of crewmen had seemed to understand English this morning, and it was extremely doubtful if the Thunder Bay longshoremen spoke any Russian. Any attempt at any communication, security or social, would simply slow everything down to a snail's pace.

"Perfect," decided Jeanne. "I should be able to get aboard with the dock workers, go below and find the girl. If I can free her and bring her off I will but if I can't I'll get physical proof that she exists, slip ashore and alert Immigration and Customs myself."

"As plans go, it's simple," observed Robin.

"I'll bet that's what Colonel Custer said," grated Jeanne. "This feels like the stupidest thing I have ever done in my life. It sure as Hell is not the way I was trained to do police work."

"Nonsense," whispered Robin bracingly.

"You'll come out of this a hero."

"If I come out of it with my hide, my reputation and my career intact, that'll do me nicely." Jeanne breathed. "In fact, if I come out of it at all I'll be grateful."

Jeanne unbuttoned the long, dark raincoat she was wearing and put it temporarily onto the black grip at her feet. Beneath the coat she was dressed in grey overalls, baggy enough to disguise her figure and dark enough to blend with shadows – but worka-day enough to pass a cursory inspection. She shoved her hair up under a knitted cap such as they had seen one or two men wearing this afternoon. With the grip swung up onto her shoulder hiding her face, she would become just another nameless dock worker or general-purpose crewman. Closer examination would strip her disguise away pretty quickly, of course. Even the most cursory glance into the grip would reveal her camera, tape recorder, personal phone and side arm.

Jeanne picked up the coat again and slipped her ID out of it as she handed it to Robin. She put the little ID wallet into the baggy breast of her overall, with her 'ace in the hole' gun in its bra-holster, as close to her heart as she could manage.

"I'll better get back to *Swiftsure*," said Robin, clutching the raincoat with sweaty hands, feeling as nervous as though she were going aboard herself. "I'll bet that security guard will check on us. And even if he doesn't, Richard'll start checking up on me soon. We have a routine."

"Yeah," said Jeanne. She reached down for the grip and hefted it upwards onto her shoulder. "I'll keep in touch," she said gruffly from beyond the black nylon. Then she was in purposeful, unhesitating, masculine action.

Robin lingered in the shadow and watched the tall figure cross the dangerous brightness quickly with an air of confidence. She knew Jeanne would keep in touch, for the number of her own little personal phone, sitting securely in her pocket now, was programmed into Jeanne's phone at the very top of her emergency contact list. Above the local police's emergency number. Above even the Mounties' emergency all-alert. She stood, watching silently, offering up mental prayer after mental prayer, and wringing the life out of Jeanne's raincoat until the intrepid investigator swung in on the end of a line of workmen going up the gangplank and aboard. Then she became lost from sight and Robin had no alternative but to turn and go back across the empty, shadowy dock to board *Swiftsure* before the security guard and Richard himself came looking for her.

Tense as she was, it never occurred to

89

Robin that, should anything happen to Jeanne, there might be other people coming to look for her as well.

Ten

That night featured among the worst of Robin's life. She lied to the security guard when he called just after she arrived aboard *Swiftsure*. She prevaricated to Richard about her lies to the security man and did it so badly that he only let her answers slide because he was too busy to follow them up. She felt redundant aboard the SuperCat in any case because the day she had spent with Jeanne had put her out of touch with the work in progress. Not even Richard had time to stop and bring her up to speed with progress and plans, though he was usually punctilious in such matters. No one aboard was going to get much sleep, it was clear. But Robin would have found sleep impossible in any case. Instead, she counted the weary minutes as they stretched out before her in a tedious wilderness of time. After midnight, she found that she was actually sitting staring at her personal phone for minutes on end, as though the force of her will could make it ring.

After the second staring episode, Robin took a big mug of tea onto the SuperCat's deck and tried to see across to *Aral*'s dock. There was little in the way of fore deck in the sleek craft's design, so she was forced to stand on the aft deck down behind the main accommodation area. The Russian freighter was invisible from this position, but the night was warm with a little wind kicking playfully in off the water. Shadowed from the city lights as well as from the brightness of the commercial docks, Robin was able to see a huge array of stars. In the end she contented herself with settling on a reclining chair and looking up at the sky, noting sleepily how a great area of darkness was slowly spreading up from the south-west, blotting out the constellations as it came.

Robin was awoken into the threatening grey of a cloudy dawn. She blinked, surprised by the change that had overcome the weather during the instant since her eyelids closed. The phone rang again and she jumped, slopping the last dregs of tea over the back of her hand. The liquid was icy. The phone rang again and she reached for it, beginning to suspect the truth. She had been asleep for hours.

"Heritage Mariner. Robin Mariner speaking." She had used her stock answer to all calls before the penny dropped. "Jeanne, is that you?"

Faintly but hoarsely on the far end of the connection, someone took a deep breath. There was a masculine timbre even to the inhalation. Robin had no doubt.

"Who is this?"

Connection was broken with a sinisterly final click.

With her mind whirling with shock, Robin punched in the dial-back number and after a moment, Jeanne's personal phone number came up on the display. PROCEED? demanded the little machine. Robin's finger hovered. Fell. What dangers might be compounded for the investigator by an unexpected call now? Robin could hardly bear to think. And yet, here was proof positive that Jeanne had just called her. Or someone had. Someone using Jeanne's phone.

Robin leaped into action. Pocketing the phone as she rose, she sprinted across the damp decking to the aft gangplank and threw herself down onto the dockside. She hit the damp grey concrete at a dead run and dashed across the expanse of it, too preoccupied to register how quiet it was now. All that occupied her mind was *Aral*.

Long before she reached the spot where Jeanne and she had parted last night, she could see that the ship had gone. She ran on, as though her mind, reeling from blank disbelief to chilling shock, was somehow disconnected from her pumping legs. As she began to come to terms with the fact that the berth was vacant, so she slowed to a walk. And by the time her toes were touching the big metal bollard which had held the Russian's forepeak mooring rope last night, she was standing stock-still, her mind empty. The infinities of speculation as to what had gone wrong with the simple plan were too wide to consider. The equally wide range of possibilities as to what might be happening to Jeanne were also something Robin did not want to even begin considering. The very least of them was that she was now in captive company with the weeping woman she had gone aboard to help.

Robin and Jeanne had skirted round this possibility in their discussions. It was something that Robin, at least, had been keen to plan for, not least because she knew herself so well – and knew therefore that if the worst came to the worst she would have to have some sort of action to get on with. Inaction would send her mad. She had, therefore, a list of names and telephone numbers in her pocket. Sam McKenzie at the local Provincial Police office, Jeanne's boss at the ViCLAS office in London, Ontario, the local office, the Harbour

Master, Immigration. And, of course, the panic numbers – the equivalents of Britain's 999 and the USA's 911 numbers. Robin looked at her watch, beginning to kick her frozen mind back into some kind of action. Just coming up to 6 a.m. local time.

When Robin's phone rang again she screamed aloud. She slammed it to her ear and narrowed her eyes as though the sound of her friend's voice would conjure up some kind of vision. "Jeanne, is that you? Jeanne?"

"Robin? Where on earth are you now? What is going on?" At first she didn't recognise the voice because it did not belong to Jeanne.

She was just about to demand, *Who is this?* when he said, "Robin, are you all right, darling?"

Not only did Robin recognise Richard's voice then; she also realised where Jeanne's rescue must begin.

"Call her," said Richard unhesitatingly.

"But she might be hiding. I could give her away, get her killed."

"But she just called you."

"Someone did. Using her phone. I'm sure it was a man."

"Call back."

Reluctantly, Robin dialled and the ringing tone filled her head at once. As she listened, she looked out at the stormy morning and marvelled how Richard could still be so full of energy and decisiveness when he hadn't slept a wink all night. Beside her fizzing, energetic husband, Captain Steerforth and First Officer Pugh seemed pale and listless. Chief Engineer Hardy popped his head round the bridge door and announced the engines primed and ready. "Right," said Richard, switching from one area of decisiveness to another. "Warn the Harbour Master and book a pilot if we need one. As soon as the full crew reports for duty we'll take her out and shake her down."

Over the unvarying buzz of the ringing tone, Robin said, "By the looks of things she'll get shaken and stirred out there today."

"She won't take huge seas," said Steerforth at once.

"We'll test her to the limit," said Richard.

"We'll have to," said Robin. "We have to know how much bad weather she can take. Richard, Jeanne's not answering. I have to alert people. This could be so important. She's at least been kidnapped, maybe murdered."

"Unless she's stowed away the better to finish her investigation. It's only a couple of days' run down to Duluth. She could stay hidden for a couple of days."

"Not with a phone ringing, she couldn't," said Robin, breaking the connection.

"Don't worry. She's probably got it switched to vibrate rather than ring."

"Then it'll just be a question of where she's hidden it," volunteered young Pugh, racily. "If she's tucked it down her under-wear—"

"We get the picture," snapped Robin. "Richard, I really don't think we can assume she's stowed away. We have to alert the authorities."

"Go down your list, then. But I'd let it escalate if possible. Don't start off with the panic button. Don't call out the cavalry until you've no other options left. Check with some of the private numbers and offices before you start dialling 999."

"OK. It's seven thirty now. Who'll be in his office at this time?"

As the crew straggled aboard and the day darkened down, Robin went through the list of contact numbers and got precisely no-where. *If Captain Mrs Mariner was certain,* suggested the Harbour Master, *he would contact the* Aral *and seek an explanation from her captain.*

No! temporised Robin. *If the Mountie were merely in hiding, that would simply alert her enemies.*

Then what did Captain Mrs Mariner suggest they do?

Captain Mrs Mariner didn't know...

The conversation was repeated several times in varying terms and never quite so politely. Sergeant Sam McKenzie was actually profane, as well as being stubbornly unhelpful. And he, in the end, struck the most telling blow of all. "Look at it practically, for God's sake. What are we supposed to do? Call out a chopper? It wouldn't get halfway to *Aral* if the forecast's right. Even if the storm holds off, it'd have to turn back at the US border unless there's a ream of clearances signed and stamped. Call out the coastguard or the navy – not that there's much of either in Thunder Bay, not with enough in the way of ships, men and equipment to board a foreign freighter. Not that we've got anything fast enough to catch her in any case. Even if we could, do you have any idea how much money that would cost? Most of our investigations budget for next year – you can bet your life on that. And how much diplomatic trouble it would make? Going aboard a Russian ship in United States waters to get some Mountie button pusher out of an unauthorised investigation? I mean, we're supposed to be liaising, and I have seen not one piece of paper suggesting that this has anything to do with the broad you fished out of the lake. Shit, I haven't even seen her initial report and case summary notes. Nobody's going that far out on a limb without full

97

documentation, chapter and verse, believe you me! If she did go aboard the freighter like you say, then she stopped being a federal officer the minute she went up the gangplank. That's not a Mountie you've lost, it's some dumb woman off on an ego-trip of her own. Did Miss Two Feathers leave you any contact numbers in the States? FBI? The Immigration Service? They're the people you want, lady. Maybe you should just dial 911 and see how far you get when you peddle this load of bull to them!"

Driven almost to tears with rage and frustration, Robin inevitably returned to the one man that she knew she could trust to help her in this situation.

"Never!" snapped Richard. "If that's what Sergeant McKenzie said then I think he's probably right. And if a province the size of Ontario can't stump up the costs and the Royal Canadian Mounted Police cannot arrange the diplomatic clout for a rescue attempt, then Heritage Mariner certainly can't! Have you any idea of how completely we could destroy ourselves here?"

"But, Richard..."

"Look at the people we could upset here!" He began to tick them off on his fingers. "The Harbour Master and Coast Guards in Thunder Bay when we deviate from our course without permission and endanger the shipping in their area. The provincial authorities in Ontario when we come out of their port to try a little piracy on the high seas. The Canadian authorities when we begin a diplomatic incident aboard a Russian vessel. The Americans in whose waters we start approaching and hailing legitimate traffic about its legal business. The Russians, of course. And, needless to say, the Foreign and Colonial Office in London. Not to mention our insurers at Lloyd's. And, now I come to think of it, several members of our company board, including, unless I'm very badly mistaken, its chairman, your father!"

Richard and Robin were not having this rather one-sided conversation in public. They had retired to an unused cabin at an early stage in the discussion, but the general situation was known, at least on the bridge. And so it was that young First Officer Pugh was able to earn Robin's undying gratitude at that precise moment, when he stuck his head around the door and said breezily to Richard, "You know, sir, our agreed course takes up along exactly the same track as *Aral* has to follow if she's going down to Duluth. And with the relative differences in our sailing speeds, we should be up alongside her in any case, long before our shakedown run is over."

Richard looked from one of them to the other. He gave a defeated bark of laughter. "All right," he said, shaking his head. When we catch up with her I'll get on the radio and ask a few questions. If we're right up alongside anyway, then I'm sure we'll be able to think of something we can do to help."

Eleven

Richard finally got clearance to take *Swift-sure* out of Thunder Bay at 9 a.m. local time and, in spite of the worsening weather, he went after *Aral* as fast as the chief engineer would allow him. The sleek SuperCat crossed the point where the Russian freighter should have been two hours later, north of Devil's Island on the outer approaches to Duluth and Superior City, only to discover that she had disappeared into the roiling murk of the gathering storm.

Caught up with Robin in the life and death tension of the chase by then, Richard gave orders to turn and pursue the errant freighter south by east. The US coastguards gave their blessing because *Aral* had effectively vanished from their system some time earlier. They did not like the thought of a rogue vessel battering about the carefully ordered Superior seaways in the midst of a storm that might all too easily turn into a ship-killer in any case.

The Heritage Mariner vessel caught up with her battered quarry two hours later still, as the winds went off the Beaufort scale and things began to get very dangerous indeed.

"How do you know it's her?" bellowed Robin over Brian Pugh's shoulder, needing to use her quarterdeck voice because of the noise of the storm.

"Look." The first officer pointed to a set of pale figures flickering faintly on the dark green field of the radar screen. "That's her identity beacon. God it's faint, though. No wonder she dropped off the Duluth Coast Guard's monitor. Something must have damaged it."

"Where is she exactly?"

"That's Fourteen Mile Point just in behind her. A lee shore in this weather. She'll have to be careful of that and so will we. And this up here is the Keenaw Peninsula up past Hancock and Houghton to Copper Harbor. All of it dangerous coast. That's where the *John Jacob Astor* went down the better part of a hundred and

101

seventy years ago – first big ship lost on the lake. And of course we're not all that far from the wreck of the *Edmund Fitzgerald* either. Dangerous, dangerous."

"They know," said Robin more quietly, looking across at Captain Steerforth in the big hydraulic command chair with his hands rock-steady on the helm and Richard standing massively behind him.

"Can you raise him?" Richard called across to Edouard Henessy, the French Canadian radio officer.

Edouard's shrug of reply spoke volumes.

"We need to get in closer," decided Richard.

"Dangerous," grunted Captain Steerforth – even as Pugh mouthed the word to Robin. "He's drifting onto a lee shore and if he doesn't start doing something about it soon it'll be too late for him."

"We have power to spare," said Richard, "even in this lot we could blast our way free from the tide-line."

"There's worse weather just behind us, though," called Pugh, glancing across from the radar to the weather monitor. "*Swiftsure* has taken everything Superior's thrown at her so far but this may be too much. If that helm was mine, I'd be thinking about using the power we have got to get round Manitou Island into the lee of the point."

"It's a good idea," Richard called back

102

easily. "But that would mean leaving *Aral* to the mercy of the storm."

"What are we going to do for her anyway," asked Pugh, "take her in tow?"

"We'll know more when we have her in sight and in contact," said Richard. "If we've time to get in for a look, then we must."

"What are they *doing*?" Robin asked of no one in particular. "Are they all asleep? Can't they see what's going on here? Don't they understand the danger?"

"You've been aboard," said Richard, his eyes focused on the grey roiling murk beyond the clearview in front of him. "How did they strike you?"

"Shiftless and evil," she answered without hesitation. "But they seemed competent enough. They'd brought her across the Northern Ocean, hadn't they? It doesn't get much worse than that."

"It may do here today," countered Pugh with grim cheeriness. "It may do here very soon indeed."

No sooner had Brian Pugh spoken than a buffet of wind, far stronger than any so far, slammed across the pitching vessel from poop to forepeak and on ahead. The wind tore the rain and spray aside like a curtain, opening up a tunnel of vision a good few miles in length. Just as it did so, the first great column of lightning shattered down out of the sky onto the distant heights behind Fourteen Mile Point. "There she is!" shouted Richard. "I see her!"

"She's running without lights," called Pugh. "What is the madman up to?"

"No lights and no power," called Robin. "The bridge is dark. There's something badly wrong."

That realisation gave all of them pause. To the extent that they had examined the problem in any detail, most of them probably supposed her to be up to something illegal. A bit of smuggling under the cover of the storm, perhaps. It was hardly unknown. It was simple enough to manufacture a fault with the ship's identity beacon. To slip out of the ordered pattern of Superior shipping. Use the cover of foul weather to sneak down to a deserted shore, safe in the knowledge that the customs choppers and spotter planes would be safe in their hangars on a day like today. It was all so exactly what *Aral* had been doing; the sort of thing a ship like her crewed by men like hers would inevitably do. And reason enough to hold a nosy Mountie aboard until the dirty deal was done and everyone safe away.

But now the stakes had changed. The whole game, perhaps, had changed.

Richard Mariner had been bred and built for moments like these. "Edouard," he said.

104

"Still nothing?"

Edouard shook his head. *Non.*

"We have to send someone aboard," said Richard.

"We've got the equipment and the men trained to use it," said Captain Steerforth.

"We may not have the time, though," said Pugh. "Especially if we get many more gusts like that last one to push her onto the rocks."

"Let's get under her lee if we can and see how things look from there," decided Richard.

Captain Steerforth pushed the throttles forward and the SuperCat roared into more powerful motion just as the curtains of rain and spray closed again. But now that they knew where *Aral* was, they could just manage to keep an eye on her as they ran in under her swinging stern.

"Can you see whether she's making any headway?" called Richard. Robin ran across to the right bridge-wing – mercifully enclosed in three thick windows – and looked down on the starboard quarter. Under the looming overhang of the *Aral*'s poop, the great blade of her rudder plunged into the wild water. Only eyes as wise as Robin's, perhaps, would have been able to distinguish between storm wrack and propeller turbulence. But when she called back to Richard, there was no doubt in her voice. "She's making some headway, but she's not under power. Her tiller's holding pretty steady, but she hasn't really got steerage way. She's under no real control at all. We have to get aboard before she starts doing some really serious damage."

"What do you see on the radar, Mr Pugh?" demanded Richard. "Have we got room to proceed?"

"Plenty of room, Captain Mariner."

"And do we have time, Number One?" added Captain Steerforth, not to be out-done.

"If we're fast and lucky," answered the young first officer, beginning to get carried away with the dashing madness of it all. It was a bit like being with the Light Brigade at Balaclava, he thought.

"Then let's get this show on the road," said Richard Mariner.

Twelve

Richard had been out in more storms on more vessels than he could readily remember. This storm was shaping up to be one of the worst. He could feel that in every bone in his body. And there were elements here that went beyond even his almost limitless experience. All the storms he had faced had been salt-water storms, creatures of deep waters and great oceans. Even those he had fought in the North Sea, in the Western Approaches, among the island archipelagos of Indonesia, had been born somewhere further out where the great waves are made. He had never faced a Great Lakes storm before and even such a simple experience as finding the choking spindrift made of fresh water instead of salt was deeply unsettling. And in all his years of sailing on generations of his SuperCats, he had never taken one out in weather like this. He found it hard to tell whether the unpredictable, unsettling motion of the deck beneath his staggering feet was to do with the strange, sharp waves or the twin-hull configuration of the vessel they were causing to pitch and yaw so wildly.

Richard looked around the little well of the after-deck as Captain Steerforth brought *Swiftsure*'s square stern round towards the steel overhang of *Aral*'s lee side. The waters between the vessels seethed like a witch's cauldron and the wind boomed hollowly against the Russian's echoing steel plates. Spray exploded over the freighter and streamed downwind above their heads. A team of crewmen were expertly at work setting up the equipment Richard would need to get aboard the freighter. Pugh was nominally in charge of them but it was Robin who was actually overseeing their work, not that she really needed to. Still, thought Richard grimly, it would give her something to do before the pair of them went up the filthy, streaming side and onto the deserted ship. Something other than worrying about what had happened to Jeanne La Motte. Other than worrying about what they might find when they started to search the derelict Russian in earnest.

No one had made the formal announcement that *Aral* was an abandoned hulk yet, but they were all quietly convinced. There was no light, no movement aboard her. There was no answer to their hails – by voice or radio. And had there been life of any kind aboard, then someone would have been hanging over the side now, asking them just what in God's name they thought they were playing at.

The first line went up and caught on the empty deck rail above. They weren't planning anything high-tech or even particularly advanced – a rope ladder swung up and secured to the safety rail where the line clung now. A quick scramble and a leg over. Had the water been calm, Richard would have been able to jump for it. He settled the equipment belt he was wearing more comfortably. The impedimenta hanging from it was the usual stuff he would need to pursue a basic search and report what he had found – torches, tools and a radio. Robin had a similar belt around her waist, making the bright yellow wet-weather gear she was wearing bag and wrinkle, sending streams of water cascading out at odd angles as though she was some kind of ultra-modern fountain. Scattering spray in a gleaming shower, she swung round and bellowed, "Ready?"

"Go for it!" shouted Richard, moving forward to her side. The rope ladder stretched upwards, its sides of unbreakable woven Kevlar and its rungs of steel, rubberised and non-slip. Richard waved to Pugh who bellowed, "They're going up now, Captain," into his radio. The two ships leaned closer together, as though trying to help the exercise along. The ladder sagged. Richard stepped up and scrambled swiftly higher. Robin came after him immediately. They both knew that there would be a counter-swing at any instant, which would throw the vessels apart and set the ladder twisting, like an electrified eel.

The wind punched Richard in the face the instant he put his head above deck-level. A wave of spray foamed into his eyes and mouth, tasting of oil and iron. The hood of his wet suit filled like a storm-sail, jerked his head back like a kick in the teeth and burst like a child's balloon. He had to hurl himself upwards and forwards, feeling as if every muscle in his long lean body was tearing loose from its tendons, to get over and onto the deck. He fell heavily but used the accident to his advantage, rolling back to give Robin a hand as the storm attacked her with equal ferocity.

Side by side, bent double and staggering across the wind like octogenarian drunkards, they fought their way up the deck. The raised edges of the tightly battened hatches tried to make them trip; the heaving of the running deck between them tried to make them slip. The whole ship, seemingly outraged by their intrusion, suddenly sought to throw them off and protect its guilty secrets. Shoulder to shoulder, they slammed against the side of the wheelhouse immediately outside the main 'A' deck door. Above them, the bridge wings stood out from the bridgehouse wall for a couple of yards, giving them some temporary shelter from the pouring rain. But no sooner had they caught their breath than the wind, funnelled under the overhang, whipped past with renewed fury. A lifeboat suspended immediately above them smashed against the steel plates with such force that splinters showered down on them like sharp wooden hail.

Richard tore the big bulkhead door open and Robin leaped over the raised section at its foot. The little wall was designed to keep the foaming river on the weather deck out of the bridgehouse itself – and it was failing. Richard leaped in behind her and slammed the door. They stood, gasping, side by side, listening to the storm clubbing the walls around them like an army of giants.

"I'll report that there's still no sign of life," said Robin after a moment. "Steerforth will have to alert the coastguard at once."

"They'll want us to try and do something if we can. We can't just leave her drifting around Superior like this."

"She'll go down onto the shore in time. She'll beach or break up. That'll sort thing's out from a safety point of view."

"Unless she's headed for anywhere inhabited."

"I hadn't thought of that."

Robin put the radio to her lips and hit the call button. While she reported in, a few terse words, Richard prowled impatiently along the corridor and back, past the silent lift and the foot of the shadowy companion-ways leading up to the navigation bridge and down to engineering. He lifted his torch and flashed it around.

As soon as Robin had finished, he said, "Let's check on the bridge. That'll give us some idea of the full situation."

As ever, he suited word with action and turned to climb the nearest companionway but Robin took his arm. "This is so strange, though," she said, her voice dropping. "It's like the *Mary Celeste*. What on earth is going on?"

"That's what we're here to find out," said Richard. "No sense wasting time on specu-lation when we can go and take a look."

"She's a bad ship, Richard."

"That's not like you, Robin."

"I know it isn't. That's why I'm so nervous. Part of the reason, anyway."

"Don't worry. We'll be careful."

The bridge was deserted; the captain's chair vacant, the helm unmanned and the engine-room telegraph set to ALL STOP – or the Russian equivalent. The clearviews were switched off, and without the unvarying movement of the wipers and the spinning disc it was difficult to see the deck and impossible to see the forecastle. What lay beyond the bow was anybody's guess, particularly as all the navigation equipment stood dark and dead. Richard strode across to the ship's hailing system. "Your Russian's not too bad," he said, resting a dripping finger on the button. "Think you can manage *Would anyone aboard please report to the bridge at once?*"

Robin did her best with the order in Russian and, although it echoed eerily throughout all the corridors and companionways, it elicited no reply at all. Almost immediately after she had stopped speaking, however, there was a squawking sound loud enough to make her jump. "It's only the radio," said Richard with a laugh.

They went through into the radio room and here they discovered that the radio had been left on an open channel. Like the loudhailer, it was running on emergency power, for the ship's alternators seemed to be on idle, like her motor. Richard flicked to SEND. "*Aral* here, over," he said.

"*Swiftsure*. Edouard. The coastguard is very worried, Captain. They think you are going to drift down onto Ontonagon. *Aral* would smash up the port there pretty badly. The harbour is full of shipping sheltering from the storm but there's nothing there big enough to tow *Aral* out of the danger zone. Nothing that big closer than Duluth by the sound of things, over."

"Do we have an ETA at Ontonagon? Over."

"An hour at the most. Over."

"Does Captain Steerforth think *Swiftsure* could turn her head enough to get her past Ontonagon? Over."

There was a moment of muffled conversation.

"Not in this," replied Edouard a moment later. "And anyway, if we could she'd just drift on down onto Chequamegon Bay or the Apostle Islands."

"Right," said Richard decisively. "Then we'll have to try the opposite tack. Send over the Chief Engineer and Mr Pugh. We'll see if we can get the *Aral* under way again and, if we can, we'll borrow all but an emergency watch to crew and con this old tub – and then we'll tow *Swiftsure* down to Duluth."

Thirteen

Robin acted as First Officer to Richard's Captain while they were getting the storm-bound freighter under way. Not that either of them took things easy. They both went back out onto the deck and helped get the men from *Swiftsure* safely aboard. The first team, as Richard had requested, consisted of the Chief and Brian Pugh – for these would be the best men to tell them whether the freighter could be powered and conned.

Robin took Chief Hardy down to the engine room while Richard and Brian pounded up to the navigation bridge. As soon as the pair of them got to the engine-control room, Hardy started to poke around with the knowledgeable authority of a man who has seen and done it all, so that not even a Russian propulsion system, labelled in Cyrillic, held any secrets for him. "Silly buggers just switched everything off and went off," he said. "Just switched it off as though it was a car they'd parked." He looked along the torchbeam at Robin, eyes narrow in the glare, clearly lost in thought.

"Swing that thing over there, would you, Captain? That's right, ah, now..."

The pool of light illuminated a switch. Hardy crossed to it and threw it. The whole room lit up. "OK," he said. "It looks as though we're in business. Tell Richard that all I really have to do is hit the starter here. In a manner of speaking, of course..."

Robin had no sooner brought the message up to the navigation bridge than the lights came on and the throbbing of the alternators began to pound through the decks.

"It's alive! It's alive!" sang out Pugh in a passable impersonation of Dr Frankenstein as the radar screen lit up. But no sooner had his words finished echoing across the bridge than all the automatic alarms began to sound. The ship had awoken to find herself in dangerously shallow water, dangerously close to shore with dangerously powerful weather spinning towards her dangerously quickly, and she wanted to tell someone about it all.

"Now that the 'A' Team's in place and at work, we need the 'B' Team over pretty quickly," called Richard.

"I'll call over to *Swiftsure* and warn them," answered Robin.

"Good. I'll go down and help them aboard," decided Richard. He paused in the doorway, dripping. "At least I can't get any wetter," he laughed.

116

"Oh yes you can," countered Robin grimly. "You can fall overboard. Be careful, for Heaven's sake."

Within half an hour, *Aral*'s motor was back in action and her propeller was beginning to give her steerage way. As though giving in gracefully, the storm, which had spent the last few hours trying to drive her onto the southern shore, swung round towards the south itself. Although it continued to intensify and the winds gusted past hurricane force, at least it was now blowing the labouring freighter out into the safer depths of the central lake. And, coming off such a close shore, it brought no great waves with it.

Swiftsure would have been in trouble, though. She was simply not designed to handle conditions like these and under normal circumstances would have used her 60-knot cruising capability to run for safe haven long ago. Even the short run to Ontonagon harbour was forbidden to her by the fearsome weather, however and in any case, her crew was needed to man the good ship *Aral.* As Richard had suggested, therefore, the crew's first act after getting steerage way was to go onto the poop and set up a towline to the SuperCat.

Into the afternoon they plunged together, therefore, punching through a cross-sea chopped into the consistency of a huge grey file by the change in wind direction. The freighter pitching and bucking, throwing up spray off her forecastle like a destroyer at flank speed, the SuperCat dancing clumsily behind, testing her towrope and the anchor points which held it with every ungainly lurch and corkscrew. Richard stood at the helm, feeling *Aral* being pushed one way by the water, punched another by the wind and jerked back on herself every now and then by the antics of *Swiftsure* in her wake. He stood, lost in some of the most difficult calculations in his long years of command. Would more power settle *Aral* more securely in the raging element beneath her – or would it push *Swiftsure* further out of control and tear the poop deck off? Would less power settle the SuperCat – or would it lose the battered freighter vital steerage way and set her helplessly adrift again?

"Any shipping nearby, Brian?"

"There's an ore freighter, *Benjamin Franklin*, five miles north of us. Inbound to Duluth. She's the nearest one of a series all on the same line. We're drifting up towards them, but I'll sing out if we get too close."

"Weather?"

Brian glanced up at Robin, who was standing beside him, watching the same screens as he was watching, then continued, hardly missing a beat, "Likely to moderate.

118

This equipment's nowhere near as good as my stuff on *Swiftsure*, but I see no reason to doubt it."

"Edouard can check with the coastguards anyway," said Robin, walking away from the Navigating Officer's station.

"Sparks?" called Richard, glancing back through the radio-room door.

"Duluth coastguard says it will moderate during the next two hours," Edouard answered. "The wind will swing east of south and continue to gust at storm ten, but it'll have died back to an easterly gale before midnight."

"That should push us into Duluth harbour nicely."

"If it doesn't blow *Swiftsure* up our poop," said Brian Pugh.

The comradely, masculine laughter covered Robin's nearly silent footfalls as she tiptoed off the bridge.

It seemed to Robin that she was the only one who had a clear view of the big picture. They had come after *Aral* because Jeanne had come aboard and vanished. Jeanne had come aboard hoping to rescue a woman trapped here. They had found out about the woman as part of an investigation into the serial murder of two women – two so far – found in the Great Lakes with a red star carved on them. And they had come aboard the Russian vessel because the first of the victims – the first at least – was Russian. And it seemed logical to assume that a dead Russian woman found floating in the St Lawrence must have come off a Russian ship. So far the chain of logic was complete, each link whole and secure. But what they had was the beginning of the chain, not the end. They needed to know why the women had died. They needed to know who was killing them. But circumstances were adding to the normal imponderables of any investigation and changing the nature of the problem. The most important circumstances of all at the moment were that the investigating officer had come aboard this ship and vanished. And then everyone aboard the ship had vanished into the bargain. How could such things be linked to the death of the poor woman Robin had helped to pull aboard the Iroquois canoe three and a half days ago? The search for answers had begun here and had stopped here. Here, therefore, was the best place for it to begin again.

Robin stood at the end of the corridor where she had met Michael Sholokov, the crewman in the white vest, and heard the woman crying. All she could hear now was the distant Armageddon of wind and water trying to tear the ship apart and, every time she corkscrewed, a range of rattles, creaks and groans. Unlike the last time she had stood here, now she had time to think, the opportunity to take her time and examine her surroundings with care and at some length.

The corridors were in the foundations of the bridgehouse, far below the weather deck. Behind her, beyond the lift shaft and shadowy stairwells of the companionways, were the engineering sections. Before her, therefore, away beyond the forward reaches of the crew's quarters there lay the coffer dam which separated the living areas from the holds. Sholokov's cabin was the furthest forward of these. Beyond it should only be the double thickness of steel plate and then the great chambers full of grain or steel, destined for Duluth. But, thought Robin, standing stock-still in the heaving, rocking rollercoaster of the ship's corridor, held in the grip of revelation, the crying seemed to be coming from forward of Sholokov's cabin. Forward and, somehow, below.

Robin turned and went back to the companionway. This was, she knew, as far down as the lift went – apart from the space below for the workings, of course. The stairway went down, though. She followed it – only to draw a blank. The stair went down six steps – to a corridor running back into engineering. Lost in her brown study, she climbed back up to the end of the corridor

121

and then went forwards with no further hesitation. She carried on past Sholokov's cabin door a further ten steps before she came to the wall which ended the corridor. She put her hand against it and felt it vibrating with the rest of the hull, resonating to the pounding of the alternators, the thrusting of the motor and the spinning of the screw, the thumping of the wind and water on the superstructure. "Damn you!" she shouted, suddenly. "This isn't right!" and she punched the metal wall with simple frustration. Then, sucking the blood off her skinned knuckles, she went back to the lift to think things through again.

The lift opened into a short corridor running from one side of the crew deck to the other. At the end of this, on her right, Sholokov's corridor led forward to the cofferdam wall. On the left, clearly, Big Vasily's corridor. Same length. Same wall.

In between, there was a painted metal wall where the backs of the cabins on her right met the backs of the cabins on her left. On that wall there was the only decoration she had seen aboard so far. It was a framed picture of the St Petersburg docks, covered in indestructible plastic and secured in a hefty frame. No one was likely to steal it, thought Robin wryly. It must measure six feet by three. And it wasn't all that exciting to look at. Seen one dock. Seen them all.

She turned her attention back to her problem. Behind that wall, the backs of the cabins met. She visualised the line of partitions reaching in front of her from here to the cofferdam. Standard ship design, she thought. Simple and cheap. Boxes backing on to boxes. Except that the first room in each side was the latrine. In order to assure herself of the layout, she crossed to Sholokov's corridor again. Yes. Cabins lay on the outer side of the passage – the first two she had looked in. The latrine was the first room on the inner side. She looked into it again. Then, struck by something almost subliminal, she paused. "That isn't right," she said aloud to the stinking stalls. The latrine was a good deal smaller than Sholokov's cabin, five doors further down the passage. She went to the next door along – another one with writing on it but one she had not opened on her last visit. This proved to be a shower room. It was no bigger than the latrine. But the next door revealed a cabin the same size as Sholokov's cabin down at the end of the row.

With her face folded into a thoughtful frown, Robin checked Vasily's corridor. It was the same story there. The latrine on this side was cleaner so she took the opportunity to pace it out, just to be sure. And she was right. The latrine and the cabin accommodated the same number of paces exactly.

But the last pace brought her to the latrine's back wall. In the cabin it brought her to the side of the lower bunk. Pipe work, she thought. Both the latrines and the showers needed water pipes leading in and soil pipes leading out. But then again ... Back to the lift she went and stood, staring forward. This time she was not imagining a neat line of partitions but a cleverly designed space, roughly twice the depth of a bunk. Maybe four feet wide. Three feet of space and a foot for the pipework.

It struck Robin then just how much the picture of the St Petersburg docks looked like a door. Without any further thought at all, she strode forward and ran her fingers down the sides. There was a *click!* that she felt rather than heard, and the left side of the frame sprang clear of the wall. In something akin to a trance, she pulled it and it swung open. She had been right. It was a door.

Fourteen

Robin burst onto the navigation bridge breathless and bursting with news. "Richard. You have to see this."

One glance at her was enough for Richard. Whenever Robin looked this excited there was something important going on. The last time she had worn that almost desperate look, he had been on the bridge of the battered old destroyer *Colorado*, the better part of twenty miles up the estuary of the river for which the ship had been named. And Robin had come to tell him there was a massive wall of water sweeping down the river course towards them.

When Robin's face burned with that particular excitement, Richard always responded at once. And he turned to do so now. The storm was beginning to moderate at last, the wind swinging east of south as predicted. The ore freighters close to the north of them were accommodatingly making a space in their pattern so that *Aral* could tow *Swiftsure* into safe haven with a minimum of fuss and delay. "Of course," he said. "I'll come at once. Mr Pugh, you have her."

As they crossed to the lift and rode it down, Robin ran over the logical steps in her thinking. Richard listened silently, secretly marvelling at his wife's single-mindedness. As the lift arrived on the lower crew deck and they stepped out into the lateral corridor, Robin asked him, "Can you see it?"

"See what?"

"The door."

"No, I can't."

"I closed it again after me. But after what I've been saying it should be obvious. Look!" She ran over to the picture of St Petersburg and pulled its frame.

"I'll be damned." He strode to her side, and shoulder to shoulder they stood looking into the darkness behind the secret door-way.

"Have you been down here?"

"No. I came straight up to get you."

"A wise move, I think. Have you got your torch?"

Richard had discarded his tool belt with his waterproof jacket. Robin still had both on her. A moment later, the beam of her torch pierced the Stygian blackness to shine on a pipe-twined slope of ceiling. As she moved the beam slowly downwards to reveal a steep set of metal stairs, so the

126

stench of the place rose up to their twitching nostrils. It was a combination of latrine, sweat and, more faintly, cheap perfume. It was without doubt a feminine aroma.

Side by side they stepped down into the black lake of darkness and odour, feeling it close over their heads with a kind of weird physicality as they proceeded. At the bottom of the steps they came to a strange area, almost like a landing. Darkness stretched away in front of them and fell away to either side. The smell was stronger than ever, sitting on the stillness of the dead air. The sound that echoed out of the impenetrable shadows was the sound of great waters rushing over distant steel. It was a strange, unsettling sound, which drowned out even the reassuring rumble of the engines.

The unnerving, almost undersea expanse of the place seemed to gulp down the puny torch-beam, so Robin shone it on the nearest walls until she found a switch. "I hope this is a light switch," she said into the echoing dark, her voice thin and frail under the watery rumble. She threw it and then she and Richard stood silently as her simple action revealed what they had found.

They were on a raised platform that stood between the foot of one set of steps and the head of another. Level with their eyes, bank after bank of dim lights came on, illuminating a space almost the same size as the laden holds above. But this was no hold. It was, if anything, a dormitory. Down each side and in a double row in the middle stretched four rows of narrow wooden pallets. Strewn around them lay a mess of rubbish interspersed with one or two bright pieces of clothing.

"One hundred," said Robin tersely, her voice dull with shock.

"What?"

"Jeanne came aboard looking for one lost girl. It looks like she found one hundred."

"How do you..." he began – and then he realised. She had counted the pallets on the filthy deck.

Without further ado, she started down the stairs into the body of the place. "Is that wise?" called Richard. "You'll almost certainly be disturbing a crime scene."

"I'll be careful," she said. "But I simply have to check to see if there's any sign of Jeanne."

Richard hesitated for a moment, his mind racing. Then he called, "Fair enough." And ran down the steps to help her.

The dormitory was only the centre of the area. Off the big room there were others. The first they entered were basic latrines that looked and smelt as though they drained straight into the ship's bilge. There were extremely basic washing facilities –

little more than cold-water hoses and open metal grilles draining in the same direction as the latrines. There were two larger rooms, much better lit, with a range of equipment in them. "Video studios," said Richard, his voice betraying shock and amazement. Behind the studios there were basic prop stores and even a little make-up room.

"Everything you need for video and still photography," said Richard.

"I wonder what sort," said Robin in that dry ironic tone with which she masked her deepest outrage.

"I think we'll have to use our imagination," said Richard. "There's nothing here in the way of tapes or photos."

"I'd rather not imagine anything of the sort, thank you."

Back out in the main area, they began to examine things a little more closely. The rubbish on the floor was the detritus of long occupation suddenly terminated. It was a litter of magazines read until they fell apart – or the remains of newspapers torn into pieces for various uses. They were all printed in Russian.

The brighter pieces scattered around were more personal – scarves, tights, items of clothing which had mostly been damaged in some way. Or, like the newspapers, used as napkins, towels, and even sanitary pads. There were shoes with broken heels and snapped straps. It was all, obviously, useless now. It had been left by women given very little time to get ready to disembark – just a moment or two for basic decisions about what could still be of some use to them and what could not. He felt a stab of ready sympathy for them. Even their obvious foreignness added to the poignancy. Wherever they were now, they would be out of their depth and helpless in the great big English-speaking world out there.

"This stuff is all as foreign as the magazines," said Richard. "You can talk about the global marketplace all you want but none of this could have been made west of the Ural Mountains!"

"These could," said Robin, straightening suddenly. She was right at the end of the last pallet, furthest into the foul place. It was one of a pair, which, for disturbingly obvious reasons, was equipped with a wrist cuff on a short chain welded to the metal wall. "Whatever it is, don't touch it," called Richard.

"I don't need to," said Robin who was crouching unsteadily, using the brightness of her torchbeam to ameliorate the gloom. "God, she's a girl scout at heart."

Richard crossed to Robin's side as swiftly as he could, more than a little disturbed by the strange unsteadiness of her voice. Was she elated or depressed? Or both at once?

130

Had she found good news or bad? Was her Mountie investigator alive or dead after all?

There on the floor beside the shackle and the pallet's thin mattress lay a pool of silken material. The label on it said *St Laurent*. On this was written a laundry number. And under that in tiny letters with indelible ink, *J. L-M*.

"She has her name on her stuff like a kid at boarding school," said Robin wonderingly. "Even on her underwear."

And then Richard realised with a shock of revelation just what he was looking at. The tiny silken pool on the shadowy, stinking deck was Jeanne La Motte's panties.

Fifteen

Richard and Robin brought *Aral* into Duluth just before midnight. They brought her into the safe haven of Superior Bay through the Superior Channel to the south, as planned, hidden in among the ore carriers. There was no long wait – they were expected.

Aral picked up a harbour pilot immediately on entry and swung up past the ore docks to sail slowly into her berth in the Duluth International seaport as though nothing at all was wrong. But in fact, just as Richard, Robin and the pilot eased the battered freighter out of Wisconsin waters and into Minnesota jurisdiction, with Minnesota Point itself close on the starboard side, a couple of coastguard vessels pulled alongside and suddenly they were up to their eyeballs in FBI officers.

The long spit of Minnesota Point protected Superior Bay from the easterly gale still battering the lake itself. The water within the harbour was calm and quiet. With Robin beside the pilot at the helm and Richard overseeing things at the side, Special Agent Abraham Sharon and his FBI SWAT team had no real difficulty in coming aboard. The minute the wiry little agent stepped onto the deck, he was at work. He introduced himself to Richard and, in consultation with the vessel's acting captain, he directed the men and women of his teams to the major places aboard where they needed to begin their work.

Then, with the dry wind gusting noisily past them to rattle the windows on the buildings up on the high slopes of the shore, the two men went straight to work themselves. Because they were on the deck, and because it was not likely to stay dry for long, they ran down to the forecastle head and started there.

"It seems quite clear what happened," Richard shouted over the thudding of the wind. "If you look over the edge here, you can see that the anchors are both half down. They're just at the water's surface, see? I've pulled them up to that level. When we came aboard they were almost fully down. I didn't notice until we started fighting to get back up through the westerly storm into the line of ore freighters and discovered how oddly she was riding. I had to pull them up, of course. We couldn't risk proceeding with them down like that. God knows what we might have hooked into. I hope I haven't damaged your investigation at all. The safety of the ship has to come first, I'm afraid.

"But the point I'm making is that the Russian crew must have anchored somewhere not far from where we found her. Most of them must have gone ashore, obviously with the women from the hidden deck – including our missing Mountie – leaving a small watch aboard. Then the storm hit really badly and she began to pull her anchor. The storm was coming out of the west then, although it's swung round since. I think it probably pushed a large enough storm surge ahead of it to raise the water level by several feet. There aren't any tides in the lake so that could well have caught them out. They suddenly must have found there

133

was too much water under them to re-anchor. And there was a worsening storm behind them, threatening to make them drift down onto a lee shore. So the watch must have panicked. They must have just switched everything off, piled into a lifeboat – there's one missing – and gone ashore. Abandoned her altogether."

"How stupid is that?" said Abe Sharon.

Because Abe phrased his observation as a question and ended it on a rising intonation, Richard answered. "It was very stupid indeed."

Abe grunted – the closest he usually came to laughter. "Damn right," he said. "Looks like it was lucky for us, though. That's quite an operation they let slip away into the lake. You want to show me this secret room you reported to the Coast Guard when you called all this in?"

The two men hurried back up the deck as the wind suddenly intensified and the next rain squall washed in over Minnesota Point. Even so, Abe paused under the deluge to look up at the vacant davits outside the 'A' deck door. "That the missing lifeboat?" he asked Richard.

"Yes. Its opposite number's mostly in splinters. Smashed to pieces in the gale."

As he spoke, Richard heaved the door open and the pair of them stepped into the 'A' deck corridor where it was warm, quiet and, above all, dry.

"Maybe they were wise to cut and run," observed the special agent. "Sounds like things got pretty hairy out there."

Richard punched the lift button and the doors hissed open. "No," he answered as the pair of them stepped in. "It was an unprofessional thing to do."

"Maybe these guys aren't really professional sailors. Maybe they don't think of themselves as sailors at all."

The pair of them were rattling downwards as they enjoyed this brief conversation. The doors slid open once again and they stepped out before Richard could answer.

The secret door stood wide open and the stairwell beyond it was a blaze of light. Men and women wearing black flak jackets with FBI stencilled in bright yellow upon them, which seemed to double as identification jackets and bullet-proof vests, were coming and going busily. They fell back respectfully as the energetic bantam of Abe Sharon walked past them with Richard massively in tow. On the half landing they paused, watching the scene of crime teams busily at work. "What do you mean?" asked Richard then. "How could they not think of themselves as sailors? What else?"

"As mobsters," answered Abe, his brown eyes busy as he surveyed the scene. "As wise guys. Goodfellas. Whatever they call the

135

Mafia in Petersburg these days. As Snakes-heads. If they'd been from Guandong where their rice cargo came from, instead of Russia, they'd definitely have thought of themselves as Snakesheads."

"And as pornographers," cut in a tall, lean, coffee-skinned woman, easily. She started speaking at the bottom of the steps but by the time she finished she was right up beside them. Her voice was full of that lazy, respectful familiarity that Richard liked to inculcate in his senior associates. "I mean, you worked out what they were taking pictures of in those rooms in back? Those little studio rooms with all the sex toys and bondage gear?"

"You're right, Beth," answered Abe, then he swung back to Richard. "But mostly as pimps. They know where the girls are going to end up. What they're going to end up doing. So these are the guys who'll get them ready in transit. No matter what it takes; no matter how much it hurts. Sailors." He gave a dry bark of cynical laughter. "That's a job description that probably ranks pretty low on their CVs. Know what I mean?"

Richard drew breath to reply only to be interrupted by his personal radio. "Yes?"

"It's Edouard. They're on again. You want me to do anything different this time? Now that we have guests?"

Every hour since they arrived aboard, the

136

radio room had received a message. Richard had spent some of the few moments he had had to spare poring over the printouts but neither he nor Robin could make any sense of them. They were Russian and looked to be in some sort of code.

"Have you got an FBI officer with you now?"

"Yup."

"What do they think?"

The connection went dead for an instant then Edouard came back on. "They can't make out anything more than you and Captain Robin. Just the call sign of the sender."

Richard turned to Abe, with Beth hovering just behind him. "That's *Caspian* calling again."

"She's in the berth beside the one booked for you guys. The harbour master says it's rare to have two Russian company vessels like this in at once. *Caspian* must be waiting for some kind of reply before she leaves."

"We'd be better to keep on with the current game plan, then, and maintain radio silence. Not that we'd know what to reply in any case," said Richard.

"That's right," said Abe quietly. "We don't want to scare them off at this stage. They've guards out all along the dockside, apparently. They're too jumpy for us to go aboard from the land side."

"But as she's a sister ship to this one, you

will want to go aboard. As a matter of some urgency."

Abe Sharon looked down at the pathetic remains of the last few months in the lives of one hundred Russian women, and the agents gently sifting through them. "You bet your life I do," he said. He turned to his right-hand man. "Beth, call a briefing, then we'll break open the armoury."

"You know, it just occurred to me," said Robin a few minutes later on the bridge as the pilot brought them in to *Aral*'s berth under the suspicious eyes of her sister ship's crew.

"What?" asked Richard, preoccupied. His eyes were on Abe and his immediate command who were hidden in the chart room while the rest of the FBI people were well concealed below decks. His mind was hoping fervently that none of the bridge party was recognisable from *Caspian* – especially as someone over there was using binoculars, and the FBI people had used the interim to plan an assault on *Aral*'s sister and to get tooled up with an amazing array of warlike hardware.

"They had a spare bunk below for Jeanne to use."

"The one beside hers looked empty too. But so what?" They were easing into the freighter's berth now. Someone would have to go onto the deck soon. Then communication could no longer be avoided and the cat would be out of the bag. Abe was planning to surprise *Caspian*'s people by going aboard mob-handed. If there were captive women aboard he wanted to avoid a messy hostage situation. If there were arms aboard he likewise wished to avoid a gory firefight. Though, to be fair, with his Kevlar jackets, the state-of-the-art hands-free two-way radios, the big S&W automatics with their red-dot sights and the lethal-looking assault rifles, shotguns, stun grenades, smoke-bombs and rams, he was ready to go to war if need be. Complete surprise was the only way of minimising the risks, however.

"So," said Robin. "They won't have sailed with a couple of empty places just in case. This seems to have been too well planned for that."

"That's right, but..." Any moment now. Richard felt a knot of tension in his gut. There was sweat on his top lip. For once in their lives neither he nor Robin were going over with the first wave. They would wait until the ship was secure and then, maybe, get invited. The knowledge didn't ease the tension inside his lean, hard body, though. Should he give the word or let Abe judge it for himself? There had been just time for a quick planning meeting and the shortest briefing session Richard had ever attended.

There had been no time for a line-management conference. They didn't even have a pecking order here, beyond the borders of Abe's tight command.

"If they had two bunks spare, then they were two girls down. Maybe the girl we found at the start of all this was one of them."

"That would tie it all together neatly enough," said Richard's lips. His mind, however, was saying *Go, Abe! Go now!*

Sixteen

"Go! Go! Go!" said Abe Sharon into the mike of his hands-free radio.

At his signal, Richard, who held the con, swung *Aral* over and allowed the sides of the two ships to bump gently together. *Caspian* had fenders out while *Aral* did not. The one set was enough to stop any serious damage to the hulls, so delicate was Richard's manoeuvre. *Aral*'s hull hardly shook, and only the man with the binoculars and a couple of deckhands on *Caspian* would have realised there was any impact at all. This was an important part of the plan, for

140

nothing could have spelt disaster more surely than to have had all the FBI agents tumbling like ninepins across *Aral*'s deck. Instead, they were able to boil out of the 'A' deck corridor and run straight across into the concealed area under the bridge wings of the two ships, leaping from one to the other with ease. As the two bridges came level, Abe abandoned all pretence. With his team at his heels he went running out through the walled section, tearing open the outer door, sprinting across the open area and leaping like a pirate from one wing to the other, three decks up. His team followed him with no hesitation at all. And their timing was immaculate, for, having bounced off *Caspian*'s fenders, *Aral* ran into the end of the dock with enough force to send the few people left on her deck staggering. The sound of the impact rang through the otherwise silent dockyard with almost enough power to drown out the first gunshots from *Caspian*.

The radio burst into life immediately. "Full reverse down here," sang out Captain Steerforth from *Swiftsure* close behind. "Can I cut and run down to my own berth now as we planned?"

Richard, winded, pulled himself up off the helm and gave a 'thumbs up' sign to Edouard who passed back, "Affirmative, Captain. Just wait for the harbour pilot.

141

You'll need him aboard even though you're only going into the next berth down the line on the far side of *Caspian*. He'll be down to you as soon as he's picked himself up. *Les Capitaines* Mariner and the rest of us will join you at *Swiftsure*'s berth in due course, I'm sure. But take care as you cross *Caspian*'s stern. They're still at war up there."

Robin didn't attempt to rise. She just swung round until she was seated comfortably on the deck, looking up at her husband. There was a wide smile on her face and a glint in her eyes. "Now," she said, "that's what I call ship-handling!"

The pilot, who was halfway out of the bridge door, turned at her words. His long, bony face split into a brief grin. "I'm with the lady," he said. "That was an impressive manoeuvre. Welcome to Duluth, Captain. I would normally advise you to wait for Customs and Immigration now, but I guess you've other fish to fry."

"And other Federal folks to fry it with," said Richard, his wind and his wit beginning to return.

A prolonged burst of automatic gunfire echoed across the berths.

"I'd go down the port side of the bridge-house if I were you," said Richard more soberly. "Keep the bulk of this ship between you and *Caspian* at all times."

"That's good advice. I'll be pleased to take

142

it. And I'd clear the bridge if I were you. You can tie up later too. Go somewhere with steel walls and wait to hear from Agent Sharon."

Richard and Robin collected their skeleton crew together and they all went down to what looked like the officers' dining area. The Mariners went through into the galley while *Swiftsure*'s people sat, exhausted, talking and smoking. Richard poked around in the lean supplies of borscht and sauerkraut in search of food for all of them. "No beef Stroganoff on this tub," he moaned. "God, don't they have anything not made with cabbage or beetroot? Look! I've found a tin with a sell-by date. Use before June 1995. Great. I bet they haven't even got goulash."

"This looks like pickled herring," said Robin from the fridge. "It's seen better days, though. Ugh! Fish soup."

"Caviar?"

"Potatoes, cabbages. Eggs. Onions. All very old by the looks of things."

"Cheese?"

"You're in luck! God, I hope this is cheese. If anything else smelt like that it would have gone over the side ages ago."

"Suddenly I'm not so hungry. Any coffee? They must have coffee aboard."

"Isn't that a samovar behind you? That

means there must be tea somewhere."

"I'll check in the cupboard nearest to it ... Eureka. We have tea. Now, who else wants some?"

"There'll be no milk, I'm afraid. It may have been the milk I confused with cheese. There should be sugar, though."

"I can live with that. Go through and see what the others want, will you, darling?"

"Yes, O my lord and master, Captain of my heart..."

But before she could obey his order, the radio buzzed into life and Abe Sharon was calling them over to him at once.

"You can all wait here if you would," said Richard to the others as Robin prepared to accompany him over the side. "Edouard, there's tea if you want to heat some water. I'll see if there's coffee when I get aboard *Caspian*."

But when they got aboard *Caspian,* coffee became the last thing on Richard's mind. As soon as he was shown into the Russian vessel's bridgehouse, he became aware of how fierce the firefight must have been. There was blast damage, particularly in the stairwells. There were bullet-holes, bullet scars and the signs of ricochets on the metal walls. The tatty lino was further dilapidated with burn marks and black-ringed holes where the hot bullets had fallen. Broken

144

glass crunched under foot and whole corridors stretched away in darkness. And as they got nearer the navigation bridge itself, there began to be smears of blood.

It was a great relief to both of them to be greeted by Abe with the words, "At least nobody's dead."

"That's good," said Richard with relief. "What can we do?"

"We're both trained first-aiders," added Robin. "My certificate's up to Accident and Emergency level. So is Richard's."

Abe gave a bark of laughter. "You guys are something," he said. "No. I need advice, not nursing. What complement would a vessel this size have?"

"*Aral* had thirty," said Richard. "I couldn't make head or tail of the ship's records, but it was clear how many names were on the various duty rosters. So, unless there were a lot of crewmen with identical names, there were thirty of them all told."

"This will be the same," said Robin. "Thirty's a bit high for a ship this size. Or it is until you begin to take account of the extra cargo of women down in the secret hold."

"That leads me onto my second request. We've been down. We've been around the lower decks. And we looked pretty closely — especially as we're missing some suspects. We're maybe as many as ten crewmen short

145

of the total. We certainly are if you're right about numbers. These ten guys have to be hiding aboard. We reckon they're in the secret hold, with or without female company, if you follow my drift. But the picture of Petersburg is a picture of Petersburg. We can't find the secret door."

Given added impetus by the thought of ten desperate men hiding among a cargo of terrified women, Robin went down to the lower deck as soon as Abe had issued her with protective clothing. Richard went with her, of course, squeezed uncomfortably into a bullet-proof jacket which was far too small for him. Abe accompanied the pair of them, with a squad of heavily armed men.

As soon as they stepped out of the lift Robin was struck by the different layout of this sister. The lift shaft still came down between two companionways, which stepped down on either side of it, so that there were stairs up and down out of the lateral crew-deck corridor. But the corridor itself was much wider. Two corridors ran off it still, reaching forward to the cofferdam wall, but these were far shorter; there were fewer doors in each and none with any writing. "Where are the washrooms?" she asked, speaking to herself as her mind raced, but one of the FBI guards answered unexpectedly, "At the foot of the stairs back there."

Robin turned, and, with them all in tow like a teacher with a school group, she went down the stairs beside the lift shaft. In *Aral*, these steps led to corridors reaching back towards the engineering sections. In *Caspian*, they led to a lower lateral corridor almost as spacious as the one just up the stairs. On the rear wall, facing aft, between the crew area and the engineers' domain, there were the four doors in a neat row. Two into latrines and two into shower rooms. Robin checked. Except that they were cleaner, they were similar to those aboard *Aral*.

Having checked, Robin came out and leaned back against the door. She was lost in thought. Her eyes were not really focused. Although she was facing forward, she could not really have been said to be looking forward. Indeed, there was nothing much for her to look at. A white-painted wall, the same as most of the others aboard. It was made of three metal panels, held in place by white-painted rivets. That was all.

And then a little seed of an idea germinated in Robin's mind. It was nothing to do with the wall at all, at first. It was merely the thought that they were a bit squashed together here. That was all to begin with. But that led her to consider that they had not been at all squashed in the lift. The lift car must be nearly double the size of the lift on *Aral*. And the wall in front of her was the back wall of the lift shaft. A wide, deep shaft that sat below the car, even when it was at its lowest setting. A shaft designed to accommodate the maintenance well for the lift – and any cable and so forth needed in the mechanism. But even so...

Robin walked forward to the central panel of the white wall. She put her nose to the join and sniffed. Yes. *Caspian* was cleaner than *Aral* – but not that much cleaner. Beyond the immediate smell of paint and metal, a little draught brought something else to her sensitive nostrils. There was still the telltale combination of latrine and un-washed flesh. And perfume. It was the perfume that gave it away. There was no perfume in the ablutions behind her.

"It's here," she said. "This middle panel's the door and leads through the service shaft under the lift and on down into the secret hold."

Abe disposed his immediate team and warned the others aboard that he was likely to engage another group of armed felons. Robin stepped forward to the panel she thought most promising – the central one. "Captain! No!" said the FBI agent urgently. "You've done enough. We'll take it from here."

Richard, who had stepped forward at the

148

side of his decisive spouse, turned to face Abe and the second he did so, all hell was let loose.

The secret door slammed open. Robin had been right – it was the central panel. The two British civilians, standing closest to it, were simply knocked aside. They fell to the ground in a tangled heap as a withering volley of fire hosed out immediately above them. Figures in FBI flak jackets danced away through doors into showers and latrines that had suddenly turned to matchwood.

Richard's first thought was for Robin. His first act was to roll on top of her. His broad back and long legs protected her from the shower of hot shell cases, spent bullets and smouldering splinters. In the confined, steel-walled space, however, nothing could protect any of them from the sledgehammer blows of sound and energy that smashed against their brains and hearts with stunning power. His mind beginning to spin into some dreamy distance under the terrible impact of the gunshots, Richard really began to suspect he must be having a heart attack. Nothing else could possibly explain the thumping agony in his chest. Even the brutal burning of the hot brass and misshapen lead could not drag him back.

The mind-numbing cacophony eased briefly. Richard gasped a breath into his blazing chest. Cordite burned his throat like acid. He realised that his eyes were streaming. He couldn't even see Robin's face, mere inches away. All of a sudden, feet thundered over him – some used the two bodies as a hurdle, some as a doormat. He clutched Robin to him as tightly as he could, but two latecomers fell over him altogether and he found himself half dragged, half kicked aside. Dazed, he tried to sit up, only to receive a brutal boot in the side of his head. He rolled back with the blow, losing sight of Robin for an instant.

Richard's long body rolled through a shattered doorway into the blood-spattered wreckage of the nearest latrine. His head slammed into the belly of an agent sitting against the end of a stall partition, looking down in dazed disbelief at blood pumping through his bullet-proof jacket. Richard found himself looking up a wall of black chest into a frowning, shockingly youthful, face. "Armour piercing," said the agent and folded forward. His flak jacket closed over Richard's face like the hand of a murderer come to smother him. Everything went black for Richard at that moment, and remained so for a few agonising instants. Hot, thick liquid pumped into his eyes, nose and mouth. Then his mind came close enough to the surface of his consciousness to warn him that if he did not move he would drown in this boy's blood.

But at the very instant he tensed his body to move, before even the first muscle twitched, the boy's body was jerked upwards. Out of a terse rattle of Russian Richard understood the words, "Two ... dead also ... Take woman ... Go..."

Boots clattered away. Blessed peace returned. Richard found some well of almost Herculean strength. He rolled over. Face down on the reeking floor, he spat out the blood and tore a lungful of air out of the atmosphere, like a shark taking a bite of a swimmer. He pulled himself to all fours, an illustration of Darwinian evolution proceeding at breakneck pace, in moments instead of millennia. Prompted by that terrifying command, 'Take woman,' he shook his head. He came near to falling once again. The ringing in his ears intensified. He felt weak and very sick indeed. But the shaking cleared his eyes and mouth. He tore another shark's mouthful of air. It was so sweet to be breathing that the stenches of cordite, blood and effluent were as nothing. He blinked his eyes clear and found that he could see.

What he could see was the toecaps of a pair of boots. He looked up, half expecting to see a Russian sailor waiting to place his armour-piercing round exactly between his eyes. But no. It was one of the FBI agents. The woman. Beth. And Beth was a strong

151

woman, as it turned out. For she reached down, took hold of his flak jacket and pulled him up to his knees.

As she was doing this, she was speaking urgently to him, but only a few of her words were getting through. Until the phrase 'They've taken your wife as a hostage' hit him and confirmed his darkest fears. That cleared his brain as though he was Saul on the road to Damascus. Two seconds later, the evolution from mindless lower life form to *Homo erectus* was complete.

"Where is she?" Richard grated.

"I'll take you. Special Agent Sharon is there. Are you all right, Captain?"

"I'll live." As Richard spat out the little cliché with yet more blood, he looked around the carnage of the place. He was about the only one down there who would. But at least no one needed immediate, life-saving attention. "Let's go," he commanded.

As they crossed to the stairwell, Richard glanced down into the secret hold. It was just as Robin had said it would be. And, mercifully, it was empty. They pounded up the stairs side by side, following a trail of destruction that spoke eloquently of a running battle and a fighting retreat. Richard's fears for Robin intensified. Some of the blood on the stairs and the walls could all too easily be hers.

"Your wife is fine," said the agent, reading his mind. "No one wants her hurt at all. Especially not the Russians."

"Think they'd take me instead?"

"Negative, Captain. Special Agent Sharon and I have already offered ourselves in exchange. They don't want to know."

"I wonder why."

"So do we."

"Where are they?"

"They're in the ship's medical facility, Captain. That's where we were holding the first contingent. Now they're all together."

They pounded into the 'A' deck corridor and slowed. The remaining FBI agents were in a defensive pattern, all with a clear field of fire covering the medical room's door. Abe Sharon, his arm in a sling, was shouting in Russian, clearly negotiating. Another voice was shouting back.

"This is an impasse," said Richard.

"Can't be. They've got to come to terms. They're in American waters with a vengeance. Where are they going to go?"

"No idea. But I'll bet they have. You think Agent Sharon will mind if I go up onto the bridge?"

"No, I don't. But why?"

"It's the nearest I can get to high ground. This isn't right..."

"OK, Captain, but take this radio, would you? It's on open channel. We can all hear it but the Russians can't, unless they are much cleverer than we think they are. And keep a watch out. Special Agent Sharon has radioed for back-up. They may come in like ninjas or they may come in like gangbusters. Just don't get caught in the crossfire, huh?"

"OK. But you keep a close eye on these Russians and what they're up to. They've been pretty smart so far."

Richard walked more lightly up to the navigation bridge, worried that footsteps above them might disturb the desperate men. He put the radio into his left trousers pocket with his handkerchief – the only pocket that didn't seem to be full of blood.

On *Caspian*'s unmanned deck, Richard hesitated, his mind racing. Just what did he suspect? Hardly anything. Nothing more concrete than that glimmer Robin had felt when looking at the picture of St Petersburg aboard *Aral*. But of course it had been that glimmer which made all the difference.

Restless and frustrated, as well as desperately worried, Richard strode across to the bridge wing. The portside wing was open, shattered by Abe's forceful entrance at the head of his men. Beyond it lay *Aral*, all lit up but silent and apparently deserted. Irrelevantly, he wondered about the men aboard her. Had they found something to eat and drink after all?

Thinking of *Swiftsure*'s men in *Aral*'s frugal galley tricked off another association in his mind and he walked back across the bridge to the undamaged bridge wing. Down there somewhere, in the next berth by all accounts, was the other lady he needed to keep an eye on. He strode along the enclosed bridge wing section and opened the outer door.

It was still a stormy night but the wind had torn the clouds to shreds and revealed a full moon just about to set. The gale buffeted past him now, knocking his breath away. "I hope old Steerforth has *Swiftsure* well secured," he thought. He leaned out over the end of the bridge wing, looking down on the poop deck and the dockside close beneath it. There was only a thin finger of concrete between that old-fashioned poop and the gleaming ultra-modern side of the SuperCat just beyond. A narrow thrust of dockside piled with crates and containers enough to make impenetrable canyons of shadow protected from the security lighting.

And as Richard looked down he saw a flicker of movement in the moonlight, running along one such canyon between one and the other. His first thought was that this must be Abe Sharon's back-up coming in like ninjas after all. Then he realised that the flicker was moving from *Caspian* towards *Swiftsure* and his heart sank.

155

Richard punched the button on the radio. "Abe, watch out. You're losing them. There must be a back way out of the medical room onto the poop deck. I can see then moving down there. They're dropping off *Caspian* and running for *Swift*—" He would have said more but at the very same instant he saw the muzzle flash and heard the BANG! of the gun. The bullet took him full in the chest and flipped him over backwards like an acrobat. He was very lucky indeed that the gun was a pistol loaded with ordinary rounds. His flak jacket saved his life. Relief was an instantaneous thing, swept away by the overwhelming pain immediately over his heart. An errant thought came – was this what the poor girl felt as her murderer completed his star by slicing through her heart itself? He hoped not. He hoped the knife would be much less painful.

Richard rolled over onto his stomach. The deck kicked up into his face with enough force to make his nose bleed. That would be Abe's men opening the sickbay door, he thought, and he came up like a drunken sprinter. The time for silence was long past so he took the stairs two at a time, bouncing off the walls, using his shoulders and back to protect his chest. Even so he hit the 'A' deck corridor like an avalanche and literally slid to a stop between Abe and the black gaping wound of the medical facility door.

"She's gone," said Abe. "Long gone, I'd say."

"Then I'm going after her," said Richard. "We'll have to move fast. They've hung onto her because they reckon on taking *Swiftsure*, I'm certain of it. If they get away in her we'll never catch them. Even a chopper would have a hard time keeping up with a Super-Cat in this. And once a Cat comes up to speed, there's no way on. You just get blown off the deck. I warn you, I know what I'm talking about. I've hopped on and off these things with the British SAS. If she gets to speed we're stymied."

"But she can't get anywhere," said Abe, following his impetuous adviser into the wreckage of the medical facility. "There's hardly anyone aboard her."

"There's the captain, the second engineer. Now that they've got someone who understands the navigation equipment, all they need is some competent sailors. And a radio officer if they want to call anyone."

Abe stopped, shaken. A frown marked his forehead, and deepened. "OK," he drawled, drawing the word out as he reassessed the situation. "Then she's all but out of fuel, surely? I mean she's been from Thunder Bay to Devil's Island then back to Ontonagon and then back here again. And she hasn't refuelled at all."

That brought Richard up short, but then

the spark of wild hope died. "No! Don't you understand?" He shouted. "We towed her back from Ontonagon. She only needed to do a little manoeuvring, that's all. She's still got enough fuel aboard to get her to the Soo Canal. To the St Lawrence Seaway, if they want!"

And even as Richard's despairing words rang out, the rumble of *Swiftsure*'s engines thundered through the night.

Seventeen

Richard never gave up. The inevitable was something he simply never faced. He had been blessed with one of those natures that never compromised, no matter what the odds against him. He had reached the position he held in life because of this. As often as not, he won his most dazzling victories during those final moments when almost everyone else had been overwhelmed by events. When they were standing, already giving in, unable to go the final yard.

Now, Richard jumped down onto the dockside in the wake of the Russians and sprinted through the shadows across to

Swiftsure's empty berth. He slid to a halt and watched the sleek SuperCat swing away, his mind racing through the possibilities for immediate action. His radio was back in his hand when Abe joined him, and he was just about to call into the open channel, pausing only to catch his breath. "They're turning north," he gasped.

"That's logical," observed Abe. "That's the shortest route out of the harbour. Through the North Channel. Along the canal."

"Under the Aerial Bridge!" panted Richard. "Is the bridge manned? Can we get them to lower it?"

"Holy..." Abe looked down at his watch. It was lost under the bandage, in the sling. "What time is it, anyway?"

"Coming up for four. Can we close the bridge, Abe?"

"It's designed to go up, Richard. Not down."

"I know that. Can we contact them at least? Even if we can't stop *Swiftsure*, we may be able to slow her. Once she's away, all we'll be able to do is to track her – if we can even manage that." His breath was returning. He could achieve longer speeches.

The female agent who lent Richard the radio in the first place arrived then, with several others in a tight phalanx behind her. Abe turned and snapped to her, "Beth, get

159

the guys who operate the Aerial Bridge for me, would you? We may need the whole bridge lowered. It could be the only way to slow down this Cat of Richard's."

As if to emphasise the point, *Swiftsure* came up towards full speed then, throwing up two thoroughly illegal fountains behind her as her massive motors hurled her across the stirring harbour at rising fifty knots.

"Wow!" breathed Abe as the big Cat pounced away. "I see what you mean."

"Can we get to the bridge ourselves?" demanded Richard as Beth started checking contact numbers and procedures. "Do you have transport?"

"Nothing out of the car-pool, if that's what you mean. No high-powered street racers."

"The local law, then. You must have liaised this mayhem with a local sheriff or marshal or whoever. Where are the local officers?"

"They're watching the perimeter for us. Back at the main entry."

"Let's go!"

"Now wait a minute here," said Abe. "I can't just leave a crime scene like that. We have a major incident here. There are men down. On both sides." He flapped his sling and winced. "I'd be less than useless in any case."

"Send Beth with me, then. Anyone to get the local people jumping."

160

"Well..." Abe frowned his *don't rush me – I'm thinking* frown.

"Are you married?"

"Yes. Miriam and I—"

"If these guys had Miriam would you be hanging around while they got away with her?"

"No!"

"Right, then!"

"OK! You win. Beth, try to stay close to him, for goodness' sake."

"Right, Abe. As close as I can. Jeez, I'd love to think my man would come after me like this."

"If you find the right one, he will."

"Not like this, Abe. This guy's a one-off. Christ! He's gone already! I'd better shift my tail here!"

Beth caught up with Richard at the gates just as he presented himself to a man from the Sheriff's Office. It was just as well that she did catch up, and just at the crucial moment. Richard had taken no account at all of his physical appearance and it was by no means guaranteed to instil confidence into a nervous stranger. He looked like an extra from *Night of the Living Dead* or *Buffy the Vampire Slayer*. His hair was a spiky crown of dried blood. His face was a mottled mask made up of at least three shades of red, from crusted dry to still

161

flowing – from his head wound and his nose. Even his teeth were red. His FBI flak jacket obviously belonged to someone smaller – and, from the sight it presented, someone recently spectacularly deceased. Even the hands he was waving so forcefully were crusted and flaking as though in the final stages of leprosy. And he stank. He stank of effluent from the wrecked toilet, of metal and oil, of cordite and blast-powder and, over all, of blood.

"Don't shoot him!" bellowed Beth as she saw the frightened officer going for his gun. "He's with the Bureau." She came in alongside him with her ID on clear display. "He's on our side," she emphasised in a gentle, calming voice.

"Thank the Lord for that!" said the officer, feelingly.

"How long will it take you to get me to the Aerial Bridge?" Grated Richard.

The young officer's eyes flashed across to Beth. His eyebrows were raised. *Is this for real?* his expression asked. She nodded forcefully. The young man suddenly broke into a grin. "How many laws can I break?"

"All of them," said Beth, feelingly. "This incident could lead to World War Three."

They piled in the back of the shaken officer's squad car and screamed off into the stormy night, climbing from the dock's main security gates up into the sparkling

162

hillsides of the city.

"You know, you're right?" Richard said, as though re-energised by the simple act of sitting down. "I hadn't thought of this as an international incident. But there are going to be some very angry people in Washington, London and Moscow. Not to mention St Petersburg. How many men did you lose?"

Instead of answering him, Beth waved him to silence as her radio began to buzz. A moment later she was talking to the men in the control room of the Aerial Bridge.

Running on an adrenaline high compounded by lack of both food and sleep and extended to the nth degree by the closest of near-death experiences, Richard was simply unable to sit quietly. He leaned forward. "What's your name, Officer?" he asked.

"Billy Young," was the answer.

"You done the advanced driver's course, Billy?"

"I sure have. Bureau trained!"

"Well, let's see what you can really do!"

Billy obliged and his big square squad car surged forward, engine and tyres screaming in the stormy darkness. He was well trained. Conversation stopped as he really began to concentrate on driving as fast as the conditions would allow. The big vehicle swung left and began to climb more steeply. Then it swung right. Richard found himself with a view over the harbour that came and went. Through the increasingly close-packed buildings, Richard could see down to the head of the bay where the ghostly shape of his vessel was hurling towards the span of the bridge, her white sides and the arching fountains of her twin wakes all a-sparkle. Under any other circumstances this would have been a sight to treasure for its ethereal beauty.

"They can't help," snapped Beth as the squad car swung hard right and started to barrel downhill again. "It's up at the moment. They're expecting a big freighter through within the next half-hour. Even if they had the authority without checking with everyone from the mayor to the Chamber of Commerce, they couldn't get it low enough in time. Probably couldn't get it low enough at all."

"Well, if we can just get there, I'll think of something," said Richard grimly.

"I really hope you are not thinking of jumping aboard from the span," said Beth. "Special Agent Sharon said I've got to stick with you, but that would be beyond the call of duty with a vengeance."

"We'll see," said Richard.

But just the way he said it made Beth whisper, "Oh, shit."

As Billy swung the squad car round hard

right at the bottom of the hill onto Canal Drive and disregarded the speed limit alongside Canal Park and the Museum, Richard realised all too clearly that they were not going to make it in time. He could see the foreshortened span of the bridge that would carry the road over the canal in a little more than a mile. But at the same time he could see the three claws of the SuperCat's bow already tearing into the black flank of Lake Superior just beneath it.

"OK, Beth," he called. "No jumping from the bridge. But do you think Abe could get anyone in Duluth to lend us a chopper?"

"You're not going to jump out of a fucking chopper, are you?" Beth's self-control was slipping with obvious damage to the cool ladylike demeanour that Abe's team all counted as the required professionalism of their job. But then again, the FBI agent had never had to deal with anyone quite like Richard Mariner in the whole of her professional life. It was weirdly like being trapped in a James Bond movie – and not at all the fun she had expected that particular dream to be. The experience was breaking down all sorts of barriers. But the thought of jumping from a helicopter into the madness of that stormy water...

"Real men do it all the time," grated Richard. "Haven't you seen *The Perfect Storm*?"

★   ★   ★

They howled to a halt just north of the bridge. This was the best place for a chopper to land, if Beth could conjure one up for them. They stood beside the huge car, listening to it creaking as its systems cooled down after the hot ride Billy had given them. Listening also to the groaning of its suspension as the raw gusts of wind tried to lift its body off its chassis. Tantalisingly close, across the stormy water, *Swiftsure* was ploughing eastwards onto Superior. Once she went out of the bright out-wash of the harbour she would be hard to spot by eye until daylight.

Richard strode up and down, as restless as the storm wind. His eyes were on his watch one moment and on the fading vision of the SuperCat powering eastwards the next. "At least she's sailing into the dawn," he told himself grimly.

Beth had leaped out of the car with the other two, speaking curtly into the radio. She had a knack of upward delegation and soon had Abe agreeing to scare up a chopper for her. Then she got onto the coast guard. And here she hit pay dirt.

The harbour master had been dragged from his bed by complaints about the war in his harbour. His natural ire came swiftly to focus on the outrageous, unsailorly and downright illegal behaviour of the SuperCat

166

Swiftsure. As he was awake, he thought he would share a little of the grief and outrage with his old friend the coast guard. By the time Beth followed Abe's call into the harbour master's seething orbit, the coast guard had already despatched a powerful Sikorsky to see just what was going on. It would be going over their heads in five minutes. Sure, it could drop down and pick them up. Anything for the FBI.

Richard and Beth scrambled into the open side of the helicopter as it settled, for an instant only, beside Billy Young's creaking, shuddering squad car. The crew oversaw the fastening of their safety harnesses as the Sikorsky swooped upwards into the blustery dark.

"Can you see *Swiftsure?*" bellowed Richard in his quarterdeck voice. The pilot may even have heard him, such was the volume he attained. But there was no way he could reply in kind. The winchman who had settled them handed Richard and Beth headsets, and during a quick-fire question and answer session they explained to the pilot what was going on and their place within the events.

"My orders are to monitor and report," said the pilot when the question and answer session was finished. "But I guess I'll have to ask Captain Mariner to come up here and act as spotter for us. We've only a vague idea of what the stolen vessel looks like. And it seems that the people on board have found a way to disable its identity beacon. The son of a gun has vanished off the radar altogether."

"What about movement and speed?" asked Richard, as he settled into a little jump seat just behind the pilot that the winchman had pulled down for him. "If you track anything going into the wind at more than sixty knots, that'll be her."

"Even if we do, she'll have to be close to us. It's still a sixty-knot headwind. That's a closing speed of one twenty knots and more. We'll have to be moving at speeds well in excess of that to catch her. We'd better find her soon or she'll be long gone. And so will the men who have pirated her."

"That's what I've been trying to tell everyone," said Richard bitterly. "And they'll be long gone with my wife!"

Eighteen

The easterly gale did more than give them a blustery headwind to contend with during the next fruitless, frustrating hour. As daylight began to slide resentfully up the eastern skies, as though angry at being hurried by their flight towards the sun, so the first rain squall arrived to wrap them in its almost impenetrable embrace. The Sikorsky dipped down to wave-top level, skimming just above the flying spume ripped off by the wind to hurl away behind them, heading for the increasingly distant city of Duluth.

"She's unique on the Lake," said Richard tensely, and not for the first time. "What she looks like, how she moves, the speeds she can achieve. It shouldn't be too hard to spot her."

"Famous last words I'm afraid, Captain," commiserated the pilot. "I can't see anything like her with any of the equipment I have in my cockpit or my head."

The next squall swung in ahead of them. The horizon drew back ahead of it, allowing a golden curtain to stretch right across the heaving waterscape in front of them. A golden curtain topped with the near-black watered silk of the storm clouds. Then the squall itself took solid shape, the rain extending the cloud base like the trunk of a huge grey tree. "No wonder the old Vikings used to think it was a tree that held the world together, hey?" said the radio operator from his seat behind the co-pilot/navigator.

Richard grunted like a grumpy bear, his eyes using the fleeting moments of natural glory to quarter the foaming expanse below, more concerned with *Swiftsure* than with Wagnerian legends.

"Sven's folks are from Norway," explained the pilot quietly. "Originally."

As he spoke, the tree of the squall caught them in its stormy branches like a lost toy kite and stole their sight again. Five more minutes passed with silence in the cockpit and mayhem going on outside it. Then suddenly Sven called out, "Hey! I have a report of a near miss! Ore carrier nearly ran down a vessel south of here. Came out of the murk like a bat out of hell. One minute she was there, the next she was gone. Missed her by a whisker. Says the vessel took off at more than fifty knots..."

"That's her!" said Richard. "Sven. Do you have coordinates?"

"Yeah. Are you getting this, navigator and pilot?" The question was routine. They were speaking on open channel in the chopper.

The ore carrier's coordinates put her fifty miles east of Manitou Island and far to the east and south of the Sikorsky. The pilot put her nose down once again and ran across the lake at full throttle but it still took nearly half an hour to reach the site of the near-collision. "Put your radar on wide screen," called Richard to the navigator as they neared the exact spot. "She can't be more than twenty-five miles away, I'm sure."

"There's not much more than that to the south of us in any case," said the navigator.

"Look for anything moving at more than fifty knots," Richard called back, forgetting he was wearing a headset in his excitement and nearly deafening all aboard.

"That's still the best idea, Steve, there won't be much capable of doing that in this," said the pilot as the navigator obeyed Richard's curt command.

"Precisely!"

"Got her!" sang out Steve, excitedly. "It's not much of an image but she's running at nearly fifty knots due south."

"How far?" called Richard. "What bearing?"

"Thirty miles down. Heading due south, with twenty more miles to go before they run up onto Au Sable Point."

The pilot was spinning the Sikorsky round through ninety degrees. Eighty noted Richard, impressed; allowing for the gusts of the easterly storm. Skimming the wavetops with his nose-wheel, he pushed the game aircraft to her limits for the conditions.

As he had with every change of status and course during the whole wild flight, Sven the radio officer reported their new heading to Coast Guard command in distant Duluth. This time, with the same excitement Steve the navigator showed, he added that they had acquired their target and were running down upon her.

"But can we catch her up?" asked Richard.

"Sure we can," answered the pilot steadily. "Where's she going to go now? There's shoreline to the south and west of her. We're to the north. At this speed, she's only got an hour of water to the east before she runs into the dead end of Whitefish Bay and the canal at Sault Ste Marie."

"And that is a dead end indeed," said Richard. "*Swiftsure*'s sister is stuck on a freighter there still waiting to get up here through the hold-up in the Soo Canal."

"But he must know that," said Beth, in one of her rare interruptions. "Whoever is in command down there must know that. What do you think he's up to, Richard?"

"No idea. He could be running in blind panic, I suppose..."

"I don't buy that. The guy who got everyone off the *Caspian* under Abe Sharon's nose is not about to panic now, just because he's got the fastest boat on the biggest lake in the world."

"You're right," admitted Richard.

"If he has a plan then he'll need to start employing it pretty quickly," observed the pilot. "He's running out of water fast."

"He's slowing!" warned Steve. "Slowing and turning east. Sven, can you call this in?"

"Is there any more shipping down there, Steve? Anything he can hide behind?" demanded Richard.

"Nothing. Everything local's in Grand Marais or Copper Harbor long since."

"Can we see him? With our eyes?" Richard cried, frustrated. As if in answer, the current squall intensified, pulling in long-distance vision to maybe twenty feet. Looking down, he was struck by how clearly he could see the waves. And then he realised just how low they really were.

"He's almost dead in the water," sang out Steve. "No. I've lost his signal. Now what?"

"But we know where he is?" insisted Richard.

"We'll be there in five minutes," the pilot promised shortly.

"You'd better watch out, then," Richard

warned. "You'll crash straight into him at this height."

"It'd be helpful to have his signal, Steve. Captain Mariner's right. If I don't know exactly where he is, I'll have to pull up and slow down."

"I've got him back," said Steve. His voice sounded a little hesitant.

It was little enough – but it was sufficient to make Richard crane forward to look over his shoulder and ask, "What?"

"I've got the signal back, but it's like an emergency ident. signal suddenly. And there's a ghost running slowly south of it."

"Hey," shouted Sven suddenly. "I've got a broad band emergency signal screwing up my communications. Where did that come from?"

"We'll see what's going on in just a moment," said the pilot reassuringly. "How close are we now, Steve?"

"Ninety seconds' flight time. I'll count you down in yards from two on my mark ... Now! ... and nineteen hundred ... and eighteen..."

The pilot glanced back at Richard, who lifted himself out into the tiny aisle and scrambled back to the security of his assigned position beside Beth. Steve never missed a beat or a yard, counting them in.

Richard settled beside Beth and they spoke quietly together, interweaving their brief conversation with all the routine business going on in the helicopter's open communications channel.

"What do you think, Richard? You think we've got him?"

"Quite frankly, I think he's slowed to push a noisy inflatable life raft over the side and then sneaked off as quietly as he could." Richard strained forwards and discovered he could still see out of the windshield in front of the pilot

"Looks that way from here as well," intruded the pilot. "You do realise what that means if it's true, though, don't you?"

"That he must have been listening to the Coast Guard channel and hearing us track him down. Yes, I know that. He's clever and resourceful, whoever is in command. That makes it more likely that this is just a trick, because if that is *Swiftsure* herself down there then he's just given up and rolled over."

"That doesn't sound like the guy we've been following so far," said Beth dryly. "You're right, Richard. It's a trick."

"But we have to be sure," concluded the pilot. "There may be lives at risk. That'd be our prime concern."

"Oh yes," said Richard. "I doubt he'd have put it over empty. It's just a question of whether anyone in it will still be alive."

"Look on the bright side," said Beth.

175

"Getting some live people out of a life raft will take us longer than reporting in a couple of corpses. He's got to calculate that. And it's time he's playing for. He may even think we'll be forced to take survivors straight for medical attention and let him go."

"Could we just pick up the whole raft and go on after him immediately?" asked Richard, but he knew it was a faint hope.

Even as Richard spoke, the bright orange of the life raft blossomed through the grey squall. So drab had been the view since that brief golden glimpse of the horizon that the colour was almost shocking in its intensity. Up came the chopper's nose and the way fell off her as she slowed to a static hover – sliding sideways across the wind to remain precisely above the wildly bobbing craft.

The winchman slid wide the long door in the side of the chopper. As the wind exploded in around them, he turned and lifted a basket free. He attached it to the cable hanging from a winch high on the fuselage and swung it out through the open doorway. Having established that there was no more direct radio contact to be had with the life raft, Sven had no more work to do as radio operator. He joined the winchman at the door and they lowered the basket towards the life raft. "Looks as though I'm going in for a swim," shouted Sven. He began pulling on a diver's headpiece and Richard realised he had been wearing a wet suit all along.

The winchman nodded and passed up a facemask to him.

"What can we do to help?" asked Richard.

"Sit tight for the moment. Either of you know any first aid?"

"I do," said Richard.

"Me too," called Beth.

"The first aid chest is in back there. Get it out but don't open it until we close the side or the contents will blow away."

Sven adjusted his life preserver and jumped. Through the gaping doorway, Richard could see him swim towards the life raft and open its zippered side. He looked inside, then heaved himself over the inflatable's gunwale, vanishing for an instant. Then he was back, standing unsteadily and gesturing fiercely.

"Three survivors. All hurt pretty badly," translated the winchman working steadily. Richard's heart sank.

The basket fell unerringly into the water immediately beside him. The instant that it did so, Sven was holding it in place with one hand and helping a crouching figure to crawl out of the life raft with the other. There was more signalling.

"They're all men, Captain Mariner," said the winchman and for a moment Richard simply did not know whether he was

177

relieved or disappointed.

When the first of *Swiftsure*'s crewmen was swung aboard, however, he soon knew just how relieved he was. The man had been badly beaten up. And he had been stabbed in the chest. Forced to open the first aid box after all to get something to stanch the blood, Richard pulled on the latex gloves, then wadded thick absorbent material into a pressure bandage. As he did so, Beth, also safely gloved, opened the man's shirt over the wound and Richard froze. There was no star – just one wound instead of ten. And on the right side of the chest, away from the heart. But to Richard's eyes, the cut could have been made with the same knife that had cut open the heart of the Lady in the Lake less than a week ago off Thunder Bay.

He had no sooner had this suspicion planted in his own heart than the second crewman came aboard, in exactly the same condition, with precisely the same knife wound. And by the time the first had been tended to and the second was being bandaged, the third was lying, beaten, stabbed and bleeding on the helicopter's running deck. Sven stepped out of the basket and was back on the radio at once.

"These men need to be in hospital at once. They'll die very quickly indeed," said Richard grimly.

"We'll have to cut and run, then. The

chase is over," said the pilot.

"That was the precise objective of whatever psycho did this," grated Beth.

"Sven?" continued the pilot. "Nearest medical facilities, please."

"Grand Marais has several local doctors listed. Beyond that there's the Plummer or the General in Sault Ste Marie."

"Get on to them, Sven, but see if there's anyone in Marais that could help first. Lay in a course please, Steve. Give me a precise heading as soon as you can. In the meantime I'll head for Grand Marais following the coast along from Au Sable Point."

The helicopter roared off due south again, dropping her nose and swooping low once more. Richard and Beth were joined by the winchman, who proved no slouch at first aid – which was hardly a surprise. The three of them made the calculatedly brutalised men as comfortable as possible, and Richard was just stripping the agonisingly restrictive latex gloves off his massive bony hands when the pilot called, "Captain Mariner, I believe we've found your vessel, sir."

The formality of the flyer's tone warned him, but he was still shocked when he looked up, for there was what was left of *Swiftsure,* seemingly scant feet below them. There was just enough of her left for him to see her and know her. She had been brutally rammed hard against the foam-white feet of the black cliffs of Au Sable Point, and she was little more than wreckage now, being pounded into kindling by the surf.

Nineteen

When *Swiftsure* hit the rocks at the foot of Au Sable Point for the second time, Robin and Captain Steerforth leaped together. They crashed onto the black ground together and she stumbled forward, slipping and sliding. Steerforth went over and fell heavily. Seeing the captain beginning to slip back down the treacherous slope, Robin ran back to help him, calling for aid. No one answered her call. Miraculously, Robin managed to keep her feet on the treacherous rock and help him up, just as the shattering bows of his command smashed down on the black rocks where he had lain. Then they ran up the slope together, racing inland away from the terrible sound of the wreck, until the guns of Captain Karpov's men brought them up short. Then they had to stop and turn.

Karpov was still on *Swiftsure*'s bridge, where he had stood from the moment he led the first of his heavily armed refugees from *Caspian* aboard to pirate and steal the

SuperCat from under Richard's nose. He was almost alone there now, thought Robin, her unqualified loathing tinted by grudging respect. He was a superb leader and a resourceful if utterly ruthless villain. And he was recklessly, almost heroically, brave. His tall, slim figure hunched forward as he thrust the throttles wide once more. The twin fountains of thrust soared like white rainbows. *Swiftsure* smashed forward onto the black-fanged, unforgiving coast. Her three-pronged bow slid, splintering, up the rock beach. The last of the prisoners and the next set of pirate guards leaped out and down, then came pounding up the sullen slope to join the waiting captains. The sound of the Cat's destruction drowned even the brute bellowing of the wind. It was almost enough to drown out the invective Hank Steerforth was bellowing at the man destroying his command. Icy rain came lashing across the eastern shoulder of the Point like the whip of a Gulag guard. Every-one on the shore withdrew into the margin of the tree line where the thickness of branches and the breadth of the deciduous leaves offered some protection from the weather. But none, thought Robin, from the brutality of what had been done, what was being done and what they all expected to be done in the all-too-near future.

Karpov let *Swiftsure* withdraw from the

shore, sucked clear of the rocks by the backwash of his last thrust. He allowed the Cat to slide so far out into the lake that, for a dizzying instant, Robin thought he must be meaning to sail off and leave them all. But no such luck. The wily pirate slid the rapidly sinking vessel back until he felt her rising on the swell of a storm wave, then he jammed the throttles full open and came racing out of the wheelhouse with the last few of his men. They paused on the buckled wreckage of the bows and waited coolly until *Swiftsure* smashed up onto the rock-fanged shore again. Then, given extra impetus by the fearsome destruction below and behind them, they leaped. As the five of them sailed through the shuddering air, Karpov himself still sprinting like a long jumper, so the murdered vessel exploded into splinters against the rocks.

Instinctively, Robin ran down the slope, out onto the hail-crusted tussocks. Steerforth went with her. But whether they were running towards the men or the vessel neither could well have said. They had only taken a step or two in any case before Karpov, who had landed as surely as a mountain lion, pulled out his pistol and they all stopped.

Behind the five Russians, *Swiftsure* was caught in the terrible destructive physics of the shoreline, the waters and the power of her massive engines. The back of the bay curved to the SuperCat's left and the outthrust of rocks hit her left catamaran hull first, swinging her to the right. The waves tumbled her across the shallows as her engines thrust her further round and further still, against the foot of the cliff itself. Here there was no beach. There was only a jumble of black rocks varying in size from a bath to a bathroom. All of the boulders were sharp-edged and vicious. The gallant vessel rode up over the smaller, lower rocks, tossing her shattered head up into the teeth of the big waves pushed by the easterly gale, round the point and into the bay. She reared right up, sliding backwards, as the wave swept under her, and then she slammed down with all her weight. All three hulls exploded asunder. The bridge detonated outward as though Karpov had left a bomb in the captain's seat. At the sound she made, even the wind faltered, as though suddenly struck with a terrible guilt – like Bill Sykes looking on the murdered Nancy. The engines had enough power to push her upward one last time, but when the next big surf came round the point, she dived under it rather than rising, for her back was broken now. And when the white water boiled away, they could all see that she was coming to pieces along the whole of her shuddering length.

"Come," shouted Karpov in his raucous, brutal English. "We go. We are finished here."

The well-armed, silent Russians herded them under the weeping trees and took them at jog-trot up the slope. Karpov ran a little faster than the rest until he was up in the lead, and then they followed his sure-footed, confident lead.

Robin and Steerforth had learned early in their captivity that talking in the ranks was frowned upon, and the terrible price that Karpov's frowns could entail. But Robin simply could not remain quiet. "We'll make him pay," she gasped. "He's done all this in American jurisdiction. Stolen. Kidnapped. Beaten; tortured; killed – probably. Wilfully destroyed millions of dollars' worth of property. And that's just in the last few hours. God knows what he did on *Caspian* when he had all those poor girls to play with. He may even be the madman Jeanne's been looking for. The way he used that knife on those three poor ... In any case, when the law catches up with him, he's for the electric chair. And I for one will really enjoy putting him in it."

"Anything I can do to help," puffed the captain. "I'd just love to see that bastard fry."

They fell silent then, and over the sound of

184

the wind in the treetops above them they heard the beat of a helicopter's blades come and go into the distance.

A short time later, the sounds of other motors began to pierce the thrashing bluster of the wind. Karpov slowed to a walk and pulled a personal telephone out of his clothes. Robin wished she were closer. The Russian had been using that phone on and off ever since he came aboard *Swiftsure*. It looked powerful enough but somehow she doubted he was talking to his masters in St Petersburg. It seemed logical to her – and she had had some leisure to mull things over during the long chase east – that any smuggling operation would only work if there were local contacts in the market for the smuggled goods. That was as true of cigarettes smuggled from Europe into her native England as it was for women smuggled from Russia or China into the United States. So it seemed logical to suppose Karpov could well be calling a local number.

Robin's chance of seeing or hearing anything was limited at once. As soon as contact was made, Karpov gestured and the prisoners were herded into the centre of a clearing so small the branches still met thickly above their heads. She occupied her thoughts as they stood beneath the dripping trees, however, with working out how she might get that local number or the name of the man whose number it was. This was precisely the kind of information Jeanne La Motte and Abe Sharon would give their eye teeth to know.

Karpov finished speaking and strode purposefully towards the group of prisoners surrounded by their armed guards. He launched into a short speech of English interspersed with Russian translation – for the prisoners were by no means the only target audience. "This is a place where we meet sometimes with other men from other ships and other people too," he shouted. "It is a place where we leave messages sometimes for each other." He strutted through some undergrowth across to the apparently massive trunk of a fallen tree. He gestured with his chin to the strongest of the guards and together they swung the body of the fallen giant aside. It revealed a shallow hole covered with strewn foliage – suspiciously fresh foliage, thought Robin.

"There is a message here," shouted Karpov. "But it is a message for all of you, not for me." He bent and lifted some foliage free, with a flourish, like a conjuror. A stir of shock and revulsion went through them all, guards and guarded alike. Under the leaves lay a dead man. He had been shot in the middle of the forehead, execution style. He had not been here for long either for his eyes were untouched. They were wide, and filled

186

with an almost apologetic surprise.

"And what did he do, this man, to merit such an end? He disobeyed his orders. He abandoned his post. He lost his ship."

Robin recognised him then. He was one of the young officers she had seen aboard the *Aral*. And all the pieces fell into place for her. This must be the man who had let the anchors slip, then abandoned ship when the storm became too fierce. She looked around the place, trying to find some landmark to guide her when she brought the FBI back here. Then she met Karpov's steady gaze and realised he was watching her, reading her mind. He gave her an icy smile and shook his head. He clearly had no intention of ever allowing her to bring the FBI back here. "Now that I have your full attention," he said, "I think it is time that the prisoners were properly searched. I will take the woman."

His personal phone chirruped as he completed a thorough but oddly impersonal search of Robin's form and clothing. He stepped back and, as he put it to his ear he looked away. Robin breathed easier with his icy eyes off her. She straightened up her clothing and said a sad mental farewell to her watch. All in all, she thought, she had got off lightly there. After the things she had seen him do, she knew he was capable of killing her – and that he would do so without a second thought if she gave him cause. But she knew he would kill her anyway when his plans required it.

For many other people, this realisation would have been incapacitating. They would have frozen like rabbits in headlight beams and been run down before they could move again. But not Robin. She shared her husband's capacity for indefatigable action. And she had been in situations like this before. She had met several men like Captain Karpov and all of them had harboured similar plans for her future. But she was still here, and none of them were, any more. She held her peace, therefore, and she laid her plans and she kept her head low, waiting for the chance that had always, in the past, come in the end.

She looked back at the poor Russian officer's body but it had been reburied. The forest lay wild and innocent once again, polluted only by the distant grumble of an engine, and the grating of gears.

Karpov broke the connection and put his phone away. "We go!" he called. The damp, depressed crowd of captors and captives began to follow him. He led them at a brisk walk out of the undergrowth to the side of a county road. The grey ribbon of tarmac wound up a hill slope until it became lost in increasingly mountainous, increasingly thickly wooded country. Downhill, it swung immediately out of sight round a bend. And, the instant Robin looked down at that bend, a big old coach appeared round it and began to toil up the hillside towards them.

A fluttering of excitement came into Robin's throat as though a skylark had escaped from its nest in her tummy. She was just on the point of seizing the main chance and exploding into action when she saw Karpov raise his right hand in salute. There was a pale flash as the driver raised his hand in reply and the coach ground to a halt beside them.

Overcome with disappointment, Robin allowed herself to be herded forward. Such was the bitterness of the feeling that she closed in upon herself, paying scant attention to her surroundings at this crucial time. She noticed that the side of the coach had been painted to look like a Greyhound Coach, but it was not. She noticed that there was a sign on the door saying *Non Stop Express*, though it had clearly stopped for them. There was another, saying FULL, though it was empty, until they were herded up aboard.

And, when she was inside, being guided roughly down to her threadbare seat, she saw the coach's destination in reverse through the backs of the signs on windscreen and rear window.

189

Seul Choix, the signs said. *Fast to Seul Choix.*

One Choice, she thought, translating with her schoolgirl French.

But then she thought of the irony of the words. For one choice was really no choice at all.

Twenty

Robin finally caught up with Jeanne Two Feathers La Motte at the place called Seul Choix on the north shore of Lake Michigan. Here she really rejoined the hunt for the girls' killer and went up towards the top of the deathlist herself, but to begin with, at least, Robin had little idea of where she actually was. And it was only someone such as she who could ever have worked the truth of the matter out.

The coach, disguised to look like any other Greyhound, ground down out of the hills and onto an anonymous, dune-swept shore a little before noon. As everything else about the vehicle had been a lie, Robin had no reason to trust the destination announced on the windows. And, therefore, she had no real idea where this place actually was. The lake spreading out in front of her like molten silver could have been Michigan or Huron or even a peaceful bay of Superior, for they had come out of the storm on the way down from the thickly forested watershed.

Robin would not immediately have recognised this low point of land, with its name that she found so sinister, in any case. Even had she been looking out of the window with any great care, there was little for her to see and nothing particularly memorable. Certainly there were no signposts to tell her that the destination really was the one on the bus's windows. The driver had taken a calculatedly bland route. Not, Robin still suspected, that he ever expected anyone to try and re-trace it with the federal authorities.

The two-lane blacktop wound down to a calm, lovely coastline, in all respects the opposite to that which they had left a little less than three hours earlier except that it too was deserted. The storm sweeping across Superior had lifted from here, and remained trapped behind the hills they had just crossed. Still, there was a restless surf, she noticed, as the coach lurched and juddered down towards the featureless, deserted shoreline, but it had nothing of the bitter power that had destroyed *Swiftsure*.

It was hardly enough to disturb the big

freighter anchored just off the point, or make the big launch powering in from it do much more than pitch and toss a little, kicking up some spray at her bow. Out in the main channel, Robin noticed with quickening interest, freighters very like the one at anchor here were sailing in and out of a nearby commercial port. They were all big ships, very nearly the size of *Aral* and *Caspian*, though she had to strain her tired mind with the effort of remembering whether there was much international shipping on Michigan or Huron, such as there was on Superior.

But then she noticed something that really made her sit up. The way this nearby freighter swung on her anchor under the pressure of the rolling waves was all wrong. Robin's sea-wise eyes narrowed. The ship was riding strangely and the freighter far behind her was labouring too hard in her steady progress through the rolling waves. They were both in the grip of the tearing force of some extremely powerful cross-current. Robin began to cudgel her brains anew. If this was Michigan, and Michigan was the most likely contender, the only currents that fierce were those passing between this lake and Lake Huron next door through the Straits of Mackinac. And that gave Robin a clear idea of where this place was. The early maritime explorers like

Champlain who named all the coastal features nearby would have called this place One Choice. She thought back to her wild ride with Richard in the big canoe so long ago at the beginning of all this. Vessels such as that, such as the early explorers used, were entirely at the mercy of wind and current. They would have stood no chance against a monster like the one running eastwards just offshore. This point was your last chance to stop; perhaps your only chance to do so. Once that current took you, you were gone.

They were in Seul Choix after all, therefore. Seul Choix on the northern coast of Lake Michigan just inside the narrows that joined it to Lake Huron. And what did she know, in all her encyclopaedic knowledge of matters maritime, about Seul Choix, the coast and the ports nearby, that could give her an edge in this situation? For she knew she would need an edge – and a very good one – if she was going to avoid the fate Captain Karpov had so clearly got mapped out for her. At the moment it was all too clearly her destiny to be found floating somewhere not so very far from here and not so very far in the future, stark and dead. Probably with a red star carved on her heart.

* * *

"OUT!"

While Robin had been lost in thought, the bus had wheezed to a stop where the road – a dirt track now – joined the end of a dilapidated little jetty. With bovine obedience radiating from every pore, she joined the shuffling line of remaining *Swiftsure* crewmen, falling into place just behind Hank Steerforth. Hank's head was also hanging; his shoulders were slumped in graphic defeat. Robin hoped the play-acting was not as obvious to Karpov as it was to her.

But of course it was. As the others climbed out into the clement afternoon and started shuffling along the creaking jetty, he stopped them. He stood at the end of the central aisle, framed in the brightness of the windshield, the driver like a featureless granite block beside him. "What you two need to remember at all times," said the Russian slowly, "is that we are looking for an excuse to kill you. You are inconvenient and unexpected. You are not part of the plan and you do not have a place in it. Your only worth is that you each might make a useful bargaining counter should anything go wrong. But that is a very slight weight on which to balance your future. The slightest thing might outweigh it. Anything you do or think of doing. Anything you try to get anyone else to do or say. Anything you refuse to do. Anything at all."

He reached down towards his belt and Robin expected him to round out his eloquent little speech by producing a gun. But instead he produced a knife. It was big, broad and wicked looking. And familiar. It was the knife he had used on the three crewmen before dumping them into the life raft. "I make myself clear, do I not?"

"Very clear," said Robin at once, keeping just a whisper of dull defeat in her voice.

"Yes," said Hank shortly.

"Very well. Let's see how long you can remain alive, shall we? It will be an amusing little game. I may even – what do they call it? – open a book on your chances. I had better do so quickly, I think, while there is still anything to make a bet about."

The launch was designed to take maybe eight. Rather than run back and forth, however, Karpov decided the prisoners would stand in the middle while his crewmen sat round the bulwarks and on the seating aft and amidships. It was an uncomfortable journey, clearly calculated to emphasise how worthless and endangered the prisoners actually were. Whether it worked for Hank and his men, Robin couldn't say. The whole experience made no impression whatsoever on her. Except, perhaps, to give her the feeling that the young man crushed

195

so tightly against her back and bottom was far too happy to be there. But then, thinking of his likely fate, she could hardly deny him a little almost innocent pleasure. He was a sailor, after all.

But that thought, the last to strike Robin on the ride out to the anchored freighter, was in stark contrast to her reception aboard. As she came up the courtesy steps and onto the deck, the first thing she heard, in gruff Russian was, "Not another bloody woman!"

The words were unexpected; so much so that they jerked her back from another calculation entirely. For she had noticed on nearing the freighter that it was called the *Beaufort*. This was a good American English name and unremarkable. Calculatedly so, she thought. But it betrayed a love for patterns too. The Russian ships *Aral* and *Caspian* had been named for Russian seas. Now here was an American associate vessel named for one of the only two seas which touched American – Alaskan – coastlines. I must keep an eye out for the *Bering*, she was thinking, when the gruff greeting distracted her. And, like the fierce current running under the freighter's keel, that short phrase in coarse Russian told her an awful lot in a very short time.

She stepped onto *Beaufort*'s deck and found herself under the gun immediately. A line of armed guards waved her fellow prisoners and herself along towards the white-painted bridgehouse. Head down, but eyes busy, she followed. Immediately outside the main entry to the 'A' deck corridor, however, where the shadow of the bridge wing gave a little relief from the noonday sun, Karpov was waiting. Like a Commandant in a concentration camp, he waved his hand. Men this side, along to the poop. Women this side, in through the door. As she stepped over the raised threshold into the 'A' deck corridor, she glanced up. Her eyes met Hank Steerforth's for a fleeting instant, and then Karpov's apparent whim pulled them apart.

The instant Robin stepped into the corridor she realised Karpov's 'whim' had actually been carefully calculated. And it fell into place with her surprising greeting aboard. For the air was heavy with the odours she remembered so vividly from the hidden decks in the two Russian vessels. A guard waved her towards the lift with the barrel of a gun. Another stood there waiting. He stepped in with her and used the muzzle of his pistol to press the button. As the lift car sped downwards, Robin felt his eyes on her, stripping off her clothing and sizing her up. There was something sexual in the scrutiny, certainly. But Robin found the experience disturbing on an unexpected level. She did not feel like some victim being sized up for ravishment. She felt like a heifer being sized up for butchery.

Twenty-One

The lift door hissed open and Robin was roughly ushered out into a short corridor. The corridor was unremarkable except in two regards. First, it was hot and smelly. Secondly, it was full of a strange, dull sound. As she walked down the corridor, her nose wrinkled and her skin prickling, Robin found that her mind was occupied with trying to work out what this murmuration could be, with its rising and falling tones, its shapeless buzzing, as dull and featureless as the drab walls all around her.

Halfway down the corridor, the guard motioned her to stop. She obeyed without thinking. It was only when he pushed her back against the wall and kicked her legs apart that the dreadful possibilities erupted into her mind. She flinched away from him, looked around the unremarkable little place and sucked in breath to scream. He put his gun against her forehead, and suddenly she

198

couldn't breathe, let alone scream. His hand patted her shoulders, breasts and belly, then slid over her crotch and squeezed. Down each inner thigh ran the practised fingers, and up each outer one. It was only when he stood back and motioned her to turn that she realised she was being searched. The relief was almost painful. The ordeal was over in a couple of moments. Karpov's less personal but far more thorough search had left her nothing of worth or note. The pair of them proceeded down that disturbing little corridor.

But then she arrived at the end of the corridor and found herself faced with an unexpectedly large door. The guard reached past her and rapped on it with the barrel of his gun. It opened at once, and the heat and the smell intensified. The dull sound washed out in a disorientating tidal wave. Only the sharpness of the barrel mouth between her shoulder blades made her move forward with any alacrity. She stepped over the threshold and found herself on a low balcony between two heavily armed guards who wore, apart from their guns, only shorts and vests. These men also waved her forward and as the door closed firmly behind her, she walked to the edge of the balcony and the top of a short flight of stairs. And here she stopped, overwhelmed by what she saw.

In a chamber little more than half the size of the hidden decks on *Aral* and *Caspian* there sat perhaps two hundred women. She saw at once that the term 'sat' was too formal. They squatted, sprawled. Alone, in pairs, in little groups. And the strange buzzing sound had been the hum of their conversations, contained, distorted by the iron walls and decks around them. But the instant that she entered, the conversations faltered. Four hundred listless eyes were turned on her. The arrival of another inmate of this particular circle of hell was noted. The conversations started up again. That was all. No one rose to greet her or to commiserate with her. Nobody cared. She was just another face, another body. Another bulk to use up precious space and air. The guard pushed her forward and she staggered a little, almost falling down the steps onto the packed and littered floor.

As Robin walked carefully among them, looking for a spark of contact, a gesture of welcome – or at least a place to sit, she began to take in the detail of the women's wretchedness and her stomach started performing some very strange gyrations inside her. They all wore underwear. It was too hot for anything more. The acres of flesh thus revealed were darkened almost universally by signs of violence and abuse. The only difference between these bodies and the battered corpse she had covered up on the canoe was that these were still capable of movement – and feeling. And none of them had a red star on her heart. The levels of bruising escalated rapidly past the blotches of casual roughness and thought-less punches to the severity of calculated beatings. The faces, by and large, had been left undamaged, but below the neck – and especially below the waist – anything went. It was no wonder, thought Robin, that even in the foreign language, the cadences of the speech were of dejection, defeat and stark terror. No wonder that she, with her scrubbed skin, creamy flesh and scented body, seemed an outsider here. Perhaps when she had suffered what these women had suffered they might be more willing to accept her. And yet, she thought, riding the sluggish wave of their rejection like a man overboard certain of rescue, even in board-ing school – even in Belsen – there had been those who would try to ease things for newcomers.

And, if Jeanne La Motte were anywhere in this hellish place, it would be with people like these.

Robin continued to walk around the big room, therefore, her actual path dictated by where she could put her feet without stepping on anyone or anything tender or precious. She did not allow her eyes to dwell too long on the women's bodies or the marks of what had been done to them. She sought out eyes and met each gaze with a slight, calculatedly helpless, smile. They all looked away, withdrawing into their groups, closing out the stranger. It was exactly like her first day at boarding school – the only day she had hated in an otherwise idyllic education. Suddenly, unexpectedly, a sensation of homesickness came, piercing her through the heart like the murderer's knife. Her eyes flooded with tears, but she did not change her strategy, she simply continued to meet the others' eyes and to smile as the hot drops scalded down her cheeks.

Robin did allow herself one invasion of the captive women's privacy, however.

She listened to snatches of their conversation, exercising her grasp of basic Russian to the uttermost. But the groups through which she passed were deeply defensive – like convicts or psychiatric patients – almost institutionalised. No group which could be identified said anything that she could hear. She, the unmarked, fragrant outsider yet to be abused or broken, was to their mind also an enemy; a spy.

The distant, unattributable snatches of conversation varied from the banal to the shocking.

" ... so I said, 'Irina, if you touch me again I'll ...'"

" ... it's the same in Archangel. They're everywhere. If you don't pay up, they just..."

" ... he's not so bad. If you do what he tells you and try to please him..."

" ... she hasn't been the same since all the officers had her one after the other in one night. Party, they called it..."

" ... for a video. They filmed it. Tied her up and hurt her really badly..."

"Of course she's a spy. Blonde bitch like that, all dressed up like a party worker on May Day..."

" ... a little accident if I can catch her when they're not looking..."

" ... I'll help if I can have that blouse of hers..."

"Don't be stupid. It would never fit you. And it'll probably be all dirty when I've finished..."

"Lady, you seem to have a knack of making enemies."

The words stopped Robin in her tracks for several reasons. Firstly because they were spoken in barely audible English. That was shock enough. Secondly, because they were so clearly addressed to her. Thirdly, because they were whispered by a woman sitting immediately in front of her. The woman was dressed in flimsy underwear like the rest of them. Her hair was filthy but tidy. Her body was as battered and bruised as any there but her face was unmarked, strong and smiling

203

wryly. She was sitting alone with her back against a wall. Immediately beside her there was a little doorway – more a hatch – clearly opening into some kind of locker or store.

Robin paused, looking around for a trap. "They getting to you already?" came the faintly mocking American tones again.

"Are they ever," said Robin quietly. Her eyes filled with tears again and the act of speaking nearly choked her.

She went to crouch down, automatically, but the other girl stopped her with a gesture. "Get your clothes off first," she said. "It'll save time. They're the only kind of a mattress you're going to get, I warn you."

The woman watched as Robin removed and folded her clothing. Underneath all her practical outerwear, she was clad in a simple, old-fashioned white two-piece cotton bra and panty set from Marks and Spencer. Even the most desperate woman in the room could covet nothing about it except for its cleanliness. "They strip-searched you yet?" she asked as Robin sat beside her, glad to be out of the all-too-public eye, her mouth open to introduce herself.

Robin snuggled back until her shoulders were resting on the wall beside those of her new friend. "Patted over," she said. "But they haven't strip-searched me."

"They will. It's where the process starts. Strip-search first. Then full internal examination."

"They have a doctor on board?"

"Nope."

Robin sat and digested this. "Maybe I'm not part of the process," she said.

"Better pray you are, lady. If you're not part of the process, then you're part of the nearest fishes' diet. And they cut you up before they serve you up, if you catch my drift."

"I know." The little confidence slipped out and Robin could have bitten her thoughtless tongue off. But then again, she thought at once, the instant this 'getting to know you' routine was over, she'd be asking questions about passing Mounties anyway.

"Aha," said the American woman, as though she had suspected all along. "And just how in Hell's name do you know that, lady?"

"I pulled one of your fish dinners out of Lake Superior before the feast had really started. Nearly a week ago, that was."

"So you're Robin. I guessed maybe. That's why I took the risk. You sure look like she described you."

Robin's whole world seemed to switch off for a second, as though reality were a theatre and God was now doing a little scene change. When it switched back on, things

205

were all slightly awry for a while. "You've been talking to Jeanne," said Robin. Her whispered voice sounded hollow in her own ears.

"Yeah. Poor kid."

"She's ... Is she ... ?"

"Dead? Not quite. It was touch and go there for a while, though. Fresh meat. The fact that she's a law officer and all the scumsuckers on both this ship and the last one have scores to settle with the law..."

"What did they do to her?"

"Lady, you do not want to know. They did some in the last place and they did a lot more over here. The last session would have killed her for certain if one of them hadn't stood up for her. Sholokov. That was his name, I think."

Robin felt a frisson of recognition at the name. Just another little sensation to add to the overload.

The American voice continued matter-of-factly, "She lisps a little when she speaks. No. You definitely do not want to know what they did to her."

"But I'm the next new meat. I may want to prepare myself."

"I kid you not, Robin. This is nightmare time. There is no way you can prepare. Except maybe to go mad like one or two of the poor bitches in here. Or get to like it, which is more or less the same."

Robin felt her face draining of colour as the savage reality of this woman's words sank in, but that sensation, unpleasant though it was, paled into insignificance itself in the face of what happened next.

The American opened the little door beside her. It folded back on itself to reveal a little locker about six feet long and a yard deep and high. In here, as though in her coffin already, lay Jeanne La Motte. She lay on her back, her eyes closed and her arms folded over the tattered wreckage of a bra which would never have fitted properly even had it been in one piece. Her face was swollen, one eye closed, one lip split, black blood crusted beneath the left nostril. The whole of her long, pale body was welted and mottled, and the marks looked livid and new.

"You know," said the American quietly, "she walked back in under her own steam afterwards. Made it right over here without any help at all. Gutsiest thing I ever saw."

Robin felt faint. For the third time in less than an hour her brimming eyes overflowed, but she did not realise. She did not really return to her senses until the American closed the door. Then she found herself on all fours, choking on vomit which her iron will refused to release because the smell in here was bad enough already. She raised her desperate face and looked the American woman straight in the eye. She did not trust herself to speak – or even to open her mouth, but such was the power of communication that went between the two of them that the American sat back as though Robin had screamed at her.

"The name's Julie," said the American then. "Julie Voroshilov. Born in Chicago, learned Russian at my mother's breast, graduated in International Business from Northwestern. Went to St Petersburg as a secretary PA to some speculator who never made the grade. Then I answered the wrong fucking job advert when the first post fell through. Like most of the poor kids in here. Boy did we all answer the wrong fucking ads!"

Robin opened her mouth to reply, when the door at the far end of the room slammed open. The guards stood back. Silence descended like a headsman's axe. Captain Karpov entered. Every eye in the room was suddenly looking elsewhere. Except Robin's. Robin was too new to know the form, and Julie, looking studiously at the deck herself, did not realise until it was far too late. But looking away might not have helped in any case – for Karpov was clearly looking for Robin anyway. When their eyes met he smiled a lean smile. He crooked his finger and beckoned her.

Like a bird watching a snake, Robin rose,

then automatically stooped to pick up her clothes. Only when she felt the movement did Julie look up and by then it was too late for her to do anything other than to grasp the warm material. "Leave all this," she said almost silently. "I don't think you'll be needing your clothes for a while."

Twenty-Two

What Robin felt as she crossed the sudden immensity of that cramped floor was unlike anything she had ever felt in all her life before. The lack of shoes was strange – a feeling she associated with privacy and intimacy. She felt shorter without footwear and, if possible, even more vulnerable. She found it difficult to walk properly. She rose on her toes and still felt ungainly.

She felt every gaze in the place scalding on the pale expanses of her naked skin and she realised, more poignantly than ever before, just how flimsy and transparent white cotton can be.

She felt sheer, stark terror so powerful that it subsumed even the acute embarrassment of all the personal things. She had not bathed in days. She had depilated neither legs nor armpits since coming to Canada, and as for her bikini region – that hadn't been seen to since last summer.

She supposed, fleetingly, that these considerations, so petty and pointless, were her mind taking refuge from the awesome horror of the immediate future that faced her now.

All of the women here have come through this, and I will bloody well do so as well, she said to herself and placed her foot upon the bottom step as though mounting a gallows.

There was a stirring just behind her and she looked back, surprised. Another woman was coming towards the steps. She must have been summoned too while Robin's senses were lost in that terrible speculation. Their eyes did not meet, for the Russian girl was looking downward, wrapped in her own unimaginable thoughts. So terrible did the poor woman look that Robin slowed automatically and was in position to catch her when her shaking foot missed its step and she would have fallen all the way back down. That simple act of care and kindness made the whole silent chamber seem to fill with a sort of whisper. Whether it was a positive reaction or a negative one she had no way of knowing. And she was sidetracked in any case by the awful realisation that the arm she was holding to support the

stumbling girl had several cigarette burns
upon it.

At the top of the stairs, the guards took the
other girl while Karpov took Robin. The
door seemed to float open and the icy lino
of the corridor slid beneath her tender toes.
The coolness of the corridor made her
nipples come to points and she knew
Karpov would be looking. She had learned
enough to keep looking down, away from
him. She focused on the floor in front of her
and flicked her eyes up only once in a while
to look for obstacles ahead.

He led her to the lift and, sobbing quietly,
the other woman followed, also led by a
guard. The doors hissed open. The four of
them entered. They turned, a little clumsily
because they were still in their pairs, to face
the doors. Each woman remained held
firmly by her upper arm. The car hissed up.
It came to a stop but Robin was away in her
dream realms of shock and did not realise
the implications of the slowing movement.

The doors opened. Shock hit Robin like
an electric current. Half a dozen strange
men were lined up outside the little car,
gawking in at her. She panicked absolutely
and wildly for the first time in her life. She
may have screamed – someone certainly
did. She turned, to hide herself; to flee.
Karpov's grip nearly broke her arm. A great

cheer went up. It was a horrible sound, like the baying of hunting wolves, full of threat and gleeful blood lust.

The door hissed closed, quietening the terrible sound. The lift jumped into motion once again. Robin realised that she and her captor were now quite alone. Karpov said, "I hope Irina is in the mood for a party. Not that she has any say in the matter, of course."

Robin began to swear at him then. She called him every name she could think of and a few that hadn't entered her head, let alone her vocabulary, since the wilder days of her youth. When he failed to respond, she lashed out at him. She didn't manage to hit him. He warded off her blows with practised ease and, when he ceased to be amused by her childish antics, he slapped her round the face. He slapped her forehand and back-hand, so hard that she would have fallen – except that he was still keeping tight hold of her arm.

So that, when the lift slowed again and the doors whispered wide, Robin was already sporting a black eye, a bleeding lip and a lividly bruised arm. Karpov pushed her roughly forward and she stumbled into a corridor. This must be the 'C' deck corridor, she calculated. 'C' was the level immediately below the bridge. It was where the captain and senior officers would have their accommodation. Where someone as senior as Karpov would have his quarters. It was more than the taste of her own blood that made her feel sick to her stomach. He came to a door and pushed it wide.

"In." He gestured. Over his shoulder she saw a good-sized room with a table and a bunk. The panic came again and she turned to run. Swift as a striking snake, he reached forward, grabbed her by her unblemished forearm and threw her inwards through the door. She ran past him, stumbled and fell flat on her face. She bruised her shins on the bunk and struck her forehead with stunning force on the edge of the table. She cried out with pain and shock, then rolled over and over, cradling her head.

After three rolls a solid pair of legs stopped her. She found herself looking up at a tall man in a white coat.

"This is the doctor," said Karpov. "He is going to examine you."

"Liar! There's no doctor on this boat." She pulled herself to her feet and blazed at the arrogant Russian. "The women told me! This is just some sick..."

Karpov slapped her again, making the shadowed cabin flicker with brightness around the edge of her hazy vision. Her head felt as though it would snap off her neck and split into pieces. Her teeth rattled and she bit her tongue agonisingly. She

213

collapsed onto the bunk and sat, leaning forward, shoulders hunched and legs spread, drooling blood onto the floor. Someone handed her a towel and she put it to her lips.

"I brought him with me from *Caspian*," said Karpov quietly. "Now he is going to give you a thorough examination, and if you fight back or call out again then I will beat you severely and he will have to treat you as well as examining you."

She looked up into the Russian's flinty face. She looked beyond him, down the foot of the L-shaped room, to where the medicine cabinets and the examination couch all stood ready. "I will be outside while the examination is being done," he said. "But consider this. Had you cooperated instead of fighting back, you would have been utterly unmarked now. When you look in a mirror you will see what you have done to yourself."

He stepped out of the door, and the doctor, snapping the wrists of his latex gloves, made an unmistakable gesture towards the examination table. Remembering Julie's sad and cynical words, Robin crossed to it and lay down, thinking, "This is better than becoming fish food."

And in fact, Irina's fate showed all too graphically that for some reason they were giving her an easy ride.

214

★ ★ ★

After the embarrassing, painful and messy process of the examination was over, the doctor gave a curt gesture towards the cabin's en-suite shower room. Robin went in without thinking, leaving her underwear where it lay on the little cabinet by the examination table. She all but had a heart attack at the sight of her face. She reached for a flannel to dab the worst of the blood with but then she paused, took a deep breath and performed a brutal reordering of priorities. She left her face alone and washed herself. At the touch of water on her tummy, she was overcome by the need to relieve herself and so she turned to lock the door. Karpov was there. She gasped with shock and stepped back. His hand pushed the door wide. His eyes remained fixed on hers. It was as though he had seen enough naked women already. "Doors open at all times," he said. "I've lost too many to broken mirrors, pills and razor blades."

And so she sat, as self-consciously as though his eyes were on her, knowing he was just outside the door discussing her most private details with the doctor. Partway through her ablutions her underwear sailed in through the door. "Hurry up," he called.

Karpov led her out into the corridor again,

215

his hand firmly round her upper arm. He said nothing more to her, but took her back towards the lift. At least an hour had passed – maybe more. Her watch was of course long gone. The corridors were not so quiet now. Men were bustling about. At this level, most of them were officers and few of them gave her a second glance. Then another reason for the activity became apparent. Robin felt the engines grumble into life with the nakedly super-sensitive soles of her feet. As they reached the lift, the ship's tannoy boomed and Karpov was summoned to the bridge. He swore shortly and looked around the bustling corridor.

Men came and went in bustling crowds, all of them clearly busy. Karpov sucked his teeth and frowned. The tannoy boomed again. Just as it did so, a crewman stepped into the corridor through a door that clearly led outside to the deck.

"You!" called Karpov at once. "Take this woman below."

Robin looked up. It was the seaman with the clean vest. The one in whose quarters she had heard the sobbing woman. She was uncertain whether she was relieved that it was he or embarrassed that he should see her like this. And she knew his name. Sholokov. That was it. Sholokov.

Sholokov came over from the doorway, his eyes busy and his face set. He was an *Aral* crewman after all. He could argue the toss against the *Caspian*'s captain if he chose. But it seemed to Robin that when he looked at her his gaze softened slightly and he came forward obediently.

Sholokov took Robin's arm from Karpov's firm grip and a glance passed between them that she could not read. Then Karpov went on up while they stood and waited for the lift car to return. Sholokov's grip was less firm than Karpov's and for an instant she felt like tearing free and running away. She glanced across at him, weighing her chances. Then her mind sprang awake. There was just the faintest smear of blood on his hand. She looked down. Yes. The smear was repeated on the otherwise pristine slope of his vest, just above the handle of a wicked-looking sheath knife.

Robin went absolutely cold. Her mind raced, replaying her memory like an old video, thinking about the manner in which he came in through the door. Had he looked startled by the number of people in the corridor? Had he looked furtive? Guilty?

Robin was beginning to regain a little self-control now and began to look about her. She recognised one or two faces, but none on whom she could possibly call for help – the nearest person to her, for instance, the first officer of *Aral* who had so nearly got Jeanne killed on their first visit aboard. He

217

saw her looking up at him and leered. Sholokov saw the look and pushed her forward a little more quickly. But as they reached the lift, so the leering officer came over. He was very much in Sholokov's line of command. But when he said to the almost immaculate crewman, "Give the arrogant bitch to me," Sholokov began to argue.

"I am sorry, Lieutenant Ivanov. She belongs to Captain Karpov. He told me to look after her and take her safely below. If you want her you'll have to take it up with him, sir."

"I'm taking it up with you, you prissy faggot. Give her to me now!"

Ivanov shoved Sholokov hard against the opening lift doors and tore Robin physically out of his grasp. She screamed, more with shock than pain, and with a good deal of sympathy for her would-be protector. He fell awkwardly into the lift car and the first officer dragged Robin forward like a forgotten puppet as he stepped half into the car and aimed a fearsome kick at his fallen crewman. It connected soundly in his ribs, the tip of the officer's boot sinking in under the crewman's solid pectoral. The last Robin saw of Sholokov, as the doors closed, was that white vest marked with a huge black smear as well as a tiny bright red one. She screamed again but nobody even looked up.

"Right, you little slut, let's settle with you like we settled with that Mountie bitch!" raged Ivanov. He half pulled, half threw her down the corridor to the doorway Sholokov had entered through. He threw her out onto the deck in the brightness of the afternoon and stepped out after her. She stood on the hot metal deck, wondering whether to fight or flee. A glance around the deck showed her that they were alone. There was nothing here but a lifeboat. One glance was enough to fix every detail of the place in her mind. Or nearly every detail.

A safety rail edged the little red-painted iron square at side and back, protecting its occupants from a tumble onto the poop behind or over the side by the boat. The inner sides were walled in white by the main funnel housing and by the bridgehouse wall. Above this wall, with the would-be rapist framed in the door, was another safety rail at the back of the bridge-wing deck. As Robin backed out into the brightness of the sun, a shadow fell on her from this height and she looked up. Someone was standing up there, made black and featureless by the sun behind him. She sucked in breath to call for help. Then she remembered where she was and how pointless that would be. And then in any case he was gone.

Robin took another step back, over-whelmed suddenly by the stench of hot iron that pervaded the little place. She staggered slightly, light-headed suddenly, and slipped. She fell heavily backwards and winded herself, striking her poor head on the deck hard enough to see yet more flashes of light before her dazed eyes. Automatically, without real thought, she scrabbled for enough purchase to get up and make a fight of it at least. Her legs parted. Her arms spread in a crucifix.

Everything stank of iron and seemed slick. She writhed, exposing more and more of herself to the officer's burning gaze, but somehow she simply could not quite get onto her feet.

He threw himself forward then, crashing to his knees between her sprawled thighs, his hands busy at his belt and zipper. He was babbling some filth at her but she could not really register what it was – especially as he was using terms far outside her meagre Russian vocabulary – and reaching down for her panties.

The instant he did so, however, a broad hand appeared like a hawk out of the sun and fastened in the luxuriant locks of his oiled hair. With no more ado he was jerked erect, not at all in the way he had planned. He was whirled around on toe-tips, like a dancer at the Kirov. His right leg swung out at the movement and caught Robin almost as painfully as it had caught Sholokov, though that may have been an accident. The impact of the blow rolled her over onto her side and she was able to scramble to her feet.

Overcome at last, by the pain, the terror, the overwhelming stench, Robin ran to the safety rail, all but throwing herself overboard as she brought up what little was left of her last meal and a great deal of burning bile. The matter behind her was settled by a couple of crisp blows and a swingeing kick. She heard, but did not see. She was looking over the side, transfixed.

Beaufort was a big ship for a Michigan freighter, but she was well laden with one thing and another. Even the 'C' deck lifeboat station was not so far above the water. She was turning across a vicious crosscurrent too, so the port side, where Robin was standing, angle a little downwards, gave an extremely clear view of the water as it rippled away into that terrifying rush down into Lake Huron through the straits.

Karpov's hand fell on Robin's shoulder, making her flinch and jump. "You are all bloody. Bloody woman," he said. The phrase brought Richard into her head just at the worst possible moment, for he called her his bloody woman when they were at odds over something. Her heart and will nearly broke then. Had Karpov not been holding her she might have slipped over into the icy

221

embrace of that safe, sleepy current. But he held her hard and continued to talk, dragging her back into the hell that the ship had become. "Where has this blood come from?" he demanded, offended.

And Robin, with the rail digging deep into the pit of her stomach with only his firm hand holding her safe – for reasons of his own she dared not fathom yet – let go of the wooden banister and pointed.

Out in the first fierce wash of the current, gone now and too far out ever to get back to Seul Choix, floated Irina, stark and dead. And, as they watched, so the water whirled her round and almost stood her up before it sucked her under.

So they both could see all too clearly the red star carved on her heart.

Twenty-Three

When Robin walked back across the packed deck and over to Julie Voroshilov, this time there were no envious or threatening comments. Several pairs of eyes met hers and she read in each a sisterly sympathy.

She felt almost as many complex irreconcilable emotions now as she had felt on that long walk out and she tried to sort them into some sort of order. She was still extremely scared. She felt less scared of the unknown and of the terrible spectre of rape and abuse, but more scared of the very real monster still cutting his bloody swathe through the soft flesh on display all around her. Well, if he was aboard, so were the women who were going to catch him and put a stop to his horrific career. She no longer felt quite so helpless, therefore. She now had an immediate mission – though little idea how to go about fulfilling it, as yet.

She felt dirty, soiled. But she knew she looked far worse than she felt. She looked as though she had suffered seriously, with her battered face, bruised arms, grazed shoulders and liberal patina of drying blood. She knew that the women around her were reacting to this above all. So she also felt a bit of a fraud.

"Jesus," said Julie with ready sympathy when she arrived beside her, "I thought they'd go easy on you."

"Why?"

"Well you're twice the age of most of the women here, and the scumsuckers seem to like them young. That kid Irina who went out with you, she's been the most popular and she's only just eighteen."

Robin sat down slowly, feeling the blood on her back crack and flake. Feeling old and stiff and sore. "Irina's not going to get any older now, I'm afraid."

"Shit! Poor kid. They kill her?"

Robin nodded. It felt as though every disc in her neck had slipped. "Somebody did. Most of this blood is hers."

"God damn them," Julie spat, glancing up at the emotionless guards by the door. "Well, I hope she died easy, though I doubt it."

"She went over the side with a star on her heart." Just saying the words made Robin shudder with the callous enormity of what was going on around them.

"My God! Maybe we'd better wake Jeanne up and tell her." Julie turned to the door, but Robin shook her aching head.

"Maybe later. Is there anyone in here we should tell about Irina first? I mean everyone's sitting in groups, which one did she belong to? It seems the least we can do to tell them what we know. Well, what I know..."

"Yeah. Oh yeah. Big Anya. She's the boss of one of the biggest groups in here. Irina was her little sister, I think. I'd better go and tell her."

"No. I'll do it," countered Robin impulsively. "My Russian's up to it, I think."

"Hey!" said Julie. "I didn't know you spoke Russian."

"No," admitted Robin pulling herself wearily to her feet. "I thought it would give me an edge. But there are already too many secrets in here."

"True. I'd better come with you, though."

Anya deserved her epithet. She was tall, muscular. She had an imposing presence even lying on her side propped on an elbow like a Roman at a feast. She had clearly taken an enormous amount of punishment but had yet to wear that hopeless, beaten look of some of the others. She was obviously acute, too. She knew what Robin had come to tell her long before the words were out.

"You saw her?" she growled in English, at the end of Robin's halting Russian

225

explanation. "You are certain?"

"I saw her over the side, being swept under in the current down to the straits," Robin repeated with the freedom of her mother tongue. "She had a star carved on her heart. She was dead."

Anya sat silently for a moment, her eyes icily distant. Then she continued, speaking in English, "A star. Tell me about this star."

But a new speaker entered the conversation at that point. "That's my job, Anya," whispered a broken, lisping voice; the voice of someone who has screamed until their vocal cords began to tear, and then screamed some more. It was a way of speaking familiar to all in here. "I'll tell you all about the star," whispered the strange voice, quietly but steadily.

Robin and Julie swung round together as Jeanne settled stiffly and wearily onto the deck beside them. There seemed to be a section of one hip which was not too badly brutalised. She settled on that and began to go through the details of her investigation so far.

As Jeanne described what had been done to the women who had been found floating in the lakes and seaways, so the room slowly seemed to fall silent under the spell of that steady, sore-throated whisper, even though it was speaking in English.

Most of these women were well educated,

226

Robin realised. They had, like Julie, answered job adverts for secretaries, PAs and the like. They almost all spoke English. And they gathered around the shattered Mountie, listening as she described the deaths of at least three of their number.

But this lecture to the whole group was a situation that could not be allowed to proceed. Robin was quick to spot the restlessness of the guards and was able to empathise with their discipline problems at least. "Hey, Jeanne, Anya, wait a minute," she said after a while. "The guards are getting worried. This probably looks like *The Great Escape* to them. They were happy enough with everyone in small groups but they'll get very nervous about all of us listening to one person. Especially if she's speaking a language they don't understand but we do. Especially if it's a Mountie doing the talking."

"Fuck 'em," said Anya roundly.

"That's why we're here," said Julie.

Anya gave a dry laugh. This was probably the most dangerous sound, short of a gun being cocked, that could be heard in this room. The guards looked at each other, frowning. "If they even report this," said Robin urgently, "then Jeanne, Julie and I are dead. Probably you too, Anya. They won't think twice. We must break back into small groups. We can talk things through and pass

227

the message round if need be. But if they think for a moment that we're trying to organise anything here, they'll take anyone who looks like a ringleader or a potential nuisance and slaughter us like lambs."

"You know she's right, Anya. Drop over in a few minutes and we'll take this further, just among us girls," Julie said in Russian and pulled herself to her feet. She and Robin helped Jeanne up and the three of them limped back to their places against the back wall.

When Anya joined them ten minutes later, the room had returned to its original pattern of small groups speaking Russian and generally staying away from each other. The guards were beginning to look more relaxed. There was still an atmosphere, however. There was still something on the air of the room made up of shock, outrage and the realisation that they could still all come together as a unit rather than being isolated by self-loathing and mutual suspicion. Jeanne's short talk had undone a lot of the brutal work the men had been doing lately. Robin, watching the well-armed men in their shorts and T-shirts, hoped that they were not sensitive enough to pick up this change in the psychic wind.

Anya arrived just as Robin and Jeanne had finished discussing general matters and had brought each other up to date with what they now knew of the background to the crimes. Jeanne was just becoming the Inspector from the Violent Crime Linkage Analysis System once again, taking Robin through the details of everything she had observed from the moment the tannoy had called Captain Karpov to the bridge. The huge Russian woman, larger by far upright than she had seemed to be lying down, sat and listened as the reconstruction of events was teased out of Robin's subconscious.

They began with the sounds. "I remember the tannoy message. I heard the conversations all around me, but none of them in detail. The engines had just started up and the sound they were making drowned out a lot of background. The sounds the lift was making. You know, the creaky, thumping sounds of the lift-gear and the car. That's it for a good few minutes. Karpov was getting worried, looking for someone to take care of me. When Sholokov the crewman opened the door, I heard gulls. The engines more clearly, of course. There were sounds of water splashing along the hull or over the propeller. Then the first officer from *Aral* arrived and the details go fuzzy. On an auditory level at least."

"OK," said Jeanne, gently, her voice husky. "What did you smell?"

229

Just the word made Robin feel sick. Her memory of the stench of hot iron – and her new understanding of what that smell actually meant – made her dizzy now. She saw again that deck, so liberally painted with bright, bright red; smelt again the iron smell of new-spilt blood.

"She's white as a sheet, Jeanne," said Julie from very far away. "We'd better give it a rest."

Just at that moment, circumstances dictated a break in the interrogation in any case. The door opened. Four men entered. Two new guards came in first, and, behind them, two men carrying what looked like an enormous tin bath. Robin had no idea what was going on here and drew back automatically, fearing some new humiliation – public bathing perhaps. Steam hung above the tub. Whatever was in it was boiling hot. She drew back further still.

But for once, all the others started forward, though none of them actually moved. With the help of the four guards, the two men brought the big tin tub down into the body of the prison room and placed it on the floor. And the most unexpected thing of all happened to Robin. After her conversation about smells – cut short by her faintness – her nose was assaulted by a real, familiar smell. "Wieners," breathed Julie, her voice close to ecstasy. And Robin realised what this was. It was no new torture. It was dinner.

The women went forward in ordered groups. Out of the tin bath, each took a rough-cut hunk of bread and a sizeable steaming sausage. Group by group, they made their own basic hot-dogs and fell to with the relish of near starvation. There was a clear pecking order, but Anya seemed happy to forgo her elevated place in the hierarchy and eat with the foreigners – who ate last. This ensured two things. First, it gave a good deal of added status to Jeanne and especially the newcomer Robin. Secondly, it ensured that there were sausages and bread left even for these lowly creatures. When the bath was empty, it was taken out while the four guards remained. A few minutes later, the men who had brought the food returned with water. All the women drank greedily for, even dressed as lightly as they were, the heat was enervating and dehydrating.

"Potty training now," said Julie. "Think it's shower night?"

"Christ, this is like boarding school," said Robin.

"A boarding school in hell, maybe," grated Anya. "They got more freedom in the gulags."

"And," said Jeanne, "there was no one in

231

the gulags running around slaughtering them."

"Except, maybe, the KGB," said Anya, with that grim little laugh of hers.

"On the other hand," said Robin soberly, "the people in the gulags really didn't have any hope of rescue or release, did they?"

"And just what hope do we have?" asked Anya, genuinely surprised by Robin's words. "Who in hell's name's coming after us, except half the pimps and pornographers in the good old USA?"

"Well, Jeanne's a Mountie," said Robin, hoping to high heaven she wasn't giving away anything damaging or important. "The Canadian authorities are coming after her, though I haven't seen any of them in action yet. The Americans have got at least one task force of FBI special agents coming after the officers and men aboard this ship – or will have when they find out which ship they're on. And I have my husband Richard coming after me."

Anya gave a cynical laugh. "Oh, that puts all my fears to rest. The Mounties, the FBI and *your husband*. We're as good as rescued already!"

But Jeanne looked up unexpectedly. "Don't laugh," she said. "I've seen the guy in action and I'd be more than happy to know he was coming after me!"

"Oh, but he is," said Robin, with unshakeable certainty. "And he simply will not stop until he's found us. That's the kind of man he is."

"Well, let's just hope we're in a fit condition to appreciate it when ever he does catch up with us," said Julie. "Being still alive would be nice."

As Julie spoke, she pulled herself to her feet in response to the signal from one of the guards at the door. The others followed suit and the four of them limped across to the steps together.

"You won't have experienced this, Anya," said Julie quietly as they limped through the other groups, "but one of the best things about being last is that the seat's always nice and warm."

"Yeah, that's a plus," said Jeanne. "It almost makes up for the fact that there's never any toilet tissue."

"I don't think you've been paying attention," said Anya.

"What do you mean?" asked Jeanne.

"She means that there will be tonight," said Robin. "Like it was with the hot dogs. There'll be plenty of paper tonight."

And so there was.

There were also no guards. The four women went into the crew's latrines – the obvious flaw in the whole design of the secretly adapted ships – and went about their business unmolested and unwatched.

"Why no guards?" asked Robin. "Aren't they afraid we'll hang ourselves from the doorframes? Stick our heads down the pans and drown ourselves?"

For once her morale-building forced levity fell a little flat. "No," said Anya, her voice flat again. "They call it 'corporate responsibility'. It's another one of their sick jokes." She turned and let Robin see her back for the first time. It was a mess of bruises and welts from shoulder to waist. "One girl I was with managed to choke herself on the paper. The rest of us couldn't stop her in time. This is what they did to us. They did it in front of everyone and it was not a very pretty sight. We keep a careful eye on each other now."

They had five minutes to the second, so conversation was brief, and this was just as well, for at the very instant their time was up, the door slammed wide. The first two guards stepped in. Two new guards were with them, one of whom was Sholokov. "Come!" he barked.

With one guard beside each, the four women were led out of the latrine and along the corridor towards the lift. "You have an audience upstairs," said Sholokov. "There are one or two questions to be asked."

Even Anya went pale at the sound of this

234

and poor Jeanne slumped sideways onto Julie, whose solid strength was all that held her upright. In the bustle of the crowded corridor the four women with their well-armed guards warranted hardly a second look from anyone.

The lift arrived. The doors hissed open. It was clear there would be room for six but not eight. Sholokov motioned the others in and then stood back with Robin. The doors closed. The bustle of the corridor swirled around them as they stood and waited.

All of Robin's bravado was gone again. The summons was so shockingly unexpected. The possibilities were so completely limitless. She thought for an instant of Richard and their twins. How would they get by without her? Would Richard be able to live with her if this was a summons to rape rather than death? Would she be able to live with herself?

But the question of living at all was moot. She was certain that Sholokov had cut the star into Irina's breast and she was sure he knew that she knew. He had engineered things so that they were alone, and the only question that remained was whether he could get away with killing her here and now. Not in the corridor, perhaps, but in the lift. No one seemed to care about Irina. No one would care about her – except, perhaps, for the unfathomable Captain Karpov. She

235

looked down. At least the immaculate crewman had a clean vest again. There was no little telltale smear of blood above the handle of that massive sheath knife at his side.

She suddenly realised that she should be running away, screaming blue murder, not standing here frozen like a rabbit in headlights. She turned. His grip on her arm tightened agonisingly. The doors slid open in front of her and he all but threw her in. She hit the back wall, seeing her own terror in close-up in the mirror there, and turned. He stepped in and pressed the button. The doors closed. The lift car began to climb. The instant that it moved, while it was between decks, he drove his elbow back into the panel and it juddered to a halt.

Robin sprang forward but, with a kind of ringing hiss, the knife sprang free of its sheath and into his big right fist. He pushed the razor point of it against her. The first millimetre parted the skin in her left breast through the tiny band of lace at the crown of her cotton bra-cup. It stung like a rose thorn and released a droplet of blood. Two inches beneath – three at the most – her heart convulsed with utter terror.

"You know," he said to her gently, in English, "that there are men aboard here who will stop at nothing to kill you now. I'm in the pay of one of them myself."

Twenty-Four

"Damn the paperwork, Captain Ball," bellowed Richard, his voice carrying easily over the clamour of the docks. "I want *Swallow* off your deck and into the water now!"

"It isn't that I don't want to help, sir," answered the captain, somewhat less forcefully. "I just don't have the power. It will take a crane a good deal bigger than anything I have aboard to shift her, as you well know. Therefore I need permission to move *Titan* over to the dockside facilities. I need permission to man a crane and lift the vessel free. I need to get a longshoreman, qualified and union recognised, to man the crane. But that's only the start. You need to show me your authorisation to put an unregistered SuperCat in American waters and to crew her and to sail her. Unless I have all those authorities, it's more than my master's ticket is worth."

Richard swung round to Abe Sharon, who was positioned just behind his shoulder. "What do we have to cover this man's concerns, Abe? You know we need to move quickly. We've been lucky *Titan* was held on this side of the Soo but the backlog is clearing fast and once Captain Ball here gets the go ahead, *Swallow* will be about as much use to us as her sister *Swiftsure.*"

"Forewarned is forearmed, Richard," said Abe. He winked at Beth, who grinned in reply as he held out his personal phone to the worried-looking Captain Ball. "I hope you can hear over the noise of the docks, sir. You are connected directly to the office of the Director. Hard copy will be spooling out of your fax within the next half-hour and, indeed the fax at the Harbour Master's office and the Coast Guard's and the Soo Pilot's office, but if you could settle your mind to immediate action..."

The captain took the little handset and turned away. Richard, Beth and Abe walked down the deck beneath the tall port hull of the SuperCat *Swallow*, being careful to step over the ropes and bolts securing her to the deck. Side by side they walked down to the forecastle and stood up on the head behind the little jackstaff there. *Titan* had been berthed in the Bondar Transient Marina while the backlog at the docks was sorted out and they now had a fine view past the SS *Valley Camp* museum ship out onto the locks themselves. All around them, Sault Ste Marie, Ontario, bustled under the late summer sunshine and the last of the big ships moved out of their temporary berths ahead of *Titan* and up into the locks.

Richard, however, was blind to the magnificence of the scene for his mind was full of gloomy foreboding as to the fate of his kidnapped wife. She was a highly intelligent and endlessly resourceful woman, who had managed to free herself from a range of dangerous opponents in the past – up to and including Filipino pirates of the most deadly and ruthless type. But somehow this was different. The calculated brutality of the whole situation, coupled with the obvious threat to a woman unprotected on the type of ship they were now looking for, crewed by the sort of men who beat women to death and then carved stars on their breasts.

Upriver, in the locks north-west of them, huge 500-ton steel doors opened and closed in sequence, allowing the water to rise and fall under its own weight, carrying the vessels with it up out of Lake Huron into Lake Superior. Richard's eyes drifted southwards looking away across St Mary's River, past Sault Ste Marie, over the Michigan countryside to where he proposed to take his SuperCat *Swallow* before darkness fell. Down St Mary's River east and south through Detour Passage into the Straits of Mackinac, then hard west past St Ignace and Naubinway, past Port Inland and Seul

Choix and into Lake Michigan after her.

Still he had not slept. Since Robin had been kidnapped, he had eaten on the move and had poured simple indomitable energy into the situation like the waters of Niagara along the waterway east of here. Beth had been forced to report to Abe Sharon on the run when the chipper little special agent had arrived. He had taxied up from the airport, having cleared things up in Duluth as best he could and caught the first flight east.

"I have no idea how he does it," she had concluded less than an hour since. "Just watching all that energy, that sheer will, exhausts me."

"He's a guy for getting things done. Have you seen his file?"

"We have a file on him?"

"Sure do. We have one with a CIA supplement and they have one with an FBI supplement. British intelligence must have a whole volume on him. KGB, too, come to that, or the Federal Counter Intelligence Service or whatever they're calling themselves nowadays. We have him documented at length. As a businessman with companies and contacts here. As an international expert on terrorism, including personal links with the PLO. On Chinese triads with contacts – personal contacts – with at least one Dragon's Head. As a possible drug smuggler with links to organised crime everywhere from Las Vegas to the Sea of Cortez. As a senior adviser and ex-Project Director with the UN. The list goes on and on. Apparently he spent the Millennium at the South Pole helping out NASA when they ran into a little trouble down there."

"You're joking!"

"I kid you not. Read the file. And his wife's file, come to that."

"Now I know you're joshing me. *She* has a file...?"

Captain Ball came up to the trio quietly, not a little shaken. He handed the phone back to Abe. "Loud and clear?" asked the special agent cheerfully, glancing out around the clangour of the busy waterway.

"Oh yes," said the captain, meaning something else entirely, "I got the message loud and clear. I'll get onto the harbour master at once. We'll have her in the water for you by four with any luck."

"Three, please," said Richard. "I'm in a hurry here." He pulled out a brand-new very advanced and extremely expensive-looking new-generation Nokia WAP personal phone with Internet access.

"Oh yes," said Beth faintly. "Did I tell you we went shopping after we made sure the men in hospital were comfortable and put the chopper crew into the Marriott?"

"Who on earth is he calling?" asked Abe,

241

beginning to see Beth's point.

"Crew," said Richard, suddenly turning the dazzling ice blue of his gaze directly on the special agent and answering for himself. "Crew for *Swallow*. And you'd better get on the blower as well if you still plan to have your own private army on her as you had on *Aral*. I'm leaving this port at three on the dot and I'm not going to stop for anyone."

Richard was as good as his word. Agent Beth Jackson, FBI, was beginning to learn that he usually was. Even as *Swallow* was being lifted high above the deck of the big freighter which had carried her over from Europoort in Holland, the first crew members were already standing on the forecastle head immediately below her twin hulls, beside Richard – while the last of them were landing at Sault's Michigan-side airport on a private jet from New York. He had been making calls for twelve of the eighteen hours he had been here, calling in favours from all over the place.

Beth was so impressed with Richard's simple command of everything and everyone around him – especially after Abe's description of his FBI file – that she was quite prepared to believe him capable of the patently impossible. So that when the courtesy chopper from the airport swooped onto the vacancy left by *Swallow* on *Titan*'s deck and Robert Redford stepped down out of it, she simply gave a mental shrug. That's fine, she thought. Maybe we need a movie star or two. That's cool. Will Smith's probably on the way in too.

Richard brought the newcomer over to her at once. "Here's someone I want you to meet," he was saying. "Bob, this is Agent Beth Jackson. She's my FBI liaison." Bob stuck out his hand and grinned. His grin was as wide as Wyoming. His eyes were a shade or two darker than Richard's – a warm California sky blue. She took his hand and grinned in return, hoping her teeth were as even and white as his. "Beth, this is Bob Stark. He's going to captain *Swallow* for me."

"Captain Stark."

"Agent Jackson."

Four words and they were firm friends.

Richard stood at Bob Stark's shoulder as he took *Swallow* across to the fuel jetty. A Soo pilot stood at the other, and Beth eased her weary body by leaning back against the throbbing wall at the back of the long, narrow navigation bridge. After the bridge of *Caspian*, this one seemed small and cramped but amazingly high-tech. Like the cockpit of a space shuttle. Windows stretched from side to side beneath one bank of instruments and above another. There were

243

more video screens there than in an editing suite. The captain's chair moved automatically on hydraulics in and out, up and down. Bob Stark seemed almost to be wearing the vessel when he occupied it. On his right sat his navigating officer. More distantly on his left, his radio officer. Down below, she knew, the engineering officers were tending the massive engines, and their voices came up to the captain on an open two-way link. Beth had simply never seen anything like it in her life.

She glanced down at her watch for the third time since three o'clock, when the massive motors had been fired up. It was still only five past the hour, but Beth had a worried feeling that time was running out too fast. She was the only agent aboard. Abe had gone off to collect the first section of the team he was hoping to build up aboard and he had not yet returned.

Beth looked across at Richard's square shoulder, and up to the set profile of the face above it. The jaw was squared and set like granite. It actually looked like granite because he had not had time to shave yet today. He was not going to change his mind, she thought. Abe was going to have to move some to catch up here or he and his men would be left behind.

But no. As the pristine hulls of the big SuperCat eased into position beside the jetty and the process of fuelling her up got under way, Beth saw the security gates at the far end of the dock open and two anonymous minibuses rolled onto the concrete pier. By the time the fuelling was complete, the FBI was solidly aboard. Beth was relieved to have them there and so she ran down at the earliest opportunity to report to Abe.

There was a side door out of the bridge that led directly onto a mezzanine deck. This level was like a balcony and it reached back maybe ten feet to a safety rail. At either end, stairs curved down to the great cavern of the main passenger accommodation area. Beyond the stair-heads, the mezzanine deck reached out down the sides, offering a second level for passenger accommodation with tables for families to gather round and play areas for the kids. There were long windows here, offering wide views almost as spectacular as that filling the clearview that reached from side to side of the navigation bridge, side to side of the Cat herself.

Swallow, like *Swiftsure*, was a passenger vessel. Around the central accommodation area, which was raised to sit halfway between the mezzanine above and the two long, low areas in the catamaran hulls, there were walkways leading to gift stores, bookshops and bars that were all closed tight for the moment.

Beth ran down the curving staircase and into the main area. The FBI shock troops looked out of place among the luxurious fittings. And so they were. The seats were wide enough to accommodate the largest passenger, but they were hardly suited to body armour. They were set out in long rows like aircraft seats and it was hard for men and equipment to negotiate them. Tables along the sides of the main passenger area were perfect for playing cards or eating a light meal. They looked a little flimsy under piles of assault rifles, riot guns, flash grenades and smoke bombs.

No sooner had Beth arrived than the Cat was in motion, swinging away from the dock and easing out into the waterway. "Back up on the bridge, Beth," ordered Abe. "You're my eyes and ears. Richard could be up to absolutely anything. I need to be watching him all the time."

But in fact Beth met Richard halfway up the stairs to the bridge as he came down to see Abe himself. "The pilot's taking us down to Detour," he said shortly. "Then we're on our own."

"That's cool," answered Beth amiably. "What are you going to do now?"

"Get Abe's people settled in. Listen to his initial briefing. Add anything I can. We'll be stopping briefly in Detour to pick up some more of my crew when we drop the pilot. If

246

Abe can arrange to get more troops there he can pick them up at the same time. Hell's teeth, look at this mess. They can't stay here. This isn't suitable at all. Beth, how many are there?"

"Troops? A dozen so far."

"Only a dozen? It looks like there are twenty of them. It must be the kit. Agent Sharon, I think your men would be better placed in one of the private areas. If you'd just follow me, please, I'll show you what I have in mind and see what you think..."

Ten minutes later, *Swallow* was living up to her name, skimming lightly along the downriver track of the busy waterway. She was as close to full speed as the pilot would allow and going faster than any waterborne vessel ever had on this stretch, weaving in and out of the lumbering Lakes freighters like a Ferrari on a freeway, bending the rules of the road.

Abe Sharon's troops were in a private lounge that was very much better suited to their needs than the public area. Here there was a solid mahogany table and sets of chairs, all of which could be moved. There was a robust suite of overstuffed furniture that accepted their heavy kit and anything that wouldn't fit there was piled on the thickly carpeted deck. The room was designed to function as a dining area or a

247

business area – almost a company board-room. It was perfect for briefings of any kind.

"You won't need to make notes at this stage," Abe was saying. "This is the first of several briefings designed to orientate the groups as they come aboard. There'll be more and more detailed briefings later in the mission.

"Firstly, the background. The discovery of two bodies floating in the Great Lakes waterway alerted the Canadian authorities to the possibility of a serial killer on the loose. Their investigations were complicated by the difficulty of identifying the dead women and, indeed, of being certain as to their actual cause of death."

A hand went up. "If we don't even know how they died, how do we know the same guy killed them?" It was the obvious question.

Abe began to explain about the red stars. About the manner in which an investigator from the ViCLAS section of the RCMP took over from local law in the case of the second murder. How this officer discovered, with the help of the FBI, that the first victim had been a Russian citizen and then the Mountie inspector herself had disappeared aboard the Russian freighter *Aral*...

Richard sat with ill-disguised impatience while Abe took his team through the escalation of the case and the realisation at Federal level that these ships, in United States waters, thousands of miles within US jurisdiction, were engaged in people-smuggling. And, more seriously still, that their serial killer was loose among the women being smuggled on the ships. His interest quickened, however, when Abe began to discuss their current situation.

With the loss of *Swiftsure*, effectively all their leads had gone cold. They suspected that the unfortunate women who had been carried on the hidden decks aboard *Aral* and *Caspian* were probably all in one place. They hoped that Inspector La Motte and Captain Robin Mariner were alive, well and with them. Logic dictated that the men who had crewed the two ships under arrest in Duluth were also with their illicit cargoes – and that meant that the man who had carved the stars on the dead women was also alive and possibly still at his bloody work. But exactly where the women and all the rest were, or were heading for, was a complete blank. Well; not a *complete* blank...

Abe handed over to Richard then, for much of the next section was about maritime matters and Richard was the better qualified to deliver the fruits of their combined wisdom. "If they're all at one place and they are headed anywhere – as opposed to being holed up ashore waiting for the heat to die down – then they must be in a large freighter," he began. "It is conceivable that they might be in several smaller craft, but the logistics don't seem to me to add up. Remember, *Aral* was lost dropping an expected cargo of women somewhere near Au Sable Point. I can see no other situation answering the situation we found. She had anchored – presumably at a rendezvous. She had drifted so dangerously that the watch aboard had abandoned. But she could not have drifted far without running hard aground. The people at the rendezvous were expecting one hundred or so women – they got the crew as well. Then a matter of hours later, they got the majority of *Caspian*'s crew too. So at the very least we have one ship with one hundred women aboard and two crews other than her own. And another ship with the first one hundred women safely dropped from *Caspian* a couple of days earlier. Alternatively, we might have one very big very tightly packed ship with all of them aboard."

"Including the guy who carves stars on girls," emphasised Beth.

"And a colleague from our sister force," added Abe.

"And my wife," concluded Richard.

That same hand went up again. "Two things," said the young agent, frowning. "Firstly, how do we know they're on a boat at all? What makes us think they are not holed up somewhere on the lake's shore, all tucked up safe and sound like Captain Mariner said?"

"We don't," answered Richard roundly. "It's a balance of probabilities, that's all. These people are desperate. They're taking these women somewhere and therefore someone is expecting them. Waiting for them. Waiting to pay for them. They're running late. *Aral* was running very late and was clearly running out of supplies, food and money. That's at least part of the reason her captain took the risk of waiting in Thunder Bay, hoping to pick up another cargo. They'll be even more desperate now – two ships down and no pay likely. They simply can't afford to wait, by my calculation. They have to deliver their merchandise, collect their wages and somehow get themselves home. Wherever they're going, they can only get in and out on the water. They're sailors to a man, after all."

"OK, say I buy that on balance of probabilities. Where are these boats of theirs? Lost among the international shipping on Superior hoping to get back into Duluth?"

"Not likely to be in Duluth. That's where we found *Caspian*," explained Abe. "But there was no report of a sudden influx of Russian women there."

"So you need a city big enough to soak up

that many girls without too much babble on the street. Further down the waterway than here – unless they've put them on a US registered boat and doubled back to a city where a Russian vessel would have raised too many eyebrows."

"That's right," said Richard. "That's our current thinking. They could in theory be as far back as Montreal or Toronto in Canada. They could be in Buffalo, Detroit, Windsor or Toledo. Or they could be heading west and south to the cities my money's on, Milwaukee or Chicago."

A silence fell as the agents digested this. Richard's brand-new, highly expensive personal phone rang. He put it to his ear. As soon as he did so, the thoughtful agent's hand went up again. "Marshall?" asked Abe.

"So the balance of probability says they're on the water – maybe even all in the same boat," said Marshall, clearly less than satisfied with the exercise of logic so far. "They're all heading to a big urban conurbation, probably in the United States. But we really don't know which of the Lakes they're actually on, and we certainly don't know where they're headed. Does that about sum it up?"

Abe opened his mouth to answer, as Richard was still listening with fearsome concentration to whoever was talking on his personal phone.

But Marshall pressed on relentlessly, "I mean, I'd like to get this clear because it might be the way they're trained to think at Scotland Yard or maybe even in the Mounties, but it's really not the way we were trained to think in the Academy."

Richard snapped off his phone and slipped it into his pocket. "Point taken, Marshall. Balancing probabilities is probably nothing to do with good police work at all. But we were right this time. That was Captain Stark patching me through to the Coast Guard. They've just taken a girl with a star on her heart out of the water off St Ignace."

"So they're in Huron, heading for Detroit, then," said Marshall, demonstrating a clear knowledge of what was where in the Great Lakes. "St Ignace is on the north shore of Huron."

"True but wrong," said Richard. "Ignace is on the north shore of Huron, but the only way a dead girl like this one could get there in the water is if she was dumped off a ship and washed down on the current through the Straits of Mackinac out of Lake Michigan. And that's where they are. Somewhere on Michigan, heading for Milwaukee or Chicago." He looked at Marshall with the ghost of a friendly smile. "And I know which one the balance of probability favours, don't you?"

Twenty-Five

"That was a close call. For a moment there I thought young Marshall was going to disprove all our precious theories," Richard said wryly to Abe as they walked side by side down the curving staircase behind the navigation bridge while *Swallow* came up to speed again, having dropped the pilot at the port of Detour on the mouth of St Mary's River. Beyond the wide windows, Point Detour swung away eastwards behind them until it was framed by the darkening sky. Up above them, they knew, Bob Stark was glaring straight into the glory of the westering sun.

"We nearly lost all our street cred as leaders and planners there," continued Richard. "That young man Marshall is shaping up to be quite an agent, if he survives."

"I'll keep a close eye on Agent Pace, watch my back and try to stay lucky," said Abe, dryly amused. But then he remembered that their good luck was the exact opposite for the poor woman in St Ignace.

"But he was right," persisted Richard. "Best guess isn't much of a way to proceed with an investigation as important as this one."

"True, but if it's all you got..." Abe completed the sentence with a shrug and a, "What you gonna do?"

"You're right. We can't stand still and wait. At least with *Swallow* in the water now we can get anywhere on the lakes at great speed. The only gamble was whether the ship we're looking for was still up on Superior. If she had been, we'd have been on the wrong side of the Soo."

"That's what I meant about the news being lucky."

"Well, at least the new information from St Ignace means we can proceed with much more confidence," said Richard as they stepped off the bottom stair into the main passenger area.

The piles of kit had reappeared. More FBI men had come aboard in Detour as planned and were waiting down in the briefing room now. More crewmen and women had come aboard as well. *Swallow* was up near her full complement, though, like *Swiftsure*, she was effectively on a shakedown cruise here.

While the new crewmembers went quietly and efficiently about their duties everywhere from the bridge to the galley, the new

FBI arrivals were with Beth Jackson, Marshall Pace and the first team who had received part of a briefing already.

"We can proceed with more confidence, Richard, just not as fast or as far. For the time being. I'm sorry," concluded Abe, as they neared the briefing room door.

Richard glanced down at the FBI man, and stopped. "We have to call in at St Ignace, do we?"

Abe stopped too and turned apologetically. "We do, Richard. I'm sorry, but it's important. I'm the agent in charge. We're flying forensics and pathology in to get the closest possible look at her, and there are liaison people from Canada coming down too. But I can't just take their reports over the blower – as you call it. I have to be there. It's expected."

"I can see that. May I tag along when we get there?"

"Sure," said Abe, bouncing into motion again. "But remember, ashore this is my show. And be warned a post-mortem can be a pretty sickening business. I've known the strongest of our recruits simply faint dead away, like one of those heroines in the romantic novels my daughter Rachel likes to read. Hey, that's a good idea. We'll invite Beth and that young go-getter Marshall Pace along, huh?"

"Fine. In the meantime, then, let's finish

the briefing." Richard was at the door now, his hand on the handle.

"Yeah. Let's see if young Marshall can earn his place right at the front beside the operating table. Did you know they take the whole face off sometimes? Cut round the back of the head and slip it all off like a mask, you know what I mean?"

"You make it sound irresistible, Abe. I can hardly wait," Richard opened the door wide.

"That's irony, right? I heard you Limeys were good at irony." Abe swept past him before he could start to explain the difference between irony and sarcasm. The second part of the briefing had begun.

"After we leave St Ignace, we will sail into Lake Michigan," Abe was explaining five minutes later. "In the lake itself, we will be the central search platform for the effort, coordinating the work of helicopter spotters and Coast Guard vessels. All the official federal boats and ships on Lake Michigan have orders to observe and report anything suspicious but they are under strict instructions not to go aboard or become involved. It'll be like looking for a needle in a haystack, of course. These guys are not fools. They are dangerous, resourceful people. There's a plus for us in that we suspect we're looking for a large vessel headed into Milwaukee or Chicago. That narrows the field somewhat. On the other hand, what is not good for us is that we have no idea what vessel we're looking for, or of her nationality, even. If they've transferred aboard an American-registered ship then we'll have our work well cut out for us because there are thousands and thousands of them. And, remember, the women will be well hidden down below, if the two Russian ships are anything to go by. Spotting the ship may well be the hardest part."

"When we've spotted her, then what?" asked Marshall.

"That's when *Swallow* comes into her own. She can actually sail at nearly eighty miles an hour. Once we have the suspect ship spotted, we'll get close to her at best speed."

"We'll not go right alongside immediately," Richard interrupted. "We'll have to be very careful. If any of the Russians are on the bridge, especially Captain Karpov, the master of the *Caspian* who pirated *Swiftsure*, they'll recognise *Swallow* as her sister and get very suspicious indeed. There are other vessels on the lake that can move nearly as fast, so the radar screen shouldn't give us away. But if anyone who saw *Swiftsure* also sees *Swallow*, they're bound to know that something's up."

"So what do we use?" demanded Marshall Pace. "Vanishing cream? Invisibility paint?

What's your best guess on that, Captain Mariner?"

Richard smiled. "I have three guesses, Agent Pace. First, if we need to move close during a flat calm in clement weather, we get the Coast Guard helicopter to buzz the boat asking about something innocuous. Official markings should drive the Russians into hiding below. Secondly, we might be able to rely on some help from the weather. We've just had days of storms in Superior. A couple of good squalls down here should let us right up alongside before they see who we are. Or thirdly, of course, we go in at night."

"Had you thought of that, Marshall?" enquired Beth, gently mocking. "We can use the Good Lord's own vanishing cream: darkness!"

"Stage one, we find the ship, then." Abe resumed with the ghost of a smile. "Stage two we get close to her. We'll be following standard routes from St Ignace to Chicago via Milwaukee in any case. And when we need to we can sail more than four times her likely speed."

"And stage three, sir?" asked Marshall more defensively.

"We'll have broken out our equipment and zeroed our arms on the approach. I see you new men brought a good deal of extra equipment with you. Thanks for that.

259

Captains Stark and Mariner here will put us right alongside at the end of stage two and in stage three we go in like gangbusters."

"Speed and surprise," emphasised Richard. "The plan turns around our very earnest desire to stop this becoming a hostage situation. I'll be right behind you to see if I can help." He caught Marshall Pace's eye just as the young agent's mouth opened. "I have done this sort of thing before. And I'm best qualified to find any hidden decks. In the absence of my wife."

"Anyone got any questions?" asked Abe.

No one had. Not even the new agents. But then, thought Richard, this was hardly rocket science.

"Right, as I say, this is an initial briefing. If there's anyone else waiting for us in St Ignace we'll bring them up to speed later. And then we'll have a full war briefing when the target has been acquired, as they say."

Richard and Abe walked out side by side. As they crossed the passenger accommodation, they could hear Marshall Pace's mocking, "Find it if we can, sneak up behind them if we're able then run in and kick ass! Great plan. Just great. I mean, welcome to the Little Big Horn, guys!"

"See?" said Richard quietly, joining in Abe's little game. "Yanks can do irony too!"

Twenty-Six

The body they did not yet know as Irina was laid out in an operating theatre lent by the local hospital in St Ignace to the FBI pathologist who had flown in some hours before. Irene lay face up on a stainless-steel dissecting table, her last shred of dignity protected by a towel across her loins. Her breast lay bare so that the pathologist could refer to the star carved upon it. And, as Abe had warned Richard, her face lay on the upper slopes of her breasts, lifted free from her skull by the pathologist.

Professor Chalk, the pathologist, had taken her scalp and face off so that the men and women there could see the damage that had been done to her cranium. The professor had executed some deft knife-work down the back of her neck past her atlas bone almost to the red abrasions that scarred her shoulder blades. She had done this in order to expand the descriptions of cranial damage into a detailed discussion of how completely her neck was broken – something that not even the post-mortem

261

scans and X rays showed with sufficient clarity.

Marshall Pace lay face down on the floor exactly where he had fallen five minutes earlier when Professor Chalk had peeled Irina's head. Richard, however, was far from unconscious. He was thinking to himself that if this was Professor Chalk then every other pathologist he had ever come across must be Professor Cheese. For Professor Chalk was beautiful. There was no other word for it. No. On second thoughts, there were several. She was beautiful, young, and chic. She even wore her operating suit as though it was by Westwood. She employed her instruments like Jacqueline Du Pré and she handled the poor deceased like Florence Nightingale. And – and this was the true revelation – she treated her audience as though they were well-qualified, professional equals with an important job of work to do.

"The central fact of the matter is this," she stated. "Death was caused by a fall from a high place. She went over something like a balcony backwards and landed with all her weight focused between the back of her head and her shoulders. I don't know what she fell off, but she landed on a metal deck, almost certainly the deck of a ship. But I'll come back to that. She would not have felt a thing. Her skull shattered, her neck broke.

Her atlas bone was crushed and her spinal cord was completely severed in two places in the neck alone." Professor Chalk moved the shattered skull to reveal the skinned area between skull and shoulders, to demonstrate the destruction of the neck bones. "She died so quickly that there is hardly any sign of the subdural haematoma at the front of the brain that we would expect to result from such a blow in such a place on her skull. At the back as you can see the damage was so extensive as to render a search for haematoma irrelevant. Her head seems to have burst. There would have been a good deal of blood and brain tissue at the site of death."

Richard glanced across at Abe. In spite of his bravado, he was very pale himself. If she kept this up, Marshall would have company in the land of Nod.

"Death was not caused by the stab-wounds to the chest. I emphasise this because I believe it is of extreme importance to your investigation. Death was not caused by the stab-wounds to her chest. Had she been alive when these wounds were inflicted, they would have killed her at once. But, like the procedure that laid your colleague there out cold, they were inflicted post mortem."

"So whoever carved the star did not in fact kill her at all?" asked Beth, frowning as she tried to follow the professor's logic.

"No. I can't say that," the professor answered patiently. "It may well have been the same person who was responsible for both acts. And I should emphasise that I do not believe her death was not homicide. It certainly was.

"Immediately before this woman fell, was pushed or jumped over the edge, she had been raped several times and sodomised at least once. She had been beaten and burned – tortured, in fact. And not for the first time. But not, I think, in the place where she met her death either."

"So she was abused in one place, brought to another, then fell to her death in a third," said Richard.

"That is correct. On the other hand, there is no matter under her fingernails such as skin or hair, so she did not fight and scratch whoever was attacking her prior to death. Or the person who brought her out onto the deck or the person who killed her, if they are in fact different people. I must add that the lack of such evidence often points to suicide. She may, in the face of some new threat or horror, have thrown herself over the edge. However, I need hardly state that even if she threw herself over the edge, it was as a result of criminal activity being done to her and is therefore culpable homicide.

"It's a while since my jurisprudence seminars, but I believe the Federal law still states that even accidental death caused as part of a criminal act should be considered murder. So she was certainly murdered.

"Then, immediately after her death, she was stabbed. Ten times in rapid succession with a knife that has a big, flat blade not unlike our own Bowie hunter's knife. Even had I not seen the results of the examinations of the two bodies found in Canadian waters, which I have, I would know that this man has done this before. Look. The star is nearly perfect. The inner and outer points match exactly. This is a swift, sure and practised hand."

"How long would it have taken to do this?" asked Richard.

"To a dead body lying still on a deck? Ten seconds, hardly more." She made the action of someone stabbing the dead girl and counted as she did it. By the time she got to "Ten!" she was finished.

They all stood silently for a moment, simply awed by the power of her re-enactment. Then Richard said, "You mentioned something about the marks on her shoulders."

"Yes, sir, I did. These marks were inflicted at the moment of death. They are part of the same complex of injuries as the damage to the skull and neck. There are more such injuries on the back, buttocks, legs, heels and elbows. There is also, I must add, a slight welt here across the small of her back that is different to the other welts in that area. It is thicker, wider. We pulled one or two strands of hemp out of it."

"Marks made when her body went over a rope-topped safety rail and landed on the deck below," said Richard.

"Quite so. But the marks themselves have significance beyond that. I mentioned that they proved to my satisfaction that she landed on some kind of deck, as Captain Mariner has emphasised. I mean by that, as I'm sure he did, the deck of a commercial vessel. The body had been in the water for some time before it was pulled out and brought here, but the abrasions are deep enough to have retained flakes of paint and other matter from the surfaces she fell over and onto. So, although there was nothing under her nails, there was something under her skin. There were flakes of red paint. Flakes of red lead-based paint or undercoat. A flake or two of rust. Some paint-covered grains of sand and silica holding just a trace of commercial fuel oil as well as complexes of rubber and leather much as one might expect and, miraculously, even a grain or two of salt, both on the sand and on the splinters of hemp."

"You found all this in the three hours

you've been waiting for us to arrive?" breathed Beth. "That's going it some."

"They have excellent facilities here," explained the professor gently and courteously. "But I also brought a complete crash team and extensive back-up. I was told that this was an extremely important case and that speed was of the essence. I'm all too aware that investigations can be slowed if forensic processes are lengthy. I've been concerned to give you the highlights of my initial work so that you can proceed on a sound basis. I will re-do it more slowly and painstakingly in due course to make sure it will stand up in court if necessary. And of course I will alert you of any new things I find as part of that process at that time. Now, where were we? Ah yes. Salt."

"Commercial salt? Refined? Iodised?" asked Richard.

"I see you are ahead of me, sir. No. Unrefined."

"Sea salt."

"Excellent, Captain Mariner. Now, would you like to build up a description of the vessel from the evidence I have just described? Your experience should allow you to see details I may have overlooked."

"Very well," said Richard. He took in a deep breath as he ordered his thoughts, then his ice-blue gaze swept over the half-dozen special agents there, over the delectable

267

professor and her assistant. "She's big. She's been ocean-going and quite recently. Salt doesn't survive for long on the Lakes. She's not been up on Superior recently or the storms would have washed her clean. So she's come in through the St Lawrence from the ocean or the eastern seaboard within the last week or two and hung around probably on Michigan. She has oil-fired engines. She's probably elderly and not too well tended. Her safety rails are made of hemp rope, not wood – as in cruisers or more luxurious vessels – or of modern polymer-based line. That means she's not likely to be in commercial service with any reputable American company. The unions wouldn't like such elderly safety equipment. Neither would competent managers or ship handlers if they had a choice. She may be foreign, though. She's rusty. Her undercoat will be showing through in places. Her decks are iron over-painted with red lead rustproofing, then given a coat of commercial non-slip paint that has been there for a good long time. And at least some of her decks are painted red. Most likely the decks of her bridgehouse. The vertical walls of bridgehouses are traditionally painted white, but these will be rust-marked and probably given a pink tinge by wash-off from the red decks. The main deck and hatch covers are not likely to be painted with non-slip, because it can be expensive and she doesn't sound an expensively maintained ship to me."

"You want to tell us her name and home port while you're at it?" asked Abe, awed by the acuity which could extrapolate so much from so little.

"It's all best guesswork," said Richard. "Professor. Have I missed anything?"

"You have gone beyond anything we had worked out, but along exactly the same line of reasoning. If I might emphasise, however, that the deck marks on the woman's back seem to me to be all from the one incident of her landing after the fall. There is very little deck-damage other than that. There is no paint, sand and so forth on the soles of her feet. Nor on hands and knees, as you would expect to find if she had been abused on the deck itself. Once again, as Captain Mariner said so succinctly, she was abused in one place, brought to a second and fell to her death on a third. In the third place, on that deck, the star was carved on her and she was bundled over the side, leaving quite a mess behind, in all probability."

"Can you tell us anything about the place she was abused in?" asked Abe, almost entranced by the horror of what was being described to him.

"Not much. It had carpets, judging from the carpet burns on her back and knees.

And there are one or two fibres there too. It had tables – laminated, wood effect, we have a splinter. A cabin? A bar?"

"That means there's almost total complicity. It has to," said Richard with a shudder of horror. "I hadn't really thought that through up to now."

"What do you mean?" asked Professor Chalk.

"Even a large ship is a closed world," he explained. "Especially a freighter. Everyone lives in everyone else's pocket. Everyone knows everything about everyone else. Secrets are almost impossible to keep. So this poor girl was taken and abused by several people. In a cabin – up in the crew's living area. Or even in the wardroom. Everyone else aboard must know about it. Nobody does anything. It's too dreadful to contemplate. But it gets worse, doesn't it? Someone then takes her out onto the deck. A high deck – the bridge wing deck or the lifeboat deck below it – the most public of places. She goes over the edge and dies. Then this person has time to go down and mutilate her, dump her over the side and leave a big pool of blood behind and nobody does anything? Nobody notices anything? Nobody else aboard even turns a hair? What sort of people are these?"

And in answer to his question, a new voice joined the conversation. "I believe I can answer that for you, Captain Mariner. Though the evidence I've brought down from Thunder Bay is worse than anything else so far."

They all turned and faced the open door. A familiar figure, to Richard at least, was standing there with his ID in one hand and a brown-wrapped package in the other. Inspector Sam McKenzie, Ontario Police's liaison, was back on the case again.

Twenty-Seven

They spent the next hour in a private room with TV and video watching Sam McKenzie's new evidence. Abe, Richard and Professor Chalk got the easy chairs. Beth and the other agents got the hard chairs brought in from a nearby waiting room. Marshall Pace got the bed, though he was awake now and sat on the edge of it, very much on his dignity.

The evidence was contained on videotape that Detective McKenzie had brought in the brown package. "These are for sale on the black market in Thunder Bay," he said

271

grimly. "Vice picked them up and a friend brought one to me because of the case. They all know I'm liaising with ViCLAS and FBI on the Ladies in the Lakes. It's not a huge force; we all have a good idea what each other is up to. I was just lucky he got it to me before I was called down here so that I could bring it with me to show you guys. I don't suppose you'll think yourselves so lucky when you see it, though."

The tape depicted the rape and abuse of a young woman. It was the videotaped reconstruction of the kind of treatment they had been discussing as they examined the body of Irina on the steel table a few doors down. The differences were that for the purposes of this video, the location had been made to resemble a medieval torture chamber. That meant of course that there was no carpet or laminated tables. There were several striking anachronisms, however. But of course the main objective was anything but historical accuracy.

"That's the studio we found on *Aral*, I'm certain," said Richard at the beginning, while he was still willing to look at the screen. He was unable to recognise any of the actors in the grim little scene, however, because they all wore masks. And, for much of the proceedings, masks were all they wore.

The victim of the medieval reconstruction

was not masked, but about halfway through the drama she was gagged. Professor Chalk sat forward at once with a grunt, her obvious concern for the poor woman on the screen compounded. "She can't breathe properly," she said. "They'll have to be careful not to asphyxiate her."

But care for the central actress was the last thing on her abusers' minds and to the shock, disgust and stomach-churning revulsion everyone was feeling a new element was added. The simple soul-deep horror of watching the poor girl slowly choking to death in front of them.

When at last she stopped struggling in her bonds, one of the men went off-shot and returned with a thoroughly modern bucket full of water. It failed to revive her.

"You're too late, you scumbag," Professor Chalk told him. "I doubt if even mouth-to-mouth will bring her back now."

Mouth-to-mouth was not tried. When it became obvious that their victim was not going to wake up, the two masked actors simply shrugged and proceeded to the end of what was clearly a practised routine on her still and unresponsive body.

"There had better be a really good point to this," warned Abe, his voice shaking. "Or the FBI part of your liaison will be terminated. I mean we knew what they were making when we saw the studios. This kind of shit doesn't do us any good unless we get an identity out of it. Otherwise we can just hold it for the trial and make the jury lose their lunch. Why rub our noses in it? That poor kid. Jesus..."

"Wait," said Sam McKenzie.

Richard looked across at him again – he hadn't been looking at the screen for some time now. This was a different man to the angry officer who had treated Jeanne La Motte so cavalierly. This was a soberer, more thoughtful man. Someone had taught him a lesson in the interim. Or he had realised just how terribly important the case Jeanne was working on had now turned out to be.

"Now look," said Sam, with such intensity that Richard was fooled into obeying.

The dead girl's body filled the screen, but her face claimed their attention. Her eyes wide and sightless, the same bright blue as her lips around the gag that had choked her. The picture froze, apparently the final shot in the sick, sickening drama. But then a shadow passed across the still, staring horror of the dead woman's face. Someone was moving around the mock rack she had been tied to, seemingly unaware that the video camera was still switched on, recording his every action. He was loosening her body no doubt for disposal. He was not like the other actors in the numbingly, bestially obscene drama. This fact was clear even though his face never featured on the screen. He was working slowly, with a dreamlike deliberation. Every once in a while he stopped and stood still, waiting for the shaking of his hands to stop before he proceeded.

"Whoever this man is, he's got trouble here," said Dr Chalk. "He's only just keeping control, I'd say."

"And he has no idea he's being filmed," said Beth. "How could that be?"

"The noise of the ship would drown the camera's motor," said Richard. "And if the studio lights were up high, he may not have seen the red recording light."

"Especially if he's in some kind of shock or strong emotion, I guess," supplied Abe.

"You just wait," said Sam McKenzie. "You'll see what the son of a bitch is in the grip of."

The man on the screen was also different to the others in that he was dressed. Neatly so. He wore well-pressed trousers and a white vest. Between the two he wore a belt and in it, a knife in a sheath. As he finished releasing the dead girl, he abruptly reached for this.

Richard realised then, at the same instant as the professor, just a heartbeat before Abe and Beth. He looked across at the professor and saw her frown, knowing that the knife was out now. He saw her flinch ten times, her eyes, already full, beginning to overflow.

Then the only sound in the room was the hissing of blank tape.

"I'll tell you," said the professor after a moment or two. Then she stopped, unable to go on. Sam McKenzie crossed to the set and snapped it off.

"I'll tell you what the worst thing about that tape is for me," said the professor with almost superhuman self-control.

"What is that?" asked Richard, his voice hoarse.

"That woman. That poor young woman..."

"Yes?" he prompted gently.

"She isn't one of the three bodies we have found. She's another one altogether."

They were running late now, well behind the schedule Richard had laid down for himself when he had looked south from the Soo. As Bob guided *Swiftsure* out of the State Docks and began to swing her round the out-thrust point and the Coast Guard's compound, Richard, Abe and the rest sat around the table in the briefing room, looking down at the cooling meal which lay untouched before them.

"So," said Abe slowly. "We now have the full pattern. These girls are lured aboard."

"Probably with fake adverts," said Sam. "Inspector La Motte was clear about that. These women think they're going to be

276

secretaries or whatever."

"As soon as they're aboard, the process of brutalising them and breaking them down begins. No means is too brutal. Beating and rape are commonplace. Expected. Tools of the trade. Torture is used on occasion and once in a while they kill a girl. Maybe on purpose, maybe by accident. But the effect is the same. They're there to change bright, sassy, intelligent secretaries into whores. That's what they're all going to be when they hit the streets of Milwaukee or Chicago, right? Prostitutes."

"That's the way it works in the West Coast with the girls that come in from Guandong and Fujian in China," said Sam. "ViCLAS and Immigration Liaison with the RCMP are quite clear about it. Almost all the illegal immigrants out of China wind up in sweat-shops, illegal industries and prostitution. Even those who have paid a big price up front for their passage find they still owe the Snakeheads so much that they can never pay it off. And being illegals, they can't come to our authorities so they knuckle under or turn up floating."

"It's the same in England, so they say," said Richard. "Half of the illegal immigrants smuggled out of what's left of the Soviet Empire end up on the streets. You can't find a whore north of Watford that doesn't speak with a Russian accent, by all accounts."

"So," said Abe, "that's what's going on. But we know already that this is a cheapskate operation. Maybe it's financed in roubles. Who knows? I'd bet that the Russian side of it probably is. And organised crime over here, which is waiting for the new supply of girls, is keeping its hands in its pockets until it sees the merchandise."

"That would explain something else, too," said Beth. "It would explain the brutality. Nowadays if you want to make a whore you get her a habit. You get her hooked on crack or whatever. It's quick, and it's cheap in the States at least. But these guys don't have that option. So they use the old-fashioned approach. Raping and beating. It's worked since the times when the dungeon on that tape was for real."

"So the sailors are hard up and desperate. They have to set up a sideline. They make movies out of what they do to the girls and flog them off to raise hard currency along the way."

"But in among all this," said Beth, "in among all this filth and perversion, we have Red Star Man. Jack the Ripper for the new millennium. Having a wall-to-wall field day. Some of it on tape."

The conversation ended there, with none of them very certain how much further their deliberations had taken them. Except,

278

perhaps, to define finally and absolutely what terrible danger Robin and Jeanne la Motte were in – unless they were already like the poor girl on the tape, floating undiscovered somewhere deep in the icy darkness of the lakes. The two leaders used the energy this simple, terrible fear gave them as a goad to action. Abe called the men and women of his shock troops to get out their equipment and their arms. Having checked their body armour and their equipment belts, they fell to stripping and oiling their weapons.

Grimly aware that he was destined to be a part of this, Richard joined them, familiarising himself with the body armour, and how to adjust it for his own huge size. Then he chose a handgun from the ones on offer – a trustworthy Glock with a red-dot sight. He chose the Glock 21, the biggest they had, with a full .45 calibre load. Then he too stripped and loaded and practise-fired it.

As he was working, with an intensity that would have made anyone unaware of the situation very worried for his sanity, he nevertheless felt *Swallow* change her attitude in the water and surge forward with a burst of power. He looked up, distractedly, to see through the long, wide windows the broad, beautifully lit span of the Mackinac Bridge swinging immediately over their heads as they sailed into the quiet waters of the Straits themselves and surged against the power of the current up into Lake Michigan itself.

Twenty-Eight

Robin looked down at the knifepoint resting on her breast. The silver surgical-steel point had made a dimple there and it stung like a hypodermic. Round the edge of her vision there swirled a void of darkness interspersed with flashes of dazzling brightness. She wavered, ever so slightly, as the dazzling darkness gathered so dangerously. She gasped, feeling her skin burst. The knife-point suddenly held a bright drop of blood. "If I faint," thought Robin wildly, "then he'll probably kill me as I fall, whether he means to or not."

Then she thought of the condition of the other dead girls. Perhaps it would be better to die quickly and cleanly after all, she thought. She could just about handle the thought of Richard being presented with a beautiful, unspoilt, unsoiled corpse. To turn up in front of him looking like poor Irina or the Lady in the Lake terrified her to the point of despair.

But her captor was almost psychic. Suddenly the knife was no longer there and the blood was a spot of aching brightness on the soiled lace atop her left cup.

She looked up, distantly puzzled, still on the verge of fainting. His eyes seemed as dark as the wild blackness still swirling round her. They gazed down at her with overwhelming intensity, almost madness. "You cannot begin to understand," he whispered, "who wants you to die and how soon."

Oh yes I can, she thought. You for a start, you mad bastard.

But then, as the lift car lurched into motion again and her head began to clear, she reconsidered. No; maybe not. For if this particular mad bastard wanted her dead, she would be laid out like a side of pork on the floor already. Butchered like poor little Irina.

So what was he up to then? Trying to scare her? Mission accomplished there. She had nearly wet herself and he knew it. Perhaps that was how he got his jollies. The others screwed with your body. Sholokov screwed with your mind. Then he carved a star on your heart and dumped you overboard. That made as much sense as any of this madness.

Or was he trying to warn her? Again,

mission accomplished in spades. She stood well warned. But warned against whom and for what conceivable reason? If he supposed she didn't know that her virtue, her life and her lily-white hide were on the line here he must think she was very stupid indeed. If he was trying to warn her, it must be against the unexpected, the secret enemy. Against someone she was not prepared against. Captain Karpov? The captain of *Aral* – what *was* his name? Zhukov. Yes, that was it. Zhukov. The captain of this tub? She hadn't been introduced to him, so he remained nameless. Any of their senior officers and crew? *Aral*'s first officer, Lieutenant Ivanov, was probably on the list – and whichever of them had called her up on Jeanne's cellphone on the night the Mountie disappeared, of course...

Typically of Robin, it did not even enter her head that he might be trying to warn her against one of the other women.

But then the time for wild speculation was past. The doors opened and the others were there, waiting impatiently. Jeanne's gaze went immediately to the red spot on her left cup. Only its brightness made it stand out. All of her underwear was pretty well smeared with the brown stains of Irina's blood already – and indeed, with some of Robin's own, also dark and dry. She looked up and saw Julie's eyes on her too; but her face was unreadable. A fleeting glance passed between them then Robin looked back at Jeanne. The battered inspector frowned and sucked at a loose tooth. The four guards marched them down the corridor and onto the navigation bridge.

The bridge was bright with the red-gold of the setting sun shining aslant from low on the starboard beam. They were heading south, then, thought Robin, storing up knowledge in the hope that some shred of information would make all the difference in the end. Like it always did for her heroes and heroines of childhood.

Do you expect me to talk, Goldfinger? demanded a familiar voice in her mind.

No, Mr Bond, I expect you to die...

I am definitely going out of my mind here, she thought, her eyes busy seeking out into the dazzling afternoon for a landmark, a ship, a sign that they were not alone in this particular circle of hell.

Three men sat behind a long chart table, outlined in red and gold. Their faces were half-hidden by shadow. Only the profile of the man at the helm was clear. And beyond him there was nothing except the lake and the sky, both almost as red as the deck of this cursed ship. Robin turned back to the three men at the chart table and wondered whether they were actually trying to disguise themselves with shadow. That would have been a hopeful sign. You only bother to hide your face from someone who might make trouble for you later. Someone still alive, for instance.

This thought, combined with the euphoria of having survived the lift-ride with Sholokov, made her feel quite light-headed again, but at least James Bond stayed silent this time.

Then Captain Karpov leaned forward into the light. "You four are up to something," he said quietly. "Tell me what it is or we will hurt you more than you can imagine."

"Nothing!" said Anya. "We are up to nothing at all!"

The guard still standing beside her swung round and drove his fist into the pit of her stomach and Karpov hadn't even made a sign. She stayed upright – just. Through what Robin's mother used to call 'sheer badness'. Karpov nodded. The fist landed again and Anya started to sink towards the deck, her mouth wide and breathless.

Karpov turned to Jeanne. "Well?" She flinched. Her recent experiences were clearly too fresh in her mind.

His eyes lingered on the shaking woman then he turned to Julie. *"Well?"* he snarled

"We were trying to work out who killed Irina," said Robin. "You've got to expect that we'll want to know. I mean she was one of us and someone butchered her and threw her overboard. Unless the plan is to turn us into fish-bait, then we've got a vested interest in getting where you're taking us all in one piece. And that means we've got to try and work out who killed Irina and try to stay clear of him. I'd have thought you'd want that too. I mean, you're the slavers of the new millennium. You're doing this for profit, not fun. You can't afford too many losses, can you? The fewer bodies fit for the block, the lower your profits, after all."

Zhukov, captain of *Aral*, leaned forward. He did not look at the two half-naked women in front of him. He gave no sign that he had met either before in another, fully-clothed, slightly saner life. The humiliation was beyond belief, thought Robin. Almost beyond bearing. "Who was Irina?" he asked Karpov.

"I've no idea. Ask her."

Zhukov's dull eyes rested on her. The level of his gaze did not rise above her tummy-button. "Who was Irina?" he asked the front of her panties.

"Irina was the name of the girl who left her blood all over the lifeboat deck this afternoon and went overboard with a red star on her heart." Robin was seriously thinking of adding more, but a choking sound from the floor as Anya recovered the use of her lungs warned her against stepping out of line.

"Ah," he said, as though a small point of no real importance had been settled.

"So that's it?" demanded *Beaufort*'s captain suddenly and threateningly in an unmistakably American twang. "You bring the whole of the Pussy Hold to silence and standstill because you and this bitch are such ace fucking detectives?"

"The women were concerned, sir. Irina was a popular girl. She was the youngest. She was like their mascot."

"Bullshit. This is all bullshit." *Beaufort*'s captain raised his fist, pointing a stubby, hair-backed index finger like the leg of a fat tarantula at her. "I think you and Miss Mountie here are planning something. And I think you others know what it is. And I think I'll just take bits out of your hide until you tell me just what the fuck is going on here. We got time for a couple more snuff movies. We can make them double-headers, no problem at all."

Karpov leaned forward then, his nonchalance masking a certain amount of steel in his voice. "I think not yet, Captain. As Mrs Mariner has mentioned the mess on your lifeboat deck, perhaps these four can go down and clean it up while we discuss matters. That will give us a chance to proceed in a more considered manner."

Robin would never have believed it possible that she would ever feel grateful to

286

Karpov. But she did now. Karpov nodded a silent order. Anya's guard stooped and pulled the choking woman to her feet. The four of them stood in line for an instant, each restrained by her guard. Then Sholokov led Robin towards the door and the others followed. She glanced back at the threshold. The captain of the *Beaufort* had slumped back into the deepening shadow beside the captain of the *Aral*. "Yeah. OK," he snarled. "Just let's not hang about here, OK? Time's awasting. It's nearly dark, for Christ's sake. And I for one think that Nancy Drew and her little friends there should be nothing more than a wet dream for the snuff and bondage set by morning."

Twenty-Nine

The thing that kept Richard sane through that seemingly endless night was being able to push himself into the thick of things. Or, at least to feel that he was doing so.

The FBI and the Coast Guard were on full alert from late afternoon, enacting Abe's simple 'search but don't stop' instructions. When no ship such as Richard had

287

described to Professor Chalk had been sighted by sunset, the search had to be scaled down for the night. The Good Lord's vanishing cream worked both ways and if darkness might be expected to conceal *Swallow* from any ship she was tracking, it was now helping the slave-smuggler hide from the Coast Guard's eyes.

But if the search was scaled down it was by no means cancelled. Richard knew that and knew he could add to the information needed, if only he could access the correct files.

If the ship could not be seen on the water until tomorrow's dawn, at least she could still be searched for in the shipping records for the Great Lakes and St Lawrence Seaway tonight. There were records of the movement of every commercial ship of any size through every waterway in the United States. With luck she could still be identified if Richard could define her most likely recent movements, present position and likely destination. Perhaps she might even be showing an identity beacon so that when they had a name they would know where she was from moment to moment and proceed without actual visual confirmation. The hope of this was enough to keep Richard up for his third sleepless night and working tirelessly until, inevitably, even his massive strength ran out.

He called up every office of every agency still manned on his new phone. He got half-hourly updates from the Coast Guard. He used Abe's security clearances shamelessly to badger the FBI, who, of course, never slept. Furthermore, *Swallow* was equipped to the highest standard. She boasted a full range of on-board computers but all of them had jobs to do – especially when the vessel was proceeding through the darkness into increasingly busy waters. And, the weather predictors began to warn them, into rapidly worsening weather.

Richard quarrelled fractiously with his steady, level-headed captain, irritated beyond measure that he could not access the sorts of records he wanted through any on-board computer. He paced up and down the bridge like a tiger in too small a cage and he demanded increasingly impossible things, completely unaware of how outrageous seventy-two sleepless hours were rendering his demands.

But Abe saved the day – or the night. He had thought to order a powerful laptop with all the other equipment he had called up. Richard had no trouble running his new phone in parallel with the machine and getting onto the Internet that way. He checked with the FBI once again, but not even Abe's clearances could get him as deep as he needed to go. He contacted the Coast

Guard next, tapping into their Great Lakes and Internal Waterways files. Then, still unsatisfied, he checked further with the Department of Transportation before focusing on the Maritime Administration, MARAD.

Still he could find no immediate information about the movements of ships through the Great Lakes at the detailed level he really needed, so, as midnight began to loom, he went back to his search engine and typed in 'Great Lakes Shipping'. It was the simplest of gambles. A mere chancing of his arm. He was so exhausted by this time that he had no idea how wasted he actually was. He had not been this sleep-deprived since his twins had been babies the better part of ten years since.

But the screen lit up with a title and a picture. Joy of joys, Great Lakes Shipping had a web page all of its own. Richard waited for it to load. Drumming on the keyboard like a caffeine junkie on a table at Starbucks. Once it was up, he dived straight in and looked around eagerly. One of its sections was entitled Ship Movements. He clicked on that and then clicked again on International Ship Movements, looking for any ships that had come in up the Seaway out of the great salt seas.

By 1 a.m. he had the last registered location of every 'salty' on the Great Lakes. By two, he had lists of all the other sizeable transports, their last registered port and whither they were bound. All in all he had called up more than sixty pages of information. And that was as measured on A4, single line spaced.

"Abe? Hey, Abe?" he called, the realities of his situation and the actual time it was far removed from his mind.

"Huh?" Abe had been hoping for a little shut-eye in one of the extremely comfortable airline seats nearby. At his side, Beth snored contentedly, and beyond her Marshall lay with his mouth open and his chin slick with drool. Beyond him, sprawled so widely that he was in constant danger of falling off the front-row chair, Sam McKenzie snored uproariously. Tomorrow promised to be challenging for all of them.

"Have you got a printer to go with this thing? Paper? Abe, for God's sake?"

"Sure, Richard. Sure. The first thing I pack when I'm setting up to go *mano a mano* with three crews of well-armed, dangerous and desperate Russian kidnappers on a ship full of helpless women and potential hostages is a really fine state-of-the-art printer and a couple of reams, A4 coloured and white. I mean, what can I tell you? It's right up there at the top of my list with the assault rifles and the flak jackets."

"See, Abe? You can do irony too. Though

you're getting dangerously close to sarcasm, in my opinion."

Abe might have appreciated this, with its fine shades of nuance between irony and sarcasm. But he was, like Beth, Sam and Marshall, utterly dead to the world once again.

Five minutes later, Richard was up on the navigation bridge watching the darkness come at him in a series of pale lines of cloud-belly above mirrored by evenly ranked formations of white horses below.

"You need the weather computer, then," he said to Bob. "That looks as though it could get nasty by daybreak. What system can you do without that will get me onto a Web site and then give me a printout of sixty or seventy pages?"

"Oh, for Christ's sake, Richard..."

They couldn't actually do without any of their computers, as the calm captain had explained to the increasingly impossible owner on several occasions earlier that very evening and began, less calmly, to explain at greater length again. But in the end, in the face of his old friend's patent distress, Bob finally relented and sent for one of the engineers to patch Abe's laptop into the weather-predictor's printer. It wasn't ideal. Richard got his information printed on a length of flimsy slightly shorter than a toilet roll and the weather-fax machine was almost out of tear-off slips – six months' supply in a night. But at least Richard was able to take the considerable column of names, ports and destinations off to get a really good close look.

It was after 3 a.m. before he came back wanting to print out a shortlist of twenty or so that looked most promising, so Bob for one reckoned the loss of the paper well worth it.

He was proved wrong at eight next morning when the Coast Guard tried to send him the weathermen's diagram of the exceedingly dangerous low pressure system whirling north of Chicago towards them and the fax was out of paper. Fortunately his first officer was able to call out the pressure gradients, the front locations and the estimations of where the worst of the squalls and the tornadoes might be expected, so he was able to get a good clear picture from that instead. But by then they were in a whole new ball game in any case.

Richard went through his list of twenty names, underlining, ticking and marking them as he went. They had come in from all over the world within the last couple of weeks and sailed up the St Lawrence seaway one after the other. They had all stayed south, away from the bad weather. Most of them had paused or lingered along the north or east shores of Lake Michigan. All of them were on the move now, southwards and westwards. He concentrated on the Russian-registered vessels to begin with, but then widened his field of search, convinced that the smugglers, cunning so far, would have disguises ready for their ships. And, as they had considered long ago, the Russians must be delivering their cargo to organised crime – and even since the days of Al Capone, the Mafia had been keen on boats.

But that was as far as he got. He was, in truth, nearing the end even of his massive funds of energy. Reality came and went as his brain began to slip into sleep. At first he thought the equipment must be playing up. But then he realised. His first reaction was to hype himself up with caffeine, but that didn't help much. Indeed, he lost half an hour between sips just after his last visit to the bridge at around four and only knew about it because his coffee was suddenly cold and his Internet access had closed down through inactivity.

Beth Jackson's long dark eyes opened a little just as he got up, wearily, to try and reload the page he had been looking at. "Richard," she purred, "for God's sake get some sleep. You need to re-charge the old batteries, man. What good will you be to her when we find her tomorrow and you're too

294

exhausted to pull your weight?"

At last, Richard saw the logic of getting his head down. He had been in stressful situations before and had always been happy to hand out the very advice Beth was giving him. It was time to take it, he thought wearily. He glanced down at the battered old steel-cased Rolex Perpetual that Robin had given him more years ago than he cared to remember, then, thinking of her, he slept. And luckily – blessedly – he did not dream.

Abe woke Richard at seven. Mariner by nature as well as by name, Richard had checked the weather and the progress of his ship through it almost psychically as he regained consciousness, so he was not at all surprised to find himself looking out into a black-skied, threatening dawn. He was surprised, however, by the look of concern and surprise mixed on the special agent's face.

Sheer terror went through him then, as though he had swallowed an icicle. The fuzziness of sleep vanished in a nanosecond. "What's the news?" he demanded, fearing the worst in spite of himself.

"It's nothing about Robin, so don't worry," said Beth reassuringly, appearing at Abe's shoulder.

"It's still a puzzle, though," said Abe. "And I'm damned if I can see the implications."

"What is?" demanded Richard, still tense from the shock he had given himself.

"Professor Chalk's just been through. She's completed her post-mortem and confirmed everything we discussed. There are still some things at the lab but she sees no reason to expect big changes when the official results come in."

"That's good, but for Heaven's sake, Abe, get to the point."

"Yeah, you're right. As part of the p-m investigation she sent photographs of the girl to our missing persons people. They've been primed to contact the Russians now as well on all of this."

"Great. So you know who she was?"

"No."

"For goodness' sake, Abe, spit it out!"

"She also sent pictures of the other girl. The one we never found. The one from Sam's videotape. They've identified her."

"Right. Good. Who was she?"

"She was Katerina Manlikovna. Special investigator, FCIS."

"Now wait a minute here," said Richard. "The FCIS is part of what used to be the KGB."

"The Federal Counter Intelligence Service. Security. Yes."

"Are you telling me that the girl in the video whom we saw being murdered was an undercover intelligence agent?"

"That's about the size of it. It's the implications I can't quite work out."

"I should say not! I mean, what would the KGB be doing mixed up in something like this?"

"Well, if you think about it, it's not so far-fetched," temporised Abe. "Since the end of the Cold War and the major reorganisations on the defence and commercial levels, even as recently as the Putin era, the Russian security and intelligence services have been focusing on the Russian Mafia. Like your MI5, Richard, spending the 80s and 90s targeting the IRA and all the other terrorist organisations working in and around the British Isles. And I think we all agreed that this was a Mafia operation. So, if it is, then the KGB or the FCIS or whoever would definitely be interested in it. Would logically want to get involved."

"It's a double-edged sword, though, no matter how you look at it," said Beth thoughtfully as Richard sat, his dark frown mirroring Abe's as his mind whirled through the implications.

Raced through every permutation of probability he could conceive of, to the one, overwhelming, sixty-four-thousand-dollar question: If the KGB had undercover people aboard, then whose side were they on?

Thirty

If the night was bad for Richard, it was ten times worse for Robin. But her anguish and discomfort were more physical than mental. She was not presented with things she could not imagine or horrors she scarcely dared consider – as he was. She took everything that night up front, on the chin, and she dealt with it as best she could. And she found strength in that.

Sholokov led Robin and her three companions down onto the lifeboat deck and here in the last of the light they were put to work. Their menial task, all but pointless in the face of the weather forecast, might have been a ploy by Karpov to get them out of the way while the three captains discussed their future – largely in terms of whether they had one – but it had another effect as well. A completely unexpected one. It took a trained investigator, her one witness and her prime suspect to the scene of Irina's murder.

As soon as Jeanne stepped out onto the red-painted deck, she seemed to go into a kind of mental overdrive. Robin, of course, quartered the northern and western horizons then scanned the sky looking for signs of other shipping, normal life. There were none near enough to count. Just a couple of freighters hull down on the horizon. But that too was logical, she thought. Karpov would never have sent them out here if there had been anyone close enough to see them and report in.

Karpov had not thought everything through quite so cleverly, however. He had sent them down here with a job to do, but no equipment to do it with. Sholokov, assuming command with habitual authority, sent a couple of the other guards to fetch buckets and mops and line. They took Anya and Julie with them. Carrying buckets was women's work, even though one of them was Vasily Bikal. The sailor stood among the biggest men Robin had ever seen, and she could not possibly have been mistaken. This was the man whose hat Jeanne and she had returned aboard *Aral* as a cover for their undercover spy mission. But, like Captain Zhukov, Vasily made no show of recognising either of them. And Jeanne was being careful to steer clear of him now, Robin noticed, with a shiver of apprehension.

Apparently casually, Jeanne began to prowl around her murder scene. Robin went with her. Sholokov and the other guard paid them scant attention, preferring to light up a cigarette each and look out at the sunset.

The low angle of the sun was perfect for defining the pattern of the dark red blood on the red-painted deck – in spite of the fact that its light, too, was red. Robin's body had made almost sensuous serpentine pathways along part of the gaudy display but had done no real damage to the over-all pattern of thickening liquid.

"You think we can talk?" whispered Jeanne, glancing across at the guards. Her guard looked across at them, but his eyes held no interest or alertness. Sholokov said something in a cloud of smoke and he looked away again.

"Look at this," whispered the inspector. "I thought from what you told me that she must have bled when he cut that star on her but that's not what this pattern says. This says she fell so hard she almost exploded. Fell from up there..."

Robin looked up and down, automatically reconstructing things. And she saw that Jeanne was right. The girl must have fallen backwards onto the deck from the bridge wing up there.

Then she suddenly remembered the shape of a man outlined in sunlight standing up on the bridge wing looking down at her. The sun had been strong enough to conceal his identity – while shining the brightest of

300

spotlights on her. She went absolutely cold at the thought. Perhaps that was the man Sholokov had been talking about in the lift, she thought with a feeling almost of revelation. Even aboard this vessel, a guilty secret like that might well explain why there was someone who wanted her dead at any price.

She realised that she hadn't even mentioned the dark figure's existence to Jeanne. And yet he would now be at least a major suspect – as well as a potential murderer of Robin herself, either in person or by proxy. Robin went swiftly across to the preoccupied investigator, her mouth open to tell her this new piece of evidence, but just at that moment the door opened and Anya stepped through with the buckets full of scrubbing brushes and rope followed by Julie with the mops.

The brief investigation was put on hold then and all conversation ceased, for the two guards who returned with the others and the buckets brought a watchful air that Sholokov and his smoking companion had allowed to dissipate. They threw away their cigarettes and turned. Under the watchful eyes of the guards, the women tied their ropes around the bucket handles and lowered them into the water, then pulled them up, slopped them over the deck and went to work. It was by no means hard work, and the evening sun held enough heat to bring warmth and even a little languor to the way they went about the task. Jeanne seemed particularly slow. She began to get in the way of Anya and Julie who had no idea that she was trying to combine her task with her investigation. But Robin worked alongside them, carefully trying to conceal the investigator's real focus. It became such an all-consuming, almost intellectual, exercise with her that she completely failed to consider the other impact of their work. And that impact was compounded when they were forced to get down on all fours and scrub the crusted edge of the dark red pattern with scrubbing brushes instead of mops. Four women, bending and kneeling, unconscious of their bodies which were seemingly naked under the pink rays of the sun, presented an enticing picture to the guards watching them, and started fantasies which the men did not have to hesitate to fulfil.

"You!" called one of the guards, suddenly, his voice harsh, even on the monosyllable of the Russian word. All four women looked up. Robin's heart fluttered. It was the huge guard Vasily. Vasily seemed to be Anya's usual minder but now he was pointing at Robin herself. She put down her brush, stood up and crossed the deck. She had no idea what Vasily wanted her for. Had he recognised her after all? Should she call over to Jeanne and introduce her as well? It would certainly be useful to have this giant looking out for them, if he could be reminded that he owed them one. At the very worst, she thought, he must be going to tell her off for working too slowly. Memories of Karpov's casual slapping came to mind. If this guard were going to do a repeat performance on her, she'd be seeing stars for a week.

But then she saw that there was no recognition in his hot gaze. He had put down his rifle, and she realised what he was doing to the front of his trousers.

She stopped, simply riven with horror.

"Hey," Vasily began angrily. He had become used to instant compliance. The possibility of a slapped face was suddenly the least of Robin's worries. Her heart twisted. She felt that whirling blackness gathering round her once again.

Sholokov stepped forward. "You can't have her, Vasily. She's mine," he said.

With a cry of frustration and rage, the guard turned toward him. The dapper man, so slight in comparison, stood his ground. When he moved, it was so swiftly that Robin could hardly see. There came that half-familiar whispering, ringing sound, and suddenly Sholokov was holding his huge Bowie knife mere millimetres away from

303

Vasily's chest. The big guard stopped. He looked across to where his gun stood against the safety rail beneath the lifeboat.

"You can try for it, but you won't make it," warned Sholokov gently. "Come on, Vasily. She's not worth getting killed over. Take one of the others."

Vasily paused. Turned. Let his gaze sweep over the little tableau of kneeling women. He pointed at Anya. "You!" he said.

Sholokov turned to Robin. "You!" he said roughly. "Get back to work."

The two women passed each other half-way between Irina's blood and the four guards. They did not look each other in the eye.

Then, as quickly as they could, the three women finished off the task Captain Karpov had set them.

Of all the things Robin wanted to do, equal even to getting off this ship alive and seeing Richard and the twins again, she wanted to apologise to Anya. But when the job was done and it was time to take the buckets, mops and brushes below for washing, Vasily decided to keep Anya with him. Sholokov and the others took Robin, Julie and Jeanne below and watched them in the washroom while they cleaned the utensils. Then they took them back up to the navigation bridge, to discover what their fate might be. Here,

304

again, there was no sign of Anya.

When Karpov, who was alone on the bridge, asked her whereabouts, Sholokov simply said, "Vasily has her."

The captain shrugged with brutal indifference. "That solves one problem, at any rate," he said.

He crossed to the long chart table and sat. Beside him, a small all-in-one TV and video rested on a pile of Lake Pilots. It was plugged into an adapter nearby and the screen glowed dull silver. Robin concentrated on that as a way of trying to escape the terrifying sense of tension in her breast.

Karpov clasped his hands together almost as though he was praying. The women stood in a line before him, their bodies clenched and shaking as though it was icy cold in the gloomy bridge.

At last Karpov looked up. "I have won you a reprieve, at least for the time being," he said. Even as he spoke, he disengaged his long right hand and raised it in a gesture commanding silence. "Don't ask me why I have done this. I have my reasons. But I must emphasise that I can allow no repetition of what went on last night. You will remain in your groups and there will be no post-mortems, no detective work. You will let the other women remain in their groups and you will not disturb them. We are overmanned. I have nowhere to put you

305

except in with the men. Ask Anya how she liked that, if you ever see her again. But in the meantime, I must be certain I can rely on your obedience. My fellow captains suggested that short of killing you I simply have you beaten into submission. But that would slow things down even further when we arrive at our destination. As you have already observed," his eyes brushed up over Robin and down again, "damaged goods earn less on the block.

"Instead I will make a little bargain with each of you. Do as I say, and these three videotapes will not be copied or released, or sold on the black market."

He held up three black boxes. The women looked at them uncomprehendingly. He slipped the first into the video slot. Julie cried out with shock. There she was on the screen. And she was by no means alone.

"You filmed that?" she hissed.

"Someone did. All of it. For the bondage market, I believe." Karpov punched the buttons and swapped the tapes.

Jeanne made a strange choking sound as her face replaced Julie's. "This was done for the extreme gore market, I believe. It's a wonder you survived..."

He hit the buttons again and Robin had to summon every reserve of strength and character. "This one is for the medical market, I assume?" she said, her voice simply dripping with icy disdain.

"No," answered Karpov silkily, with the hint of a salute to her strength. "I did this one for your husband. It was your husband, wasn't it, who conned *Aral* up beside my *Caspian* and who worked out how I was making my escape? Who then came down onto the dock behind us and was there again by the aerial bridge, and, no doubt, was also in the helicopter I had to decoy at such a dangerously inconvenient moment. I've a feeling I'll need an edge over him should we ever meet again."

"If you ever meet my Richard, you won't need an edge, Captain Karpov, you'll need an undertaker."

"I've no doubt one of us will," he said, rising to signal that the interview was over now. "Perhaps all three of us will. And soon."

Thirty-One

They came for Jeanne at midnight.

Robin, who was beside her on the floor where they had fallen asleep while quietly discussing the inspector's theories as to Irina's death, insisted on going with her, no matter what the risk. The look on the poor girl's face simply made it impossible for her to do anything else – especially after the price Anya had been forced to pay for her hesitation earlier.

In the face of Robin's insistence, the leader of the guards who had come to fetch Jeanne shrugged. The two women began to cross the room together in the wake of the phalanx of men. Robin caught Julie's eye and gave an infinitesimal shake of her head – no sense in all three of them getting involved in whatever horror this was. All the rest of the women on the floor appeared to be asleep. None of them was. Robin looked again for Anya, as she had on a regular basis up until exhaustion had claimed her. But there was no sign of the poor girl.

There was a fair to middling chance,

thought Robin queasily, that she and Jeanne were off to join her now. Up the stairs they went and out through the door. An almost silent sigh seemed to follow them – relief from most of the others that they remained unmolested for tonight at least.

In the corridor outside, they were met by Ivanov, the dangerous first officer of the *Aral*. "They didn't send for you," he said at once to Robin.

"She said she had to come, Lieutenant Ivanov," supplied the guard.

"They didn't send for her." The supercilious young officer appeared unusually hesitant; shaken, even.

"Inspector La Motte doesn't speak much Russian," said Robin a little desperately, her own command of the language dangerously slippery. "I can help her understand..."

"Every woman understands a stiff prick," sniggered one of the guards, but the officer silenced him.

"They might need to communicate with her," he decided. "You'd better come along."

Robin followed the group of men, her mind and emotions in the familiar turmoil. She would never walk barefoot on lino again, if she survived, she told herself. She would always associate that particular sensation of slightly yielding icy softness on her feet with

309

the intensity of this terror. Of knowing that anything at all might be about to happen to her, without limits, without even the safety nets of logic or reason. The only certainty was that whatever might happen was not going to be pleasant. And yet on she went, having volunteered for the duty. To stand beside a woman for the simple reason that the woman would be destroyed if she was on her own. It was sheer madness. Like crawling through the wire into no man's land on the Somme, to pull in a wounded comrade from under the machine guns there.

But she wasn't going to get a VC for this. No one else would ever know, except for these men and whatever others they were taking her to see – and none of them would care a tinker's damn. What had the brutal captain of the *Beaufort* said? "Might as well make it a double header..."

That was likely to be one of the saddest epitaphs anyone would ever receive – and she had asked for it herself. Insisted upon it. Argued her right to throw her own stupid life away.

She had just begun to call herself all the names under the sun when they arrived at their destination. Robin looked around, shocked and surprised. She had been expecting to be put in the lift up to the officers' quarters. 'They' so far had always been the captains and she had assumed 'they' were this time too. But apparently not. This was a dingy corridor in the crew's quarters. She began to shiver with deepening dread.

"You can go," said the officer to the guards, and all four of them walked off down the corridor, leaving the two women standing behind him as he turned and tapped at the door to one of the crew's cabins.

This is it, you stupid bloody woman, thought Robin to herself with the venomous bitterness of someone who has done the right thing – but at far too high a cost. *It's party time.*

Captain Karpov opened the door. "What's she doing here?" he asked at once, looking at Robin, who stood frowning, her mind racing with shock and sudden speculation.

"Translator." The officer shrugged.

"We don't need a translator, you imbecile! I speak fluent English. God! It's no wonder *Aral* was such a disaster."

First Officer Ivanov opened his mouth to say something in reply, but Karpov raised his hand.

"OK. Fine. I apologise. That was uncalled for. You've done your best and you've done well. Off you go. And remember. Keep this quiet, especially from your own people. And that includes Captain Zhukov." Karpov waited while the officer sidled away sulkily down the corridor.

In the time it took him to do so, Robin smelt that familiar, cloying metallic smell and realised that this wasn't about sex after all. "Anya..." she whispered.

Karpov said, "Come in."

And in they went.

As soon as he stepped back and Robin could see through the door, it was clear that the cabin was an utter mess. It looked as though its entire contents had been trashed. The impression of utter destruction became overwhelming even as she approached the door.

"Mind your feet," warned Karpov as they stepped across the threshold. "There's glass everywhere."

Robin looked down. The floor was a sea of silvery shards around several little islands of safer darkness. She trod very carefully, breathing shallowly and carefully for the air was foul.

The cabin had not only been trashed, it looked as though it had been hosed with blood. There was blood everywhere, sprays of it splattered over the upper walls and up onto the ceiling. Streams of it slithered off the lower walls, collecting into pools on horizontal surfaces like tables, chairs, and the little basin in the corner. Rivers of it

312

flowed across the floor and gathered into lakes around their feet. It was the main reason that the islands among the smashed glass looked so dark. It was cold to the touch of Robin's feet but was still just liquid enough to slop, tinkle and drip.

Had Robin had any lunch during the last few days she would have lost it now. Bile burned in the back of her throat and a sense of overwhelming loss and guilt. She looked at Jeanne. The inspector's face was so white you would have thought that much of the blood around then had been hers.

But the true source of all this terrible redness lay on the bunk concealed beneath a pile of sopping red bedding. As soon as the two women were safely in, Karpov closed the door behind them and, without any hesitation or even a second thought, he heaved the pile of blood-soaked bedding aside. Both of the women screamed aloud.

The giant Vasily lay sprawled on his back staring directly at them with an expression of shock and outrage. He was naked. In his right hand he held a three-foot length of heavy electrical cord. Its white plastic coating looked almost as white as the skin of the fist it was wrapped round, except where it had been smeared with blood and except where its end had been cut back to make a multicoloured three-line whip ending in a vicious-looking tangle of copper wire.

313

In the middle of his surprisingly hairless chest there was a bright red, five-pointed star. But unlike the others in the case so far, this had obviously been the primary cause of death. Out of each of the ten gaping, black-throated gashes, great sprays and gouts of blood had come. As though each cut had literally exploded open.

"You need the police," said Jeanne automatically. "You have to send for the FBI."

"You know that's not possible," said Karpov, unexpectedly reasonably. "We could keep him to show the FBI in case they catch up with us. But until that happens you're the only trained investigator we have. I really do need to settle this as quickly as possible. We all do." For the first time in their brief acquaintance, Robin got the impression that Karpov's 'we' included herself and the women below.

"The crewman in the white vest. The one who guarded me this afternoon. Sholokov," she began.

"Yes?" he prompted.

"He and this man had a fight on the deck about ... About..."

"Over your favours and future. Yes. I know. The fight continued briefly a couple of hours ago up in the bar. It was packed up there because all the men are watching the Russian-American games on the television. Vasily here crept up behind Sholokov when

314

the American and the Russian were neck and neck in the hundred-metre sprint and laid him out with a rye whiskey bottle and ran back down to his cabin. It was a quart bottle and made of extremely thick glass. Sholokov is in the infirmary out cold with concussion. Under guard, for his own protection. Though I suspect he's safe enough now. Safe from Vasily, in any case."

Jeanne had finished looking around the cabin – her first careful examination without moving – or even touching – anything. "Where's Anya?" she asked quietly, as though she expected to find the woman also in here somewhere. Robin looked around again, suddenly struck with a chilling thought. There was enough blood for two.

Karpov looked at the investigator with an expression of mild surprise. "That's why you're here," he answered. "It must have been Anya who did this. And now she's disappeared. I really think you had better try to find her before she does it again. Or before Vasily's friends find out about this and start taking it out on whoever is closest to hand.

"Don't you see how dangerous this is? *Beaufort* is an overcrowded ship in an extremely explosive state. You may not have noticed the tensions between the captains and the crews but they are real and they are dangerous. It's bad enough that the

315

Americans all think the Russians are brutal and sadistic rapists – which some of them are. Or that the slightly saner Russians think they have been forced to brutalise these women because the Americans don't have the balls or the backbone to do their own dirty work. It's bad enough that girls keep dying on us – or, more precisely, on *Aral*'s crew. And now this. It's the spark that will set this whole tinderbox alight."

"So what?" said Robin. "Just so fucking what? Do you really expect any of these girls to care one little bit if you all tear each other to shreds? There isn't one man aboard this vessel who doesn't belong in Hell, and the sooner the better."

"That's as may be," said Karpov, still so unnaturally calm and reasonable in the face of her righteous anger. "But remember, you women are the most expendable elements in all of this. If we go down, so will all of you. I'll save you two until the last if I can because you're the only real bargaining counters we have aboard to insure us if anything else goes wrong. But you'll die before I do, and all the women down in the hold will be dead long before either of you two. In fact, you know, you're about the only hope they've got of staying alive for the next day or so until this is all over and keeping the blood-bath at bay."

Thirty-Two

After the little pep talk, Karpov left them to get on with their investigation with the parting words, "Your first deadline will be on you soon. The men up in the crew's lounge will be coming down within the hour. The sports broadcast ends at one. You'll need to have finished your investigations down here by then or you may be invited to remain for the rest of the night. And remember, only Vasily and Sholokov had single cabins so if you get caught it'll be party time again."

Jeanne's training suggested that they try to reconstruct what had gone on. To reconstruct the crime, as she put it, though they were both aware that Vasily's death was less of a crime than it may have seemed, given what he was doing when he met his untimely end. Robin allowed that this was a good way to proceed at first but she kept emphasising that the main thrust of their enquiry was not to establish what the murderess had done, or how – but where she had gone; so that they could find her and protect her. And do so in less than an hour before they needed some serious protection themselves.

They quickly satisfied themselves that, during a beating with the electrical cable, Anya had managed to catch up a piece of smashed mirror – may even have smashed it herself – and used it as a dagger. Her attack had been unexpected, devastating and effective. Ten stab-wounds later, with the cabin just so much bloody kindling, she must have closed the door and fled.

"The corridor – indeed the whole area – must have been deserted," said Jeanne.

"They were all up in the bar watching the games on TV, the same as they are now," Robin reminded her.

"She'd have been covered in blood. Where could she have gone? There are no marks on the floor or anything. No blood-shod footprints."

"I know where I'd have gone," said Robin. She walked up the short corridor no more than twenty steps to the door of the shower room. She pushed this wide. They went in together. The atmosphere was steamy enough to tell of recent use. Everything smelt of metal in any case, for the stalls and the floor were made of it. But that was enough for Robin. Jeanne was on her way into the stall to check for blood in the outlet but Robin stopped her. "We know enough to go on to the next step," she said. "Where would she have gone from here?"

As she asked the question she turned. Standing behind the door was a bucket on wheels containing a mop. It was half full of reddish-brown water. "She tidied up the corridor – easier than getting Irina's blood off the deck this afternoon. That's what happened to your footprints. But then where? Where?"

They stood side by side, lost in thought. Then, "That piece of cable in Vasily's hand," said Robin. "How much damage can it actually do?"

"A lot," said Jeanne. She half-turned her back and pointed to her shoulders with an ungainly hand. The darkest of the marks there had strange flattened endings and Robin realised with a literally sickening jolt that the marks conformed to the cut-back end to the cable in the dead man's hand. "Well," she said, "if he had used it much on her then she would have needed to go to the infirmary."

"I needed to," said Jeanne simply. "And I was lucky they let me. That was Sholokov, you know. He stopped them before they killed me and got me to the infirmary. He gave Julie some stuff from there to put on the worst of my wounds."

"Sholokov," said Robin. "He's responsible for keeping a good number of us alive and

319

out of trouble. Not least me. But..." She paused, remembering that smear of Irina's blood on the whiteness of his vest right above the handle of his knife. His threatening, terrifying words to her in the lift. His Bowie knife with its point cutting into her breast. "But he's the fly in the ointment this time," she concluded a little lamely. "She can't have got into the infirmary with guards in there keeping an eye on him."

"Unless they weren't paying all that much attention," said Jeanne. "The infirmary is just down the corridor from the crew's lounge."

Their deliberations were brought to an abrupt halt at that moment by the sound of approaching voices. Neither woman had a watch so they had no way of knowing that the broadcast had ended early. Not that it mattered, particularly. The gathering sounds gave them plenty of time to step back into Vasily's blood-spattered cabin and they waited here until the voices died away again.

"If we're lucky there'll be a couple of minutes' quiet between the time they get to their cabins and then come out again to clean their teeth or whatever. If we can make it to the lift we can get up to the infirmary and check there," whispered Robin a little breathlessly.

But in fact they did not need to test their

luck at all. Karpov appeared, opening the door so suddenly that he nearly gave the pair of them heart attacks. "I thought you might get trapped," he said. "Come with me now and I'll get you away from here."

"Take us to the infirmary," said Robin. "She must have gone there. She might still be there."

"As you wish," he said amenably. "Those bloody guards were a waste of time, by the way. When I went back to relieve them I found they'd sneaked off to watch the TV anyway."

Behind his back, the women exchanged a knowing look.

"I'm needed on the bridge," he told them as he led them upwards. "We're heading into some very nasty weather. Very different to the storms in Superior, I think you'll find. But when you're finished come and find me. Now that the crews are all out and about you'll need an escort wherever you go. This is the last night, remember. The final chance for some of the men. They've unfinished business and unsettled scores. Some of each with the women. That's why I've doubled the guards on the extra hold."

"You don't want the merchandise damaged any more," said Robin, her voice oozing cynical sarcasm.

"They're going to get damaged, all right," he said. "You know, they were all well

321

broken in before you turned up. Never a word of disagreement. Never a hint of refusal, no matter what. Just, 'Yes, sir, yes, sir. How high do I jump, sir?' Then you come along and suddenly I have sailors getting their chests cut open." He swung round and skewered Robin with a coldly steely gaze. "When these women get where they're going, they'll have to be broken in all over again. They'll get things done to them that will make your Mountie's back here look like a love-bite. And that's entirely because of you."

"Typical chauvinist fucking logic," snarled Robin, unaware of just how much damage this experience was doing to her normally ladylike vocabulary. " 'I'd knocked them down but you helped them stand up so I'll have to knock them down again and all the pain is your fault.' That sort of logic-chopping makes me sick. It's like dealing with Hitler or Stalin, for God's sake. I can just hear him fitting in perfectly with Beria and all those bastards in the Kremlin. 'If all you millions of people weren't so politically untrustworthy, we wouldn't have had to set up the Gulags and work you all to death. You only have yourselves to blame!' Jesus. Welcome to KGB World!"

"And welcome to the infirmary," said a gentle, mocking voice.

Jeanne went straight to his bedside. "Sholokov," she said. "Captain Karpov said you were in a coma."

"I have a big headache. That is all. Karpov does not know everything. Nearly, but not quite everything. Why did he bring you here?" Sholokov struggled into a sitting position. His head was swathed in bandages, but Robin hardly gave them a glance. He wore his pristine vest in bed, too, she noticed. But that was obviously of more interest to Jeanne, who ought really to have been thinking more clearly.

"There's been another death," said Robin.

"Vasily. Yes I know."

"Well, that really is clever. Considering the lengths Karpov is going to in order to keep it quiet," said Robin. "Are you psychic?"

She was thinking that if Sholokov was not as badly hurt as he seemed and if the guards were not, after all, at his bedside, then he was back in the frame again. She was simply certain that he had carved the star on Irina. And that put him on the shortlist for the others too. And it was a shortlist of one, in her book.

"Not psychic, no. Let us say I am well informed. What is it that you say in England and America? *I have it from the horse's mouth.* Is that correct?"

"It is if you came out of your coma to find

323

a badly beaten woman helping herself to medication," said Robin.

"Well! And are you psychic yourself?"

"Where is she?" demanded Robin, less than impressed with this grim humour, given the situation.

"You know where she is. I'll bet you a fortune you know."

"All right. If you know about Vasily then you've talked to her. If you've talked to her and you haven't turned her in then you've agreed to help her. If you're helping her from up here then you'll have told her she can go to the only single cabin below other than Vasily's."

"Are you by any chance related to Hercule Poirot?"

"Sherlock Holmes, actually. Look, can you stop all this Chekov comedy routine and take us down to her? She's still in terrible danger, you know. You can't begin to believe she's going to be safe down there for long."

"You're right and I apologise. Consider it my concussion talking. Let us go down at once." He heaved himself out of the bed and Jeanne took his arm to steady him. "Do you think it was murder?" he asked. "I'm just looking for an opinion from someone trained in American law."

"The first wound was justifiable homicide," she said. "Given what he was doing to her at the time. The other nine will have to

324

go to diminution of responsibility. Temporary insanity should cover it, why?"

"I'm just interested. Should it ever come to law. Which, I'm afraid it never will."

"Why is that?" demanded Robin.

"Think about it. She was the strongest of the original women. She was the natural leader. The one most difficult to break. But if she could be broken, of course then the others would all fall into line. She is the key to the whole cargo, really. Or rather, breaking her is. Pain and humiliation could not do it. Nothing they could do to her would do it. But murder might. If she believes she will go to prison for thirty years, or even go to the electric chair, murder really just might break her. And if it doesn't, then nothing will. And, of course, in that case..."

Sholokov was standing between them now. He was steady enough to draw his finger across his throat to show what Anya could expect if she was not broken in during the next twenty-four hours or so.

"We have to get to her," said Robin.

"Indeed you do," agreed the light-headed Sholokov. "Not least because, after her, you two are next in line."

Anya was on Sholokov's bunk. She was lying face down because her back and bottom were such a mess. All three of the rescuers recognised that moving her to a place of security was of the highest priority, but Anya herself wanted them to rub the soothing unguent she had found in the infirmary into her most damaged areas. She could not manage this herself because her hands were also cut from clutching the glass dagger. But, noted Robin with some relief, the wounds were not too deep. Clearly she had not had the opportunity to protect her palms and fingers before she started using a dagger of broken mirror glass on Vasily, thought Robin grimly, but she would be able to handle everything from a keyboard to a concert grand piano within the week. But these wounds more than anything let Sholokov off the hook. For this killing and this killing only.

It was Robin who dressed Anya's wounds, for she held the most current first aid certificate. Even so, it took the better part of an hour to do the job properly. But as she worked, they were all busy trying to work out where on earth upon this overcrowded ship she could hide a naked, damaged female murder suspect for the next twenty-four hours. Well, during the hours of impending daylight at any rate. And it was Anya herself they were worried about – not Karpov's powder keg of a situation.

"Sholokov," she said at last. "You must have some ideas?"

"None. I have no ideas either. I have been

aboard only hours longer than you and I
have nothing like your experience in shipping matters. Is there no crow's nest or
some such?"

"Don't be silly. They haven't had crow's
nests for years..."

The door burst open.

While the panic was still burning through
them like the lava through Pompeii, Karpov
said, "I thought I'd find you here. When I
came off duty at four and discovered that
our patient was not quite as catatonic as I'd
supposed. And here is Jill the Ripper also.
Excellent. Can we all move quickly? I have a
hiding place, but we'll be lucky to get to it in
time. Dawn is coming and I don't want us
to be observed except by the men I have
briefed."

Karpov led them up one deck then out
through the 'A' deck door onto the weather
deck outside. *Beaufort* was sailing with all
the expected lights under a stormy but
brightening sky so they were able to see
their way down the deck towards the
forecastle head. The dawn was warm but
blustery. Robin's sea-wise senses told her
there was nasty weather brewing, and
even had she not known that, the way in
which the lines of pale cloud bases in the
lower sky echoed the ranks of white horses
on the upper water would have been

327

threatening enough.

The ship was beginning to buck, not liking the set of the water. Spray spattered up over them as they came to the forecastle head. It was uncomfortably icy. "Where are you putting me?" asked Anya nervously.

Robin, for once, was fooled by her superior knowledge. There could be several safe havens up here – not comfortable but serviceable. A ship of this age and size might conceivably have some crew accommodation up here. At the very least there would be chain lockers – safe enough until the anchors went down, if Karpov had brought up some blankets, dry clothing and supplies.

And even as this thought occurred to her, she saw, right out on the port side of the forecastle, a pile of darkness which might very well be supplies and dry clothes. There was a tall figure standing beside it – Ivanov, *Aral*'s first officer. Robin looked across at Karpov, feeling a very genuine sense of gratitude. He was a strange man, who worked by his own rules. But he seemed just that important little bit better than the rest of this scum. And he was going to take care of Anya after all.

But then a brief and errant gleam of light escaped from the strange cloud cover; perhaps from the setting moon. It shone on the pile that Robin had assumed to be bedding, clothes and supplies beside the port rail at the first officer's elegant feet. The pallid brightness glinted off Vasily's wide, accusing eyes and shone dully on drying blood on his clothes and bedding. Anya froze, then turned. For an instant she was a thing of silver like a Cellini cast. Truly beautiful.

Then Karpov shot her with the silenced pistol he had conjured from his pocket. The bullet was heavy enough to spin her right and carry her backwards until she slumped beside the corpse of the man she had killed a little earlier that evening.

"Well," said Captain Karpov into the gusty near silence that even the shot from his gun had hardly disturbed, "that's settled that problem. Now, let's get this mess cleared up and dumped safely over the side before the really bad weather hits us, shall we?"

Thirty-Three

It was Richard who spotted the bodies. He was back up on the bridge, staring gloomily out at the morning, still trying to work out the implications of Abe's revelation about the Russian Security Service having underground operatives aboard *Aral* – and, presumably, aboard whatever ship they had all ended up on now. Unless the unfortunate woman on the video had been working alone, which seemed frankly unlikely. The bottom line, as far as he could see, was that it only mattered a two-penny damn if the Russian agents were ready, willing and able to find some way of telling them where they all were and which way they were headed. Without that information, Richard and his rescue mission were effectively on their own and with their backs against the wall. Especially in the face of this weather.

The gathering storm was the last thing on earth Richard wanted or needed and he was beginning to feel that his legendary luck might just be at the ebb. The rapidly worsening conditions would make it much more difficult for the searching helicopters to spot whatever ship they were chasing, with or without the help of any Russian agents aboard. And, in any case, the weather would soon force a reordering of their mission priorities. Some women perhaps at risk on an unknown freighter with Snakeheads, slavers and secret agents were less important than someone actually in trouble in the water, when push came to shove. And the same was true of the Coast Guard vessels also involved.

Richard pulled out the list of ships and descriptions of their movements he had printed on the last of the weatherfax's paper in the early hours and stared down at it for perhaps the hundredth time. A dozen names stared back at him, arranged in alphabetical order. His target could be any of them. It was just a list of names, ports and movements with half a dozen pictures of vessels in various anchorages. On the Internet, the pictures had been bright and colourful. The weatherfax's printer was black and white. He stared at the names as though the intensity of his gaze could somehow make them communicate with him. *Asian Star, Avoco Transporter, Beaufort, Bering* ... He got no farther than the Bs before he gave it up again. It was useless. He all but crushed the paper into a ball to cast aside. But, careful always, he folded it carefully instead and slid it into his pocket.

With his list away and his thoughts darkening by the instant, Richard walked right, behind Bob's shoulder, then behind his first officer's and out to where the forward-facing clearview met the side window and he could stare out into the stormy day with an uninterrupted view. The weather matched his mood. Perhaps it even dictated it, to an extent. Both were dark, brooding, and very dangerous.

It was just at that moment when the thickening cloud and the gathering light balanced each other to perfection. Soon the day would begin to darken again and the gloom would give birth to squalls and worse. This was the north-eastern end of tornado alley, after all. And this was the tornado season. Away in the distance a light gleamed, achingly bright. The light at Rock Island, or Porte Des Mortes, he reckoned – unless their long night's run had brought them down as far as Kewaunee or Two Rivers. He hadn't bothered with charts yet this morning. All that citrine spark served to do was to emphasise the manner in which the black jaws of storm clouds and storm swell were grinding together upon it. It sparkled for an instant and then it was gone. Richard allowed his gaze to follow the surging ranks of the waves as they marched towards him like an infinite grey army. As though the ghosts of the South were still shattering themselves and their world on the slopes of Gettysburg.

And there, on the back of a long wave, rolling up and over, less than a hundred yards away Richard saw the two bodies, entwined like lovers.

"Bob!" He was in motion and voice at once, torn out of his moment's apathy into instant, decisive action. "There are people in the water. One hundred yards off the starboard quarter. Swing west and you'll give me some protection while I go out after them."

Bob opened his mouth to discuss matters like safety and likely survival with his importunate employer. But Richard was long gone.

Richard ran down the curving staircase, calling over Abe's briefing, "Abe, there are people in the water. I'm going out after them. Are any of your men boat-trained?"

"All of them. That's why they're here."

"Good. I want your four best. Sergeant McKenzie, you too if you want."

"Let's make that Sam, shall we?"

"OK. Sam it is, then. Abe, is any of this kit life preservers or anything like that?"

"A good deal of it. We're preparing for ship-to-ship transfer."

"Break it out and follow me."

Richard ran through the aft section of the passenger lounge, past the closed shops and the open toilet facilities into the bar. By the time Abe caught up with him, with Sam, Beth and several laden agents in tow, he was out through the entertainment area and onto the after deck. Here, the SuperCat's wake stretched away between the twin fountains of her water jets. A straight white line chopped the grey ranks of the waves in half for as far as the eye could see, but as they arrived, breathless, they saw the white line curve suddenly, as Bob brought the vessel round across the wind.

The instant this happened, Richard was off again, up the outer companionway onto the little square of deck beneath the lifeboats. He hit the release button on the nearest inflatable and it soared out into the stormy water, trailing its security line behind it. As it flew, like a clay pigeon out of its trap, it split apart. The bright plastic protective sections flew away – but not too far: strong lines held them like wings close to the boat as it emerged from its chrysalis, inflating automatically, still in the air. The safety line jerked taut and snatched the flying inflatable out of the sky, smashing it brutally onto the water.

None of them had stood around to watch this. They had followed Richard's whirlwind passage back down to the after deck. Here they had strapped on the life preservers and prepared themselves for action. At a fast trot, Richard led them to the starboard side, forward of the falling arc of water from the easing jet. Here, at the foot of a short safety ladder, the inflatable bobbed, as though by a miracle. A miracle of brilliant design, thought Beth, as she looked down, simply awed.

Richard led the way once again. Over the side he went, swarming down the safety ladder to step into the fully inflated boat. He clipped his safety line in place. No sooner had he done so than he turned and was pulling in a bright red line attached to one of the plastic casings. Even as Beth stepped aboard, he wrestled the casing alongside and reached down into it. He pulled out a sizeable box that had been secreted in a waterproof section there. "First aid kit," he bellowed, dumping it into the bilge. He pulled out another, more oddly shaped. He began to unfold it like a child's transformer toy. "Motor," he shouted, and, seeing that she was safely clipped in as well. "Pull in the other. There are oars and more life jackets in it. Radio, beacon. Lots of survival stuff. Hurry!"

By the time the others were in place and clipped in, Richard had secured the Tinker-toy motor to the only solid section of the air-filled boat and was trying to make it start. Beth had pulled in the other plastic section and opened doors and drawers in that as well. The oars were telescope design. The life jackets were inflatable. Everything, just as Richard had described it. And, in the final section, what looked like a tent. Or a sail. The metal rods that went with it looked as though they could make a frame or a mast with equal ease. This isn't so much a lifeboat, she thought, it's a Swiss Army knife afloat!

The engine spat into life. "Cast off," bellowed Richard.

Abe reached to obey.

"Anyone running a timer on this?" Sam asked breathlessly. "Because we're going for the record with a vengeance."

Richard brought the inflatable round in a tight semicircle. He was guided more than anything by the position of *Swallow*. Bob would be bringing her across the storm to be upwind of the two in the water. Richard aimed to be exactly in the lee of her starboard side, therefore. A little way out from the centre of that he would find what he was looking for. But in the meantime he ordered, at his loudest command volume, "Keep a lookout there. Two people, holding onto each other."

"Alive or dead?" wondered Sam.

"In this?" asked Abe, with a *What hope have they?* shrug.

"There they are," called Beth.

Richard's mind was racing. He held the handle of the little motor, guiding the inflatable in towards the pair in the water, and he had spent some hours practising this in this type of boat, so no one would do it better. But at the same time, he wanted to be there at the side, ready to pull them aboard and check for vital signs. He did not for a moment think that they were anything to do with his desperate search for Robin. He simply wanted to be sure he had given them the best hope for survival that he could.

A wave crested under the little boat and he saw them below, wallowing in the trough. A tiny mirror image of *Swallow*, he sat the inflatable lengthways on the foaming crest above them and let the weight of her slide them down. "Watch it," he shouted, unnecessarily.

As luck would have it, one of the agents was sitting, unemployed, beside Richard just at the moment that Abe, Beth and Sam were filling the starbourd side, letting the inflatable tilt just enough so that they could slide the bodies in the water aboard. "Take the tiller," Richard ordered, and was there to welcome them.

They came in together, so tightly were they wrapped around each other. It seemed at first glance that they must have loved each other almost beyond belief, to die in each other's arms like this.

But then, as they wrestled the woman free, Richard got a look at the man's chest. One glance and he knew that his life-saving skills would not be needed there. Such was his concentration that he put aside the form of the obviously fatal wound and turned to the woman with no further thought. She, like the man, had been massive and muscular. Like him also she had met a violent and untimely end. A bullet hole pierced the outer swell of her right breast and an exit wound marred the lithe power of her muscular back. Or would have done so had the back not already been beaten to a pulp. Grimly, motivated by habit rather than hope, Richard checked the woman for signs of life. Her flesh when he touched it was marble-cold and stiff if not solid. He thrust his fingers firmly into the top of her neck, forcing them resolutely beneath the point of her jaw.

And what he felt there caused him to turn to the young agent holding the tiller, his face as white as chalk. "Get us back to *Swallow* as fast as you can," he shouted. "This woman is still alive."

Thirty-Four

Richard sat looking down at the woman's pale face. It had been an hour since he had carried her aboard. She had been cleaned, tended and bandaged. She had been tucked down beneath the warmest duvet aboard, with a collection of hot-water bottles heated just to blood heat and changed every half-hour or so. She had clearly lost a good deal of blood, but there was colour returning to her cheeks as she began to warm up.

Swallow's medical facility wasn't up to hospital accident and emergency standard. It was little more than a tiny room with two beds – one occupied by the living now and the other by her dead companion, and some basic first aid equipment. There were no X-rays or scans available. But Richard was pretty certain that the bullet that had made the ugly wounds front and back of her torso had followed the line of her ribs without penetrating her thoracic cavity, in sharp contrast to whatever had performed the rudimentary open-heart surgery on the dead man.

Certainly, once Richard had sucked a couple of pints of lake water out of her lungs with his gentle but powerful mouth-to-mouth, she seemed to be breathing easily enough.

As he waited by her bedside, Richard's mind had been prey to all sorts of speculation about her and her strange, strangely deceased companion. But he would simply have to wait for her to wake up to settle some burningly crucial matters.

In the meantime he had occupied himself with working out the manner in which she had managed to survive in the water. The large man's corpse had been wrapped in a mess of sheets and clothing, which seemed to have been covered in blood. The man's own blood by the look of things. It had all gone by the board as the pair of them were pulled out of the water, so he would never be certain now.

This clutter had managed to trap a good deal of air and rendered the corpse quite buoyant. The woman had derived flotation and some heat from her grim companion, therefore – but even so, she could hardly have been expected to survive in the freezing, stormy water for more than an hour or two – especially wounded as she was.

The importance of that fact was overwhelming, for the ten wounds on the man's

chest proved to Richard's absolute satisfaction that the pair of them had been
thrown overboard from the ship he was
looking for. There could not possibly be two
sets of people sailing the Great Lakes
carving red stars on each other's hearts. He
needed to talk to this woman so urgently
that it was only Beth's gentle presence
behind him that stopped him shaking the
survivor awake at once.

The instant she began to stir, however, he
was ready. Among all his other thoughts and
speculations, he had prepared for this
moment most thoroughly.

So that, when Anya blinked her eyes wide,
extremely surprised to find herself alive, the
first thing she saw was a photograph of
Robin Mariner.

"I know her," she said at once.

"Damn!" said a deep, booming voice.
"Does anyone aboard speak Russian?"

"It's all right," said Anya. "I speak English.
I know this woman."

"She's my wife," said the man with the
deep voice as he lowered the picture. "Is she
well?"

"She's alive," said Anya wishing a little
wistfully that a man as good-looking as this
might one day come so powerfully after her.

Richard did not pursue the distinction
between being 'well' and being 'alive'. The
fact that there needed to be one showed

341

how short the time had become. "What ship were you being held on?" was his next question. It was, in his opinion, far more important than any other. All he wanted to know – all he really cared about among all the death and destruction – was where his Robin was and how he could get her back.

She shook her head. "We never saw the name. We were taken aboard in the dark and held below decks for most of the time. I saw a lifeboat once, but the name had been painted out."

"All right. Don't worry." He took a deep breath, then he went through the relaxed, real-world courtesies of introducing himself, explaining where she was and finding out her name. It was all so normal that, after everything she had gone through since leaving St Petersburg, it almost made Anya break down. But she saw how desperately he needed her help, and something deep within her subconscious told her how unreservedly he had offered her his.

Anya kept the firmest of grips upon herself, therefore, and tried her absolute best for him.

"Can you tell me anything about the ship and her crew? The men who were holding you?"

Anya described what she could, but it was clear that she had had other preoccupations besides noting the details Richard was hungry to know. She described the accommodation, the routines and some of the abuse. She described what she had seen of the inside of the bridgehouse and the crew's quarters. She described the showers, the latrines. "The decks are painted red," she said.

She described the crews in detail from Sholokov to Vasily Bikal who lay dead beside her, but she skirted round the star on his chest and how it had come to be there. She did not know the names of their ships, however. Richard filled them in from the sequence of events she described to him; she had not been on *Aral*, but *Caspian*. She had been transferred onto the new ship a while ago and had come to know the three sets of crewmen increasingly intimately.

She described the girls. Old, new and just arrived. She described Jeanne the Mountie and the treatment she had received from Vasily and the rest. She described Robin but glossed over the more brutal treatment she had received, reading all too accurately the desperation in his eyes.

She described her last few hours aboard and Robin's part in them.

Then she stopped, as though she had run out of words. She realised she had just confessed a brutal murder to an absolute stranger. She, an illegal alien in a strange, forbidding land.

Richard sat and looked at her, his mind full of ready sympathy, but still burning to know any tiny detail that would give him even the ghost of a clue. He re-examined his options and decided not to ask her whether she had any idea that one of the dead girls had been an FCIS undercover agent and whether there was still a Russian security officer hidden aboard. Abe would want to debrief her and put her testimony, thoughts and advice into his final war briefing. That would be time enough, he thought. His main priority was still to work out what ship the girl had been on, where on earth it was and how he was going to get Robin safely off it again.

Gently but insistently, Richard took Anya back over the final hours and minutes. Slowly, she acquiesced to his gentle insistence, once again hiding only her part in the murder of the monster Vasily. Among the candour of the rest of her statement, the lies about the monster's execution sounded trite and hollow in her own ears. But Richard didn't even seem to notice. His examination instead ended with the question, "Well, then, do you have any idea precisely when you and the dead man were thrown overboard?"

"I didn't have a watch on me."

"Of course not. But can you remember whether it was dark? Light?"

344

"In between. It was dawn. Yes, that's right. The moon was setting and the sun was coming up. I could see them both through holes in the clouds."

"It's just after nine in the morning now. Sunrise was at six this morning. So you were in the water for two hours. You won't have drifted any distance. Only the storm wind and the waves pushing you eastwards. And you've only been aboard *Swallow* an hour, while we've been moving west and south. Whatever the name of this ship you were being held aboard, she can't be too far away. Have you any idea at all of her course? Where she was heading for? Where they were taking you?"

"Somewhere big. A big city. Somewhere more than a hundred girls could vanish onto the streets."

"It has to be Chicago. Well, we're on course for the Windy City. It will be a good deal windier than usual today, by the sound of things." He laughed, self-consciously, but Anya was wise enough in the ways of men to see that he was talking while his mind was whirling because he was so worried. And he was making his feeble jokes to cover up his concern.

"But you have no idea of her name?"

"Whose name?"

"The name of the ship you were aboard."

"Oh. No. I am sorry. I too wish we could

contact the authorities and help."

"We have the authorities with us." He explained she was on a vessel packed to the gills with FBI officers and she paled again so rapidly that he thought her wound must be haemorrhaging.

It looked to him as though he had reached the end of the line with his questions for now. He tensed himself as if to rise.

What simple bad luck it was, he thought, that in their efforts to get the two bodies aboard they had lost all that bundle of bedding and clothing they had been wrapped in. I'll bet there would have been something to help us in the dead sailor's pockets, he thought, glancing across at the mountain the dead man's naked body made beneath the blanket on the other bed.

Then he sat down again, the penny dropping and his mind lighting up with revelation and hope. Pockets. It was as simple as that. She hadn't seen the ship's name – but she had seen the ship. Even in outline, even in the dark no two ships are alike. And he had something in his own pocket that might very well help Anya to give him a good deal more than a clue.

"Would you recognise her if you saw her?"

"Saw who? Saw her how?"

"Richard," warned Beth, who had been fussing quietly in the background all through the interrogation, "you know you

346

can't take her up onto the bridge to go ship spotting with you."

"Don't worry. That's not what I had in mind. She doesn't have to leave the bed at all. I did all the legwork for her late last night. I just hadn't realised...

"Anya. Look at this piece of paper. Do any of these ships look as though they might be the right one? Look at the names. Look at the pictures."

Richard unfolded the last list printed on the weatherfax and handed it to the exhausted woman. Her eyes drifted dully up and down the page until, suddenly, they blazed into life. She brought the paper closer to her face and squinted, clearly trying to read the name of one of the pictured ships. "Yes!" she said. "Yes, this is her I am sure. What is her name? *Bering*? Yes. *Bering*."

Thirty-Five

"I've found her!" said Richard, breathlessly, on the bridge two minutes later. "She's on a freighter called the *Bering*. Where is she?"

"Has *Bering* got an identity beacon?" asked Bob. "Jack? Anything on your radar?"

"According to the Web site last night, she should be somewhere between Beaver Island and Milwaukee, so she's not that far away from us," said Richard, crossing to Jack's shoulder and looking into the screen of the radar. Like everything aboard here, it was fed in and enhanced through computers. It came up on square, vertical screens. Richard was used to the bowls of the Doppler collision alarm radar systems on his tankers. Sometimes he could not get used to looking up as opposed to looking down.

Jack's fingers danced across a keyboard below the screens. His hand reached occasionally for the mouse. The image on the screen shifted. The colours changed. The coast of Lake Michigan brightened. It became acid-green shore and islands in a royal-blue wash of water dotted with bright golden schematics representing ships; boxes of symbols and numbers, like aeroplanes on a flight-controller's screen.

That was another thing. Richard was used to simple green blips on expanding circles in a black background. This stuff was so high-tech it sometimes made his head ache. It could even give you a 3D display along or across any heading, with little ships, each sailing along beneath a little cloud of codes and numbers giving identity, speed and heading.

At the foot of the display there was a little box with the word SEARCH in a familiar grey button graphic beside it. Jack typed in *Bering*, grabbed his mouse and pushed the button with his cursor.

On the royal-blue sea, beside the acid-green coast, two ships' identity numbers blazed briefly. Then one died, while the other remained bright. "There she is," said Jack proudly. "The good ship *Bering*. She's heading for Milwaukee right enough."

"How far away?"

"Forty miles south-south-west. Hang on and I'll give you a bearing. Ha! A bearing to the *Bering*. That's a good one."

Richard missed this witticism, though it was on the same level as some of his own. He was talking to Bob. Or rather, he was listening to Bob, for *Swallow*'s captain knew his old friend well enough to answer his questions even before they were asked. "We can be up with her within the hour," he said. "Richard, the conditions are worsening fast. *Bering* may be running into Milwaukee just for shelter."

Richard remembered Anya's description of the men in charge of the ship she had been trapped on. "I doubt it," he said. "These are desperate men on a desperate mission and they're running out of time. They expect to be at their destination today, come hell or high water."

"Well, it looks like they're going to get both," warned Bob. "And so are we."

"Hey!" called Jack. Both men swung to look at him, but he was talking to his machine, not to them. "What are you doing, you useless lump of tin? How could she be coming from Milwaukee and going to Milwaukee both at the same time? Jesus. Get a grip, would you?"

"Within the hour?" repeated Richard, swinging the weight of his near-frenetic excitement back to Bob.

"Weather permitting," said Bob.

"Within the hour," said Richard to the assembled agents. "So we'll make this fast. Special Agent Sharon and Sergeant McKenzie have gone to interview the survivor, Anya. They need to sort out one or two

350

details that could have an operational impact when we catch up with *Bering* and board her. So you should get kitted up at once. We'll try and arrange a chance to zero your weapons from the after deck, but it'll be pretty wet out there..."

"It's going to be wet all over," observed Marshall Pace. But, since his performance in the pathology lab, no one found him quite so amusing.

"Then we can come back in here and soak my expensive carpets during final briefing, Agent Pace. Is all that clear? Good. Then off you go."

Richard ran up to the sick room, where Abe, Sam and Beth were in deep conversation with Anya. "The list of crimes she's describing is just horrific," said Beth, meeting him at the door, her eyes wide with shock. "It's even worse than Abe feared. Worse than that list he gave you on *Aral* before the assault on *Caspian*. Sam's making notes for the Canadian authorities just in case but if you're right about catching *Bering* within the hour, they'll all face charges here. I cannot believe they thought they could get away with it."

"We're not preparing our day in court here, Beth. We're seeing if we can sort out the good guys from the bad guys and work out where they'll be and what they'll be doing when we get aboard."

351

"They'll be all over the place trying to blow us back into the sea by the sound of things," said Sam grimly, looking up from his notes.

Richard and Beth went closer to Anya's bed and prepared to join in her conversation with Abe. She was dead white now and her voice was a hoarse whisper. She was clearly exhausted. Abe was taking her over the ground she had travelled not with Richard earlier but with Jeanne and Robin two days ago. Each of the people involved had their own focus and that slanted where their questions came from and the nuances of fact they were looking to explore.

Richard wanted to find the ship and rescue his wife – and Jeanne and the girls they were with if he could.

Abe wanted to establish the pecking order on board; to discover who was in charge, who had any links to the reception organisations ashore. He wanted to try and work out who were the Russian undercover operatives, his opposite numbers and respected colleagues in the brave new world of global crime networks and global policing. He wanted to know which of the officers to hit with the stun-gun if he could.

But Anya kept on drifting off into the investigation Jeanne and Robin were pursuing, for it was Anya's Holy Grail as well. The women all wanted to know which of the scumsuckers around them was carving red stars on their hearts. But she already had her firm convictions as to the truth.

"It's that Sholokov," she told Abe, causing no little confusion in the agent's mind, for he was asking who she thought might be an undercover lawman, and she was telling him who she suspected of the carving. "Robin was certain that he was the only one who could have cut Irina when she fell down onto the lifeboat deck."

"So that was Irina," said Beth. "But she died of a broken neck. We found her. We examined her. Her skull was shattered by the fall."

Anya cried out then, as though she had been struck. "What is it?" asked Beth.

"She was my baby sister."

In the little silence that settled after that the wind hit the window like a sledge-hammer. Richard looked up. That was nasty, he thought, inconsequentially. And we haven't reached the squall line yet. It hasn't even started to rain.

"Your sister," said Beth, her voice desolate with shock at the pain she had unwittingly caused. "I'm sorry. I didn't know. But the professor said she couldn't have felt a thing. It would have been instantaneous. Like a light going out. It's true, I promise. If it helps."

Anya drew a juddering breath. *"Da,"* she

said. "It helps. I have been driving myself crazy thinking what it must have been like for her to die as he carved up her heart."

All of them made a mental note of that sad, sad admission, in case Vasily's murder ever came to court.

But then Anya asked the sixty-four-thous-and-dollar question. "If she was already dead, why did he have to cut her?"

"Maybe that's how he got off," said Beth. "At least one of the other women he cut was already dead as well."

"She was the Federal Intelligence agent I told you about," supplied Abe gently. And then, remembering the video, he asked, "This suspect of yours, does he wear neat white singlets?"

"That's Sholokov," she said. "Always with the clean white vest, the perfectly creased trousers and the great big knife. There was only one like him aboard."

"Has to be," said Beth. "We've got him dead to rights."

"Except," said Abe slowly, "that we don't have any actual proof that he's actually killed anybody. He seems to do his knife-work only upon the dead. They die, they go over the side, in the few moments in between he carves a star. Like the lady says. Why?"

"A message?" suggested Richard.

"What?" said Beth, more than a little

outraged. "A *message*?"

"Think about it," said Richard quietly. "It certainly got our attention, didn't it? And the attention of every major law-enforcement agency in the St Lawrence and the Great Lakes, along the route this terrible traffic was taking. We wouldn't have noticed any of this except for the stars."

The soft chimes of the tannoy sounded just at that moment. "Calling Captain Mariner. Will Captain Mariner please come to the bridge at once..."

"What?" demanded Richard.

"We seem to have a problem," answered Jack.

"What's that?"

"*Bering*. Her course descriptor read that she was coming out of Milwaukee and going into Milwaukee at the same time. I thought the machine was playing up. But it's an expensive machine. State of the art, but well prepared. There should be no bugs. So I called the harbour master at Milwaukee. And the machine is right. *Bering has* just left the port. And she *is* just coming back. Don't you see? She was there last night, left this morning but she's running back into shelter now. Coming out of and going back into the same port, like the computer said."

"But that must mean *Bering* was in Milwaukee docks last night."

355

"She was. Safely moored. For thirty-six hours, in fact."

"Then it can't be the same ship. The ship this woman has just described was out on the lake last night. She was shot and thrown overboard, for Heaven's sake. That didn't happen in Milwaukee harbour."

"No," agreed Jack, sadly. "It looks like we're back to square one."

But Richard wouldn't give up. He had come so close. He knew it. Anya had been so certain. So positive. He had seen her recognise that photograph, and he had seen the revelation in her eyes. She had *known* it was the right ship. And no two ships ever looked absolutely identical, even in outline.

He swung around, like a massive marionette, in the grip of emotions beyond even his gargantuan control. He would go and get Anya to look at the picture again. She had made a mistake. Perhaps she would be able to correct it with a second look.

But no. He simply couldn't badger her again, no matter how important his questions were. She was grieving for her sister, deep in shock and slipping deeper.

Grieving for her sister.

It hit him then. How simple his mistake had been. Of course there were ships that looked identical to each other. Sister ships.

Sister ships were identical.

356

He made another mental leap forward even as he turned back to Jack and his machine. "When you keyed in *Bering*'s name, two ships lit up," he said, his voice trembling with simple tension. "Why was that?"

"It happens sometimes. Two ships have call signs or ID signals that are identical except for the last letter or two. Sister ships, usually."

"The sister," said Richard. "Can you find me the sister ship?"

"I can try. But I'm going to need a name, I'm afraid."

Richard reached into his pocket and brought out that precious piece of paper he had so nearly crushed and thrown away. And there she was. The small name so easily overlooked beside the picture of *Bering*. And Richard shared that moment of revelation that Robin herself had experienced nearly forty-eight hours earlier. How the sisters had so neatly been named after seas. *Aral* and *Caspian*; *Bering* and...

"Find me the *Beaufort*," he said.

Thirty-Six

Beaufort swung across the storm and rolled uneasily, then she swung back into the wind and steadied for a moment. She was well to the south of *Swallow*, less than two hours from safe haven, and the worst of the weather was spinning out of southern Wisconsin, leaving only a long tail twisting into northern Illinois. The waves were high and conditions were worsening, but things were easier down here nearer Chicago. Easy enough for helicopters still to be out and about.

"What on earth is he doing now?" asked Robin of herself, feeling the ship turn and begin to roll. She slid off the bunk and, catching the guard's eye to signal that she was not doing anything he need worry about, she looked out of the window. On the second bunk, Jeanne stirred and whispered something in her sleep. They were, according to Karpov, in the last place of safety aboard. It was certainly the last place of safety Robin would have thought of. They were in Karpov's cabin. There was a guard on the door outside and another on a chair inside. Both were big men from *Caspian*'s crew, carefully selected for the job. Neither of them seemed to speak any English and neither of them had shown any reaction to the long talk that Karpov and the women had had before the captain went away about his duties again. It had taken all of Karpov's diplomatic skill to calm the two shocked women and come some way towards convincing them that he had acted for the best. Desperately, yes. Brutally, perhaps. But for the best.

Robin for one was neither as convinced nor acquiescent as she seemed. But she was all too well aware that, for the moment at least, Karpov was the only thing standing between her and death. And that, after all, counted for something.

As Robin crossed to the window, *Beaufort* swung back and steadied. And there, right ahead of her, a chopper dropped out of the low, drizzling cloud and settled to squat on the deck. A lone figure jumped out of it and, crouching, ran back towards the bridgehouse. Halfway there, he was met by a windswept welcoming committee. The clatter of the aircraft's departure woke Jeanne.

Unlike Robin, Jeanne had the ability to spring from deep sleep into instant wakefulness. She sat up. "What's going on?" she asked.

"We have a guest. An important man with an important mission, I should guess, from the reception he's just been given and the fact that he's out at all in weather like this."

"I wonder who it is."

"It's the money man. It has to be. It wasn't Coast Guard or Customs. Not in a private helicopter. He was wearing a coat and carrying a briefcase, so he's come to check the stock and prepare to complete the bargain. It's the Mafia. Well, I guess the captain and crew are American Mafia just as the Russians are Russian Mafia. But this guy's the next step up. Godfather, close relative, family accountant – something like that."

As Robin spoke, she crossed to sit on the bunk again, facing Jeanne. "Clearly, they've got some final tying-up of loose ends to do before we go into dock. It will require quite a bit of organisation to get the girls off the ship and onto the streets. This is the start of that. I can't think of anything else it could be."

"Loose ends," said Jeanne, a little queasily. "That includes us."

"Yup. So now is the moment for our best thinking and some ideas for survival. Time, as they say, is running short."

"How can you be so flippant? They're going to kill us, Robin!"

"It's a way of coping with absolute terror.

360

The only way I've got short of curling up and whimpering. What can we *do*, Jeanne? There must be something. Think!"

As *Beaufort* ploughed steadily through the deepening murk towards distant, rain-shrouded Chicago, the two desperate women re-examined everything that they had worked out about the case so far. This time they did it with a new spin – looking not for the identities of the men who murdered and carved up the girls, but for weaknesses in their enemies' positions and strengths in their own. For secrets they had discovered which it would be advantageous to reveal when the going got tougher still.

"Even if Sholokov is the one carving stars on the girls," said Robin towards the end of their discussion, "he's working for someone. He told me in the lift."

"What did he mean by that?" asked Jeanne thoughtfully. "Is he working for somebody but cutting up the girls for his own reasons, or is he working for somebody and cutting the girls for them?"

"I don't know," said Robin slowly. "I hadn't thought it through like that."

"Is he working for just one person, do you think? Or could he be working for more than one?"

"Why?"

"Well, he's involved with so many people, isn't he? He does seem to be the key to this.

Look. He didn't kill Irina. We're certain of that. The pattern of blood on the deck proves she died in the fall. Therefore the man you saw on the bridge killed her. And yet Sholokov still seems to have cut her – because you swear that she had in fact been cut – and no one else had the opportunity."

"That's right."

"OK. Now let's suppose Sholokov doesn't kill any of them. There's someone else who kills them and uses Sholokov as his house cleaner."

"And Sholokov likes to decorate them before he disposes of them?" Robin's eyes narrowed thoughtfully as she asked the rhetorical question.

"OK. You saw the man that murdered Irina, and Sholokov has warned you someone wants you dead. Logic suggests that's the same person, right?"

"Yes."

"But it's not Sholokov. Sholokov might have been bribed to kill you but he hasn't done so. In fact he's been helping protect you."

"Helping who to protect me?"

"Captain Karpov. If Sholokov's the key, Karpov's the wild card in this. Captain Karpov wants us kept alive. He wants us all to get through until the deal is done and he is safely away. At the very least we are his insurance and so he doesn't want us dead."

362

"I think Richard made him nervous," said Robin. "Something he said to me made me think that he's really quite convinced Richard will be coming after me nonstop, no matter what it takes. And he won't stop until he's got me or the people who do anything to hurt me."

"And is that true? Is Karpov right to be nervous of Richard?"

"Oh yes. Yes he is."

"And is that sufficiently powerful motivation for a man like Karpov? Is he so scared of Richard catching up with him?"

"Well, he said he was," answered Robin a little huffily.

"OK." Jeanne let it ride – much as she had after talking to Karpov earlier. "So Sholokov works for the murderer. And he works for Karpov. But Karpov can't be the murderer. One, because he hasn't murdered us..."

"He murdered Anya."

"Yes. And he'll go to the chair for it if I have my way. But we've been through that already. He told us why he did that."

"To keep peace aboard. All right; let's say we agree with that..."

"And Anya was the only one who went overboard without a red star. Secondly, Karpov was on *Caspian*, and there's no doubt, is there, that all the dead girls are from *Aral*."

"You're right again," admitted Robin. "So

363

it's someone senior aboard *Aral*. Someone who gets carried away. Or simply gets a kick out of going over the line. They start brutalising a girl as part of the training, but they get so much sick fun out of seeing them suffer, they just keep going until the poor girl dies. Then they get Sholokov to clean up their mess. He carves the star and over the side the victim goes."

"Now, a lot of the brutalising goes on in public. In the bar, in the shared cabins. It's part of the process, I guess. So does this person, this mad man who kills the girls, does he do that in public too?"

"No. We've skirted around this. But I've been thinking. There must be a line. Doing too much damage to the merchandise, as Karpov calls it. The crew don't cross it. The murderer does. But he does it in private. People can suspect but only Sholokov knows. Because if everyone knew the truth, why should he bother tying to kill me because I might know who he is?"

"But you've only got Sholokov's word that someone's trying to kill you."

"Well, I believe him. And I think Karpov knows and believes him too. Sholokov has told him who the murderer is and he's powerful enough that Karpov can't confront him without starting the war he's so worried about. I think that's why Karpov's been looking after us. Why, apart from Sholokov,

364

we're always surrounded by people from *Caspian*. People he knows he can trust."

"You know what you're saying, don't you? The only men with that much power on *Aral* are…"

"The captain and the first officer. Yes. It simply has to be one of them."

At this moment, even as the two women were sitting, staring at each other, shaken by what they had discovered, the door burst open. The captain of *Aral* stood there, tired-looking, rumpled and grey. Emotionless, characterless, almost featureless. "You are wanted on the bridge," said Captain Zhukov. "Come now."

The two women hesitated, looking from the captain to Karpov's guards. Then the slim, arrogant shape of Lieutenant Ivanov, *Aral*'s first officer, stepped forward, and behind him there was a gang of ill-kempt but extremely well-armed *Aral* crewmen.

The atmosphere on the bridge was every bit as threatening as the gathering storm outside. "This is one of the biggest screw-ups I have ever come across," the newcomer was snarling. Not a man who ever needed to raise his voice – that was worrying, thought Robin as she was shoved in over the threshold. "You're late," continued the accountant's diatribe. "You're below numbers. Half a dozen below at least. You've lost two fucking ships. You should thank Christ fasting that those were not financed by us – though if you've got kith and kin in Petersburg you'd maybe need to worry a bit.

"You got a trail of dead broads floating every couple of yards between Chicago and the Atlantic. You got the FBI all stirred up. You even woke up the Mounties, for Christ's sake. What is this, amateur night in Hicksville?"

He swung round to look at the two women standing in front of him. "And you got these two. The Snoop Sisters. Well, take them out and fucking kill them, will you?"

"Wait," said Jeanne clearly. "Before you do that you should know..."

Lieutenant Ivanov smacked her along the side of the head with his gun and she went down like a log.

"He's the one killing your women," said Robin. "He's why you're six girls short."

Because she wanted to make most mischief she pointed at the senior suspect: *Aral*'s captain. Zhukov stepped back, white with shock, his face a grey picture of horrific guilt.

The American caught his expression of stunned and guilty horror and gave a laugh that was hardly human. "Well, that settles that, Ivan. I hope you got a great retirement plan all set up because you are out of a job and they're all coming out of your pay packet. Every single dead girl. Now take these mouthy sluts out and fucking waste them before they can do any more damage."

"Sir," said the *Beaufort*'s navigation officer, calling across to where his captain sat between Karpov and the newcomer behind the chart table, "we have a fast ship incoming. She's going quicker than the radar can register. More than seventy—"

"That's my husband!" shouted Robin, tearing her throat. "And he'll have brought the FBI with him."

"So what," snarled the newcomer. "He'll be too late. He'd have been better off bringing a team from the morgue." He gestured, a brutal chopping motion, the side of his hand. Steely fingers fastened around Robin's arms.

"Wait," called Karpov, rising with utterly unexpected forcefulness. "She's right. This man will never stop. If you hurt her he will do you serious damage... "

"Oh, for fuck's sake shut it, Ivan. The women die now. Your only choice is, do you die with them?"

Karpov drew himself up still further. Robin looked around the bridge and realised for the first time how alone Karpov actually was here. Not even Sholokov was in evidence. "Then I must tell you," he said, "that I am an officer of the Russian Federal Counter Intelligence Service. You should all consider yourselves under arrest!"

The American gave a howl that trembled between outrage and laughter. As though he could take no more of this comic opera bungling. "You cannot be serious!" he yelled.

The gunshot blasted Karpov backwards. Blood sprayed from his shoulder. The concussion of the sound in the confined space seemed to wind them all. Robin saw a bright brass shell case sail out of the side of Ivanov's gun. Two captains down. Promotion beckoned the elegant, icy first officer. The ricochet took out one of the port bridge windows.

"No, not in here, you fucking dickwit," screamed the American. "Get them out onto the deck!"

The men from the *Aral* bundled the three of them out of the door. They had to drag Karpov and Jeanne, and they had to restrain Robin, who was fighting, kicking, shouting and swearing. The shaken Captain Zhukov and the fuming First Officer Ivanov followed on behind. They bundled the three into the stairwell and they all rushed down in a kind of rugby scrum together. Down the second flight. Down the third, along the 'A' deck corridor, through the 'A' deck door and out onto the red-painted deck where the blood would remain invisible until the downpour washed it away.

But as they stepped out through the 'A' deck door into the disorientating grip of the storm, so Sholokov appeared. He had gone on ahead, thought Robin, numbly. He had worked out where they would be coming and he had hidden in the best place of all and waited to spring his trap.

And he had clearly gone right off the rails at last. Running with rain, but moving like a robot, he stepped up to the startled crewmen holding Karpov and his knife flashed like lightning. The men slumped forward and Karpov staggered free, clutching the mess of his shoulder. Sholokov did not pause. He came for Robin, slashing wildly with the knife, his face utterly calm; totally at peace. Like the face of a saint at prayer. The guard at her right staggered back, dropping his gun as he clutched his red-spraying throat. Robin caught it up as she twisted free and ran for her life out of the terrible mêlée, feeling the familiar shape of a solid automatic settle into her grasp. She had no idea what sort it was, but life had contrived to give her a better than average idea of how to use it.

Halfway across the deck she stopped and swung round. Taking a deep breath to steady her breathing, her heart and her hands, she levelled the solid handgun and flicked the little lever she took to be the safety. Sholokov stood squarely in her sights

369

still hacking at Jeanne's guards. Dead and dying men lay all around him on the deck. She began to squeeze the trigger, slowly and smoothly, letting out her breath in a steady stream, just as she had been taught to do.

"Not him!" shouted Karpov from out by the port rail. "Robin! Not him. Sholokov's on our side."

Robin swung back to look at the Russian, her face blank with simple disbelief. She realised, with a shiver of shock, just how badly he had been wounded. She saw him stagger and slide to his knees, the whole of his right side streaming with red.

And she saw, there, just behind him, running in out of the rain at breathtaking speed, the white hull of Richard's big SuperCat *Swallow*.

Then there was a sharp report that made her swing back again. Jeanne was lying flat out on the deck and Sholokov was sitting in front of her. The white of his vest was spoilt at last, for there was a great gout of blood across the back of it with a massive area of darkness at its heart. Ironically, the huge red mark was almost star-shaped.

Then Sholokov slumped backwards and Robin saw with horror that Captain Zhukov and First Officer Ivanov were stepping out onto the deck, armed to the teeth and clearly looking for her.

Thirty-Seven

Richard stood at Bob's right shoulder for the last time as *Swallow* came down upon *Beaufort*. That way he could keep an eye on Jack's screens as well. Abe had convinced him that he would be better placed up here to begin with at least, but his real intentions were clearly demonstrated by the flak jacket strapped securely to his upper body and the big Glock 21 .45 calibre automatic holstered at his waist.

"Any minute," sang out Jack over the alarm chimes warning of imminent collision. The golden numbers representing the quarry they had been racing down upon for a little more than an hour glowed urgently well within the red box indicating their danger area.

"We should fit this system with engine cut-outs in case some madman tries to ram things on purpose with it," said Jack, tensely.

"Some *other* madman, you mean," grated Bob grimly.

Richard was oblivious, raised to another

plane by fatigue, desperation and the nearness of violent action. In spite of his blueblack, Celtic hair, there was still something of the Viking about his eyes. Something of the berserker now.

"There!" It wasn't even Richard's voice any more, the carefully modulated boom of it given a grating, desperate edge. "There she is!"

The rain was snatched away and *Beaufort* filled the clearview immediately ahead. Bob swung the speeding SuperCat round to port, while Jack's shout of surprise was still somewhere between his lungs and his throat. The captain cut the engines while the mate's shout was still echoing on the air.

"Brace!" yelled Richard and Bob with one voice.

Richard's hand closed on Bob's shoulder with a grip that cracked his collarbone.

There, on *Beaufort*'s deck, Richard could see dead and dying strewn about already. Two faces flashed white ovals at him, framed by the doorway to the 'A' deck corridor. One raised a gun and shot at the leaping SuperCat. At this man's feet there lay a woman and she seemed to be dead as well.

Then, away on the far side of the deck he saw another movement and another head was raised. Another woman's head. And even in the dullness of the stormy day, her hair gleamed like golden guineas.

A weight such as he had never known was lifted from his heart, for only Robin's head in all the world had ever gleamed like that.

The two ships came together with a mighty impact. But they were big ships, well found and strongly built. They survived.

Some of the people inside them were not quite so fortunate. Everyone on *Beaufort*'s deck was knocked down and slid away. Living and dead alike. And those aboard *Swallow* fared hardly any better, braced and ready though they were.

Even as *Swallow* was still shuddering along the length of her target, Richard was gone. Out through the bridge door he came, onto the upper level above the curling staircases. He swung left and ran toward the ship's starboard side, past the head of the stairs and on. He pounded along the length of that upper balcony past the family tables and the children's facilities, his eyes looking through the long windows there, whose lower sills were exactly level with the freighter's deck. Right at the back there was a door containing a porthole at eye level, and he opened it, hurling himself out onto the little deck from which he had launched the lifeboat.

The deck was full of Abe's men, as was the deck below, with more men boiling out of the entertainment area beneath their feet.

The lifeboat was in the air again, trailing its tightly secured line behind it. Someone had flung it bodily down off the deck to make more room.

They were just one good jump below the level of *Beaufort*'s main deck, and, even as Abe gave the order to fire grappling hooks, Richard, like a pirate of old, had taken a great flying leap upward and out and across.

Beaufort's safety rail took him in the lower stomach but he had calculated this. He folded forward across it, gripping the lower rail with one broad hand as he swung his legs up and over like an acrobat, dropping to a crouch beside the gaping door and the girl surrounded by corpses.

His Glock came into his hand almost of its own volition as he pushed his left index finger into the crook of her throat. He glanced down at her. It was Jeanne, though her face was so battered it was hard to recognise. OK, he thought, his eyes busy again, at least she was alive. She stirred at his touch. She wasn't too badly hurt after all. He grabbed her and dragged her roughly but swiftly along the deck, slipping and sliding on the blood, the red line of his laser sight sweeping through the thickening rain like a Jedi's light sabre.

Richard left Jeanne propped at the front of the bridgehouse, well clear of the hail of grappling hooks. Then he ran out across the deck to where Robin had been. She was no longer there. He would have paused and looked about for sign of her but the shooting started then and, judging from the sparks suddenly brightening the metal at his feet, some of it was aimed at him. He rolled forward and hid behind a hatch cover, all too well aware that this wouldn't give him much cover if his attackers were more than one deck above him. But it was a perfect place to pause and get his bearings. And to try and work out where in hell Robin was.

Robin had used the confusion sown by the impact to get a move on. Barely able to keep her feet, she had run up the starboard side into the shelter of the starboard bridge wing. Now she peeped into the 'A' deck corridor through the porthole in the closed door, just in time to see *Aral*'s senior officers go scrambling back upstairs. Good, she thought. She swung the portal wide and stepped in, silently, and gun first, just in case. She felt a fleeting regret that she had not thought to get more shells from her dying guard. She had no idea what type of gun this was or what load it carried. Well, if her luck stayed good, then she'd be able to pick up another one. If her luck went bad then it really wouldn't matter.

Down the stairwell she crept, with her bottom whispering against the banister and

375

her shoulders sliding against the wall, holding the gun out in front of her, pointing regularly upwards and downwards in police-standard two-handed firing position. When she came to the bottom step, she took a deep, silent breath and, keeping her back to the wall she stepped down and round the corner. Into the corridor she came, spread like a spider, swinging the gun round.

The guard on the door into the women's quarters looked up and saw her there. The rain had rendered what little she was wearing almost as transparent as cling film, and such was her stance that, jaded, shaken and nervous though he was, it was obviously not her weapon that he noticed first. He didn't get to notice anything second because she shot him right between the eyes. The gun was surprisingly light and easy to use, she thought. And it was very, very accurate. In the olden days, before her experience aboard *Beaufort*, she would have tried to talk him into surrendering. Used feminine empathy and reason. And some-time in the future she would have night-mares over this, especially about the way the whole back of his head seemed to come off, spraying thick redness with the gaudy abandon of Vasily's cabin and Irina's death on the deck. But right at this moment, that was all she thought: that this was a good gun; she liked it.

The dead guard had another gun identical to Robin's and a couple of boxes of refills ready to clip in. They each held eight shells. She took the lot and tapped on the door with the strong metal butt. "Open up," she called in gruff Russian. "Move! We've been in a collision. I think we're sinking. All hell's breaking loose out here."

The door opened at once, thrown wildly wide by one of the younger, more excitable guards. Robin stopped his excitement and his ageing process simultaneously and abruptly with a bullet through his heart. Heart shots were much less messy than head shots; she would have to remember that. She stepped over him, eyes busily checking the chamber for more guards. There were none. The women all sat, nervous, defeated, depressed and expecting the worst. Most of them were too downtrodden even to panic at what was going on all around them. They were clearly missing Anya's leadership – and that had probably been a part of Karpov's calculations too. Karpov the secret agent. It beggared belief! She stopped wool-gathering by an effort of sheer will and looked around again. At least they had been told to dress themselves while she had been away.

Robin suddenly, unaccountably, felt embarrassed by her near nudity. The feeling was compounded because she was up on

377

the balcony between the top of that short flight of stairs and the doorway just behind her. It had a solid floor but wide-spaced safety railings. She was very much on show in this position and she could hardly present an edifying sight, prancing around up here in transparent knickers.

But the new Robin had little time for finer feelings. "I have come to tell you," she said in her gruff, slightly garbled Russian, "that the FBI are here."

There was a stirring of near panic in the room. She really had not expected that. The spectre of deportation was almost as bad for these poor girls as the threat of prostitution on Chicago's streets and in the Mafia's brothels.

"Wait," she shouted, improvising with an acuity even Karpov would have been proud of – fighting to keep cooperation high and panic low. "You will be well treated. You will not be arrested or deported at once. The American authorities have been working with your own Federal Counter Intelligence Service. There have been undercover officers watching at all times. They wish to destroy this terrible trade both where it starts and where it ends. You are a part of that now. The court cases could go on for years."

She had their interest now. "What shall we do?" called Julie Voroshilov from the far side

378

of the room.

"Barricade yourselves in. Guard the door. Wait for the FBI to come," she said. "I will wait with you here and help you fight if you must."

"But it's far too late for that!" spat a supercilious voice behind Robin. And First Officer Ivanov kicked the door with all his might so that it slammed into Robin's back and sent her crashing into the railings. Captain Zhukov piled in after him, followed by all that remained of their crew. But Robin really saw none of this, for she was unconscious. The last thing she saw with any clarity was the sight of her two new friends the automatic handguns taking flight like steel birds away across the room.

Richard stuck his head up from behind the hatch cover. He stuck it up sideways one ear and one eye first. It filled his ear with rainwater but it was apparently the safest way. Someone Richard had once known in the SAS had told him about it, sometime in his gaudy past. It's better to lose a bit of your ear, the SAS man had said, than the top of your skull. One eyed, he scanned the deck and bridgehouse. Whoever had squeezed those shots off at him was long gone now. Abe and his men were boiling out of *Swallow* and disappearing into the port side 'A' deck corridor like black stout down an Irish throat. Richard sat up so that his FBI flak jacket was on show and then he legged it up the deck to join them.

They were doing exactly what Abe had planned in the briefing. Establish a secure area. Expand it. Check arcs of fire, lines of retreat, infiltration and incursion. Hold and expand again. From the 'A' deck door, they took the 'A' deck corridor. Then they secured the openings to the companionways, going up and down. As they did this, a team disabled the lift in case of surprises, hampered only by the restless tossing of the ship, which had lost its way since the collision and was falling more firmly into the grip of the storm.

As Richard arrived, Abe was sending the first team upward to secure the staircase to 'B' deck.

Marshall Pace was due to lead the next team, downward into the engineering sections. "I'll go with Pace, Abe," said Richard. "Down there is where the hidden decks will be."

Abe nodded.

"I'll go with Richard," said Beth. "Liaison and communications."

Beth had a point. Alone of all the SWAT-trained people there, Richard had run on ahead without a communications headset. There were no spare ones to give him now. And she was the member of the group in charge of the spare laptop.

But Abe saw that there was more to Beth's simple request. She had come to like the big Englishman on a more than professional level. "Liaison, communications and bull-shit," he said, gently. "But you can go too. Good luck."

They moved off, and he leaned over the banister to call quietly, "Stay back, though, both of you. Let Marshall and his men do the work."

Then the first serious rips of automatic gunfire started just above him and he jerked back into command mode.

It was Richard who noticed the stairs were wet and added two and two. He did not realise that some of the water beneath his feet might also have come from the two men who had run in off the deck at the moment of collision. Marshall's men were moving in total silence so Richard hissed to Beth, "Tell Agent Pace my wife has just come down here."

To Richard, knowing Robin, this short message meant one clear thing: watch out for another gun. To Pace, as is the danger with Chinese whispers, it meant something else entirely: there's a woman in trouble down here. And that, as it turned out, was lucky.

The FBI team went round the corner into the corridor very gently, as steadily as the increasingly restless stirring of the *Beaufort* would allow, with Marshall Pace at their head. The first thing they saw was the dead guard. The next, as they moved silently and slowly forward, was the door into the lower hold, very slightly ajar. By the time Richard and Beth stepped into the corridor, Pace's men were arranged in a practised disposition, with an arc of fire covering the whole of the corridor, to the door and beyond. Marshall himself went forward on his belly, covered by his men but taking the point position bravely.

"Wait!" hissed Richard. "I'll go with him! She's my wife!"

Before Beth could even broadcast the words on her headset, Richard was flat on his belly worming forward along the rocking passage floor up to Marshall's side, past the restless remains of the guard and up to the creaking, gently stirring door.

It was as well they went forward flat on their bellies, for the instant Marshall's hand pressed the door back, a barrage of automatic fire turned it all to kindling above them. Women started screaming wildly.

"How can we see into the hold?" asked Richard. "Got a periscope?"

"Better!" came the answer.

Within moments Marshall had a camera there on the end of an articulated metal rod capable of twisting in any direction like a snake. He pushed this through the wreckage of the door, and the fish-eye lens put a picture of the entire hold onto Beth's laptop. The floor was littered with the detritus of recent occupation – and this time there were crowds of listless, battered women lying among it.

Richard rolled through the door, slicing the beam from his big Glock from side to side. One or two of the women screamed and he froze, looking down. Fearful that whoever had shot out the door was still hiding among the women, he slithered swiftly down the steps and lay on the little platform, his eyes busily searching for the golden hair he loved so completely. Even before the others joined him on the little platform, he could see that Robin was not there after all. If she ever had been, she had vanished now.

No. Not vanished. Richard rolled up onto his knees and looked along the length of the hold. There, at the furthest end, was a set of pull-down ladders exactly like a loft access or a fire escape. And right at the top of these a final, masculine, pair of boots was climbing upwards. Richard looked up. His sea-wise eyes measured impenetrable layers of metal with ease. They're climbing upwards onto the weather deck, through the forward hatch, he thought.

As though to confirm Richard's calculation a cascade of water thundered down through the opening. The women on the deck of the hold below screamed again and wriggled away from the icy shower. "Do you see," he yelled to Marshall, "they've taken some of the women as hostages and dragged them up on deck?"

"I see, but I don't understand why. They're in just as much of a trap up there as they were down here. And it's wet and stormy up there."

"They're in a trap wherever they are aboard unless they expect to win the gun battle..."

"In which case we're the ones in the trap..."

"Or unless they're planning something we don't know about yet."

"Like what?"

"Let's go on up after them and find out, shall we?"

No sooner had Richard finished speaking than he was in action. With Marshall, Beth and the others close behind, he ran down the length of the hold, picking his way through the crowd of women. As he moved, he was giving one last desperate check for Robin here before he followed the route up to the deck where, in his heart of hearts, he knew that she would be.

Robin came to, beginning to feel like a very

old woman indeed. Her back hurt from atlas bone to coccyx as though she had suddenly developed lumbago. Her arms and shoulder joints had a burning almost arthritic pain in them, making her twist forward and hunch over, and all her muscles ached rheumatically. But their pain was as nothing compared to the violent throbbing in her head. She was so tired. Her skull felt as though it was full of cotton wool and she could hear almost nothing because the blustery roaring in her ears was making her very deaf indeed. Her teeth were all very loose and she was really quite worried about the continence question because she seemed to have wet herself. How she was still on her feet was beyond her. Someone emptied a bucket of water over her and she opened her eyes wide in shock and outrage.

Robin found herself on the fore deck of the *Beaufort* at the back of a sorry-looking crowd of girls. Many of her aches and pains were explained by the manner in which the two men holding her were twisting her arms to keep her upright. Another douche of cold water came as *Beaufort* slammed her head round uneasily into a tall wave. Water exploded upwards over the two officers and more than a dozen crew surrounding their fifty or so best-preserved captives, armed to the teeth and desperate.

"Of course it was wise," snarled Zhukov.

385

"If we had remained down there we would have been trapped. Cut off. Unable to retreat. And you saw that they were already coming in through the door after us. Had we been quicker to barricade ourselves in things might have been different. But at least up here we can see what is going on. We can make decisions and look for ways out."

"What way out is there for us, you psychopathic old fool?" yelled Ivanov. "Unless the American crew fight them off then we are finished."

"No!" cried the captain, wildly. "I will think of something!"

The whole of the clearview window right along the front of the navigation bridge exploded outwards then, hosed all along its length by a steady swathe of automatic fire from inside the bridge itself. "Well, you had better think of something quickly, old man," raged Ivanov. "That was the FBI taking control of the bridge, I think!"

Desperation lent the *Aral*'s captain a touch of cunning if not of genius. Looking wildly around the deck, he saw *Swallow* bumping uneasily against the port rail, apparently forgotten and deserted. "Look!" he exulted. "Look! Anything that bastard traitor Karpov can do, we can do too! We'll escape in that. It is well we dragged the dead weight of this bitch along. She knows how to control such vessels, or so Karpov said."

They were off across the deck at a run, the crewmen herding the women like bedraggled sheep, the two desperate officers half carrying the increasingly wide-awake Robin. They had reached the port rail in a trice and they crowded back to the point where they could step down past the empty lifeboat-launching catapult onto the little deck. Because of the stormy conditions and the relative speed of the ships on impact, *Swallow* had slid quite far forward now, dragging the FBI's grappling hooks along the safety rail. The step down into the SuperCat was halfway down *Beaufort*'s deck, well forward of Abe's carefully constructed areas of control in the bridgehouse; far beyond his reach.

Richard stuck his head out of the hatch top and got another earfull of rain. Automatically, he looked up towards the bridgehouse for that was where logic suggested they would be. The clearview windows were still falling like occasional hail, the last shards sucked out of the metal frames by the blowing and sucking of the wind. The deck appeared empty, so he straightened up and looked around more widely. And he saw at once what was going on. He leaped up onto the deck and, governed by reason just for a final instant, he crouched, saying to

Beth, "They're going for *Swallow*! Warn Abe at once." Then he was gone.

Beth repeated his words to Marshall Pace and leaped out of the hatch herself. Marshall tensed to go with them, but looked down at his men. He could only go if they could follow. And they could only be spared on Special Agent Sharon's word. Marshall crouched in the open hatchway, therefore, and watched Richard and Beth throwing themselves across the deck like sprinters from the recent Russian-American Games. "Agent Sharon," he said forcefully into his mouthpiece. "This is Marshall Pace, Agent Sharon. Come in please."

But the only answer he got was from Sam McKenzie. "Agent Sharon's down, Marshall, and he's by no means alone in that. He got hit in a firefight releasing some guys from *Swiftsure*'s crew back here. It'll be a while before he can talk to you. And in the meantime, we could do with more bodies up here, if you can spare them. It's like Alcatraz on the guards' day off."

Marshall Pace looked across at the flying figures of Richard and Beth Jackson. He shrugged, seeing all too clearly where his duty – and his best hope of promotion lay. "We're on our way," he said to McKenzie.

Richard and Beth had gone when he looked again. They really were on their own now.

Thirty-Eight

Richard slid across the slippery deck and hit the rail hard. But, winded rather than wounded, he jumped over and leaped down. Beth came over behind him, also slipping and sliding. Not a moment too soon either. The last of the Russians aboard had pulled all the grappling hooks from *Beaufort*'s port rail and the two vessels were drifting rapidly apart.

The pair of them slammed across the little lifeboat deck, their boot-soles still slippery and slick. Then they crouched side by side until Richard had peeped in through the door to make certain their arrival was unsuspected. Only because of the noise of the storm could that much thumping and banging go unnoticed.

The Russian sailors had the girls assembled outside the door into the navigation bridge and Bob Stark, his eyes on Robin and his face grimly pale, was standing with his hands in the air. "We've got to turn this round somehow and settle it quickly," said Richard more or less to himself. "If these

389

people seriously get control of this vessel, God alone knows where it will end."

"But where are they going to run to, Richard?" asked Beth quietly. "They're on a lake, for Christ's sake. There's no way out. Even if they take this vessel too, how much fuel do they have? Where in Heaven's name are they going to go?"

Richard swung round to look at her, his face pale and lined, his eyes deep-set in bruise-dark sockets, like blue stars peeping through cloudy skies. "It's not where they're going. It's how much damage they'll do on the way there. We can't let this thing go on. We have to think of a way to stop it now."

Desperately, his ivory brow furrowed in the deepest of frowns, he looked down. Looked down and reached down. Reached down to slide his fingers across the deck and lift them. They were smeared in thick, deep red. That's why the decks had been so slippery. Both *Beaufort*'s deck and now this one were smeared in blood. But the red marks went far beyond what they could have carried on their boots. "Did you notice any of the women bleeding badly?" he asked Beth.

"No. They all looked battered but OK to me. They chose the strongest and least battered by the look of things."

"Any of *Aral*'s crew?"

"Nope. Far too fit and well by and large."

"That's what I thought." Said Richard. His frown cleared and he gave a tight grin. "Then we have a wild card aboard. Let's see if we can find him."

Beth looked down at the blood for a moment. "That shouldn't be hard," she said. "But he won't be much good when we get to him unless he's found a way of stanching this blood."

"Good point," said Richard. "And I'll just bet he knows that too."

They came up to the door of the little infirmary like a shadow and a ghost. But they needn't have bothered. Covering their movement there came an announcement from the captain telling the stewards to evacuate the galley areas and report to the main passenger area. As they approached the doorway, their movement was further covered by Anya's voice, weak from her wound though it was. With the booming of the tannoy, this would have covered the approach of a small cavalry charge. It was only because the infirmary was away from those parts of the passenger areas currently under *Aral*'s control that she had not raised the alarm. She was too weak to move much, and this too was fortunate, for she had a score to settle and she would have been settling it at once if she had possessed the strength.

Richard came through the door with the big Glock already pointing its red dot squarely between the Russian's shoulder blades, though only its brightness distinguished it from the red that drowned its colour. He moved quietly enough so that neither the croaking woman nor the silent man heard him. And when he spoke, his voice was quiet too. "Well, Anya, it seems you will be able to introduce me to our guest."

Captain Karpov turned slowly, far too well aware of the damage that sudden movement might do to the shoulder he was trying to fix. "I knew you'd come," he said.

"And what did you think I'd do when I got here?" Richard had not moved the Glock. Its red dot now sat over Karpov's heart. The Russian didn't seem to care much.

"You'll do what you've been doing all along. You'll fight to get her back."

"Right. Do I go over you or do I go round you?"

"I am an officer of the Russian Federal Counter Intelligence Service, assigned to the Anti-Mafia section. I do not have my identification papers with me at present because I am working undercover. But if you will help me do something with my shoulder you will go beside me. It is my quest also to see these women free."

"*Free*, you KGB bastard? You *shot me*, you

son of a bitch!" whispered Anya venomously. "How is that going to make me *free*?"

Having got the women aboard *Swallow*, the men from *Aral* were uncertain what to do next. They turned to their last remaining senior officers, but First Officer Ivanov clearly thought that Captain Zhukov was really beginning to lose his grip. And he had good reason. Captain Zhukov was looking around increasingly wildly, hesitant and indecisive, and he was muttering to himself. They all understood very clearly the points that Beth had mentioned to Richard, though that conversation, like Karpov's resurrection, remained a closed book to them. Their main motivation was simple, from the psychopathic captain to the simplest of his command. They wanted to avoid being arrested now. They simply wanted to run away.

Zhukov jammed his pistol against the side of Robin's head, bringing a trickle of blood to her ear. "Where to?" repeated Bob. "Where do you want me to take you to, Captain?"

"Where to?" shouted Zhukov. "I don't care where to! Just get us away from here! Now!"

Bob Stark turned slowly back into the navigation bridge. As he went through the door he heard, "Go and keep an eye on him,

Ivanov. Make sure he doesn't start playing some game with his engineers. Our men down in engineering will shoot at the first sign of trouble. And they'll shoot to maim! Men with no testicles or kneecaps can still run an engine!

"And, while I think of it, tell him to get anyone else aboard up here where the crew can watch them. The rest of you take these sluts down into that area down there and watch them. Watch anyone else that appears."

Ivanov paused on the threshold. "Where will you be going, Captain?" he asked.

"I'll be searching this vessel to see if there's anyone hiding out or whether there's anything we can use." As Zhukov answered, he pulled the gun away from Robin's head and slid it down her shoulder and round her ribs until it pushed viciously into the outer swell of her breast.

"There'll be plenty of equipment, sir, the FBI won't have taken all their supplies with them. There'll be plenty for you to look at. Leave the woman here with me, Captain. The bridge is quite secure. I could keep an eye on her."

"No. You stay here and guard the bridge. I can trust you to do it alone and I need the others to guard the other women and the crew. I shall keep this one with me. She knows about vessels like this. She might be a useful source of information."

"Very well, Captain, but think what more you stand to lose – what all of us stand to lose – if she should become a source of pleasure instead."

At Ivanov's words, Zhukov paused. He looked up at his officer and then down at the woman he was holding. He moved the gun infinitesimally, then thrust it back into place, shoving her forward with a brutal new viciousness and pushing himself more securely against her. As he did so, he began to mutter again, and she did her best to close her ears to the things he was saying as they began to move through the bowels of the heaving vessel.

Much of the equipment and all of the arms that the FBI had left aboard lay in the briefing room. Richard knew this and planned to get to it as fast as possible. Once he had bandaged Karpov's shoulder and made sure Anya was comfortable, he led his little three-man unit out of the treatment room and into the public areas. There were no passageways or corridors on this level of *Swallow*. Everything was open plan and easy access. Only Richard, familiar with every curtain and corner, could have led them through without being detected. And even he was only able to do so because the Russian crewmen had made the mistake of putting the women in the middle of the public area and then making an inward-facing ring around them in order to guard them. The exhausted, nearly defeated men only looked up or out to motion the dribs and drabs from the stewarding team into their guarded circle.

Richard's team made no sound at all as they moved down to the briefing room. It had a new door with well-oiled hinges so it opened silently before them and closed silently behind them. As they went through the arms and equipment there, they simply had to engage in a whisper of conversation. "What is your plan, Captain Mariner? It will affect the selection of equipment."

"You're right. I plan to contact the engineers first. There should be half a dozen of them. A powerful force if we arm them well. The stewards may not all have obeyed Bob, so we might gather up any of them we meet. All these people can be found in the passages below. The passages themselves will be easier for us to work in than these public areas. Noise also will be contained down there. We might even get away with a shot or two before we cause serious alarm."

Robin's mind raced coldly and desperately. Her main thoughts focused on escape. How could she break away from this man? She was certain that he was sliding out of control very quickly indeed and it was getting increasingly like holding hands with Jack the Ripper. But Zhukov had no intention of letting her go. He held her carefully and kept his gun against her at all times, making a sick game of pushing the weapon into ever more painfully intimate places. They moved quickly but not silently, for he kept mumbling to himself a drone of Russian that she could not really make out interspersed with loud, clear questions and directions. That presented another problem for her. Where should she guide him? How much should she show him?

They started in the public area, walking around the group of women and their circle of guards. Fortunately, the second wave of FBI men had left a good deal of their surplus supplies here. The captain examined these and, while finding little of use, he was nevertheless convinced that this was probably all there was. He pushed Robin forward, and, as Richard led his little team past the starboard toilet passage, so Robin led him into the port one. By the time the ever-cautious Richard was locking the briefing-room door, Robin and her muttering captor were in the passage leading past the infirmary. Robin, of course, had no idea at all that there was anyone within it.

Anya heard him coming. The mad drone of

Russian gibberish speared into her mind like pure adrenaline, for she knew Captain Zhukov's voice all too well from her hellish days on *Aral*. Simple terror made her twist and turn, to use the pain in her side as a way of waking herself up. And it worked. She sat up, feeling the bandages tear free. She looked around for somewhere to hide but the room was small and stark. She heard his footsteps at the door. "What's in here?" he rasped.

"Infirmary, I think," answered another familiar voice.

All Anya could think of to do was to pull off the rest of her bandage and slip it under her pillow. Then she lay back, pulled her sheet up over her face, closed her eyes and played dead.

The door opened, they came in. Anya held her breath. "What's this?" he said.

"I don't know."

"We'll take a look." Footsteps came closer, right between the beds. "Pull the sheet back." There was a rustle. Anya heard Robin gasp. "Vasily," purred the dead man's captain. "So that's what happened to you. But how in God's name did you come here? Pull back the other one."

Anya was given just enough notice to compose herself. She kept her eyes closed. She stopped breathing. The sheet came off. "Karpov shot her," said Robin. "Your first officer helped him throw them both over-board; didn't he tell you? *Swallow* must have picked their corpses up. She was close behind."

Anya felt him approach to look at her. She was right at the edge of her self-control now. If he should touch her she would crack, she knew. His breath moved against her breast as he looked more closely at her wound. Her control went slipping away, and...

There was the sound of a muffled shot.

"What was that?" He snapped erect. Anya heard Robin hiss with pain as his movement twisted her arm tighter still.

"A shot, I think." Robin's voice was hoarse.

"We go and look. Now!"

Anya lay as still as death until her heart-rate slowed into the low hundreds per minute and then she sat up and started trying to fix her bandage back on. As she worked, swiftly and silently, she looked around for something to put on. She had been lying around in here for long enough, she thought. She had things to do. Scores to settle.

There were two guards overlooking the engineering section, and, like many of *Aral*'s crew, they were sloppy. They were watching the men at work in the compact engine control room in front of them and they were not watching the corridor at their back. They were standing side by side in the doorway, their automatics pointing inwards at the end of a little corridor perhaps ten feet long. Richard, Beth and Karpov stood silently at the corner of the lateral corridor less than three steps away, communicating in a few silent gestures. Beth was better qualified than Karpov to take a man with Richard – as well trained and unwounded. But he was Russian, KGB at heart, sexist and proud. He would not hear of it. Richard and he ran forward side by side, therefore, their guns raised to act as clubs. Richard's blow went home neatly and powerfully. The Glock was more than two pounds of solid steel. His man dropped without a sound. Karpov's target started to turn. His gun caught on the doorframe and the Russian captain smacked him on the temple as hard as he could with the Smith and Wesson 1076 he had garnered from the store in the briefing room. As this was even heavier than the Glock, it should have been effective, but the seaman staggered back, swinging his gun upwards. Karpov squeezed the trigger. Nothing happened. "De-cock it," called Beth desperately.

"It's on safety," snarled Karpov.

"No! De-cock. There's no safety…"

"What?" yelled Karpov, but he was already too late. The guard was already squeezing the trigger.

Then Richard's red dot flashed on the Russian's heart and the big .45 calibre bullet went exactly where the red dot glowed. The sound was deafening. The effect was explosive. It was lucky that there was no important machinery behind the Russian sailor or that would have been blown open into the bargain. "You two keep watch," Richard said at once. "I'll sort out these engineers. And, Beth, show him how the gun works, will you?"

All Anya could find to put on was a white robe. It was far too big, and so shapeless that it made her look very much like a ghost. That was apt enough, she thought. She certainly ought to have been a ghost by now. She couldn't even tighten the belt because of the pain in her side, so it all swirled eerily around her as she crossed to the door and peeped out into the corridor beyond. Her plan was quite simple. She was going to find her girls. Precisely what she was going to do then she had not thought through, but, she thought, that at least would be a start.

But Anya was terribly aware of two further things, and both of them terrified her almost beyond measure. The first of these was that the mad captain was out there somewhere, muttering and shuffling and leading Robin Mariner around. And the second was that she had no weapon what-soever to fight him off with if he found her. She not only looked like a ghost therefore. She moved like one.

But it did her no real good in the end, for, as she came round the corner out of the bar area into the port toilet corridor, she felt the cold steel of a gun barrel pressed against her neck. She nearly fainted with shock. Her knees actually began to buckle. She would have staggered, perhaps fallen, but a firm arm closed around her waist, below the bulge of the bandages and took her weight for an instant.

"What are you doing up and about?" asked the voice of Richard Mariner in a near-silent whisper.

Five minutes later, Julie Voroshilov looked up listlessly from her endlessly twining fingers and started to scream. She was seated at a table facing forward, with a clear view of the balcony outside the navigation bridge. And there, with her arms raised and her mouth wide, stood Anya's ghost. In an instant there was pandemonium. The women leaped up wildly utterly out of control. The guards leaped up as well, as shocked as their victims, too slow-witted to know how to react. Then she was gone, but the screaming did not abate. At the sight of their dead leader the women had leaped

402

from apathy to hysterics. First Officer Ivanov burst out of the bridge. The elegant Russian was waving a gun and yelling at the top of his voice but he could not begin to make himself heard. Instead, as he stood up there shouting and gesticulating, a single report rang out and he flew backwards against the bridge wall and slid down it, his face switching instantly from arrogance to shocked surprise. On the wall behind him, he left a bright smear of redness almost as wide as his shoulders. By the time he was sitting sprawled upon the deck carpet, he was silent and dead.

A flicker of white flew past him and through the gaping bridge door. Suddenly Anya's voice rang over the tannoy. It was weak and sepulchral enough to belong to a ghost but it was also amplified by the system to overwhelming volume. "Sisters," it said. "Take their guns. Take the scumsuckers' guns."

Moving as one, the women did as Anya said. There were nearly fifty of them and there were a dozen guards. The men suddenly seemed to realise how terribly outnumbered they were. One desperately swung his gun down and squeezed off a shot. Miraculously he hit nobody, but the report of his gun was echoed at once by the gun that had killed Ivanov and he flopped backwards like a landed fish and was trampled underfoot. The others turned to run but found that they in their turn were surrounded by a circle of grim-faced, well-armed engineering officers. "Lay down your arms," bellowed Karpov over the din. But none of the men had any arms to lay down any more. The women had them all.

Robin had contrived to lose herself and Zhukov in a maze of passages towards the after part of the engineering section. This was doubly dangerous. On the one hand her captor was getting angry that they had not, as promised, found the engine control room, where he thought the sound of the gunshot had come from. On the other hand, she was taking a dangerous, sadistic psychopath further and further away from everyone else aboard. When the shooting started up again she knew she had made a serious error. While his muttering became wilder and wilder and the twisting of her arms and the poking of the gun barrel became even more calculated, she tried not to panic and look for some way of getting him back to civilisation. A small puddle of icy wetness beneath her foot coupled with a chilly drop of water on her shoulder gave her some inspiration. She looked up. There, immediately above her head, was a sealed hatch up onto the aft deck. It was designed for emergency use and had an electrically operated fold-down ladder.

"Captain," she said gently. "We can go up there. That will take us straight up onto the deck."

He looked up. He stopped muttering.

"It will take us up," she repeated. "Just as it did on the *Beaufort*. We will be able to escape."

Zhukov shoved her roughly across the corridor. Sniggering to himself he tried to push the switch that activated the device with her right breast. When that proved too soft, he used her forehead. At once the ladder began to unfold. As soon as it was firmly in place, the hatch unsealed and slid back, releasing a waterfall upon them. Laughing derisively and muttering still, the captain pushed Robin upwards. Coldly she still tried to calculate some kind of advantage to be gained, some edge that would let her get away. But he was well practised and cunning. She mounted the steps as she had climbed out of the *Beaufort*'s hold. She went first, with one hand free to steady her and the other firmly in his grip. He climbed just behind and below her, so close that she could feel his breath on her buttocks. And he wedged his gun barrel immediately above the line of her panty waist, the cold 'O' of its mouth against the inward curve of her coccyx. She never really stood any chance at all.

Up they came into the maw of the storm. The sky was low and immensely threatening. Great bolts of lightning struck down onto the water disturbingly close at hand. Of *Beaufort* there was no sign and even Chicago had shrunk to a distant glimmer, unnaturally full of lights in the early afternoon. The SuperCat was swinging round now, heading in towards the welcoming calm of the distant harbour. *Swallow* pitched and bucked, liking neither the wildness of the weather nor the set of the sea. In spite of the enormous power of her engines, her speed began to fall away. She wallowed uneasily, as though she feared something hidden in the low-whirling overcast. Robin and her captor were thrown right and left but he clung to her as though they were Siamese twins. The effect of it all came close to disorientating Robin. What it did to the madman whose grip on reality was already so fragile, she could hardly imagine.

Robin looked desperately around the streaming, wind-torn little deck, still seeking some edge or weapon to turn against her captor. But there was nothing. All she could see ahead of her was the reflection of them in a pair of big glass doors, which stood closed across the main entrance to the dark, empty entertainment section. Such was the nature of the light that the glass, backed by absolute blackness, effectively became a huge mirror. And Robin stared into the depths of this, so her wide eyes were tempted beyond the staggering figures of herself and her captor out over the wild water behind them.

Her wild gaze jumped past her own hunched shoulder and away. Out to where a whirling point of cloud was reaching with majestic inevitability down towards the water beneath it. And the water was rising in answer creating a vortex like a swan's neck whipping towards them with terrible speed.

For the first time in her life, Robin began to scream. Full blooded, sea-trained, at the top of her lungs, the sound was unnervingly loud. It shook even the madman crushing the life out of her and screwing his pistol into the side of her tummy, just above the jut of her pubic bone.

Something moved in the blackness behind the big glass doors. There for an instant stood Anya, terrifyingly ghostly, with the wildness of the waterspout writhing across her. Robin's screams reached a new intensity, as though all her years of being calm, sensible and controlled had allowed her to save up for this. Anya's dead face twisted in horror too. Then it jerked away in an explosion of shattering glass as the captain, who had also seen her stark, stone dead less than half an hour before, began to empty his pistol into her.

Robin hurled herself aside with all her might and simply tore her slick body out of his grip. She seemed to fly through the whirling air, aware of a great, roaring suction as the first winds of the waterspout took hold of the air around her. The glass from the shattered doors did not simply fall down; it flew out and backwards, sweeping over her. As she hit the deck, she rolled and saw the wave of shards and splinters break over the staggering figure of Zhukov. He flew backwards against the safety rail, then bounced forward again as the vagary of the wind reversed its terrible force. Still clutching his gun, and screaming every bit as loudly as she had done, he slammed forwards onto his knees and skidded over towards her. His cheeks were like crystal porcupines, bearded with long clear splinters. His white glass hairline reached down to his thick black brows, but he had thrown up his arm at the last minute and his eyes were clear and mad. And looking straight at her.

Robin pushed herself backwards until her shoulders hit the side of the engine housing – an act that lasted nanoseconds. Then he was upon her, his face showering glass and blood in equal measures. He struck at her and clawed at her, too far gone, apparently, to remember that he even had a gun. But then the waterspout, still stalking them and

408

every bit as mad as he, demanded his attention. It did this by snatching up the inflatable out of the water behind the SuperCat and slamming it round on its too well anchored safety line into the little deck at its back. Robin saw it coming and shrank down. Zhukov recognised something in her eyes and threw himself aside. The inflatable crashed into the engine housing immediately above her head and then slammed down onto the deck. The steel shaft of the engine, which held the propeller, slammed across his thigh and the sound it made was a crunch, not a snap. His howling became every bit as wild as the wind's. Robin rolled sideways but his left hand caught the slimness of her ankle and fastened there. She should have kicked out, twisted free, run away once more, perhaps. But instead of doing any of these things, she simply threw herself back at him. Ready, willing and almost able to tear him limb from limb herself.

But just before Robin landed upon the crippled madman, she realised her fatal mistake. Her shoulder blotted out the brightness of a red dot immediately above Zhukov's heart. *I'm in the line of fire*, she thought, fighting to get out of it again at once. She succeeded in twisting round, half turning over, just in time to see the unmistakable form of Richard standing just behind the hatchway through which he had followed them up onto the deck. Behind him, terrifyingly close at hand, the slim, almost elegant curve of the waterspout leaped in. He was taking careful aim, as though at a shooting range, waiting, she knew, for her to move just a little more. But she was tangled in cordage from the little lifeboat and simply couldn't move quickly enough.

Then the Russian's gun arm came down over her shoulder and his gun began to thunder in her ear. The bullets thumped directly into Richard's chest, hurling him backward over the rail and into the water-spout's path.

Robin spasmed as though the bullets had all hit her. Such was the power of her reaction that she did manage to move the tangle of cordage. A strong plastic cover-section slid up beside her hand. With no further thought she grabbed this and slammed it round into Zhukov's face. The impact drove the glass fragments deeper through the thin bones of his skull and his howl went up an octave and several decibels. He dropped the gun and clutched at his face. Robin snatched it up at once and pushed it against the clenched fingers, pul-ling the trigger. Nothing happened. He had emptied it into Richard.

"Allow me," came a distant whisper. She

looked up and saw that Captain Karpov was standing there, right beside them. She flung herself back at the moment that he fired. Zhukov's head exploded out from behind the hands and the crippled body spasmed beneath the inflatable's motor.

"Once more, on behalf of your friend Jeanne of the Mounties." He shot again, though there was obviously no need to make sure.

"FBI trained," he said wryly.

Swallow surged forward then, her great water jets biting and hurling their huge white rainbows right into the base of the waterspout. The movement threw Robin back and she rolled to her feet, grabbing the inflatable's safety line. "Help me," she shouted at Karpov and within the instant he and Robin were running aft. Beth had joined them before they reached the after rail. Then the two women leaped overboard with the tough little life raft while he pulled the safety free and ran back in to warn the captain that both his owners had gone overboard.

Robin pulled herself into the boat and began to look around for Richard even though she was reaching down for Beth at the same time. There was no sign of him. She swung Beth aboard and pushed her down towards the motor. "Can you use one

411

of these?" she asked.

"Yes!"

Both the women were shouting because of the thunderous howling of the waterspout so close behind them, and Beth's eyes kept being pulled away to the wild whirling whiteness of it. *Swallow*'s jets seemed to have thrown it slightly off balance, for it was beginning to twist away and it was thinning even as they looked. But the water all around them was fizzing like champagne and the spout itself seemed to have sucked it up into quite a hillock. Beth got the motor to catch and sat back, powering the game little vessel in the waterspout's fizzing wake. Robin sloshed and wriggled up into the very front, reaching down between her wide-spread knees to grab the safety line. Then she rode it like a cowgirl on a bronco, her eyes busy among all the fizzing, foaming madness up ahead, searching for the slightest sight of him.

Away behind and to the right of her Bob Stark was giving *Swallow* full throttle, swinging the SuperCat round in a curve far tighter than her design specifications promised. Karpov stood in Richard's usual place. And Jack, who was a Kansas boy, was shouting and hollering at the sight of the waterspout sweeping across the clearview. But Karpov's hand came down on his shoulder as they saw the tiny speck of the

412

life raft bobbing desperately close to its foot.

"Closer!" Robin was screaming. "He went right in under it!"

"I daren't!" yelled Beth in reply. "It's going to take us. Can't you feel the boat beginning to lift out of the water?"

Robin could, but she didn't much care. Richard had never let her down. He had come for her, against all the odds and never stopping across the length and breadth of the Great Lakes. And just at the very instant he had found her she had lost him. If she failed to find him now it would simply be too much to bear.

"Richard," she screamed, her throat raw and aching after her screaming when she first saw the waterspout. "Richard!"

Something moved in the fantastic buoyancy of the wildly foaming water. She signalled Beth and they were beside it in a heartbeat. She caught it as it fishtailed and slipped down the columns of bubbles, heading for the bottom of the lake. She pulled it out of the water, glanced at it and threw it aside into the bottom of the boat. It was a flak jacket with FBI marked on it and the straps on maximum setting. In the puddles in the bilge it lay behind her, its breast marked by the great pits where the bullets had gone into it.

Gone in, but had not gone through.

"ROBIN!" Robin looked back to see Beth

wildly gesturing. She looked back and raised her eyes above the surface, which she had been so carefully searching. The waterspout was turning. It was coming back for them.

But then, in that kind of bow wave just in front of it, she saw a hand thrown up above the foam. That was all. Just a hand. She signalled to Beth who saw it too. The inflatable turned and headed directly towards it, back into the wilderness where the wild winds were. Robin angled herself further and further to the right as they came up towards him, hoping her weight would stop the wind from snatching them up out of the water before they could reach him. The spray came horizontally and stung like the lash of barbed whips. Soon Robin was spread out flat along the gunwale fighting to hold it in the water, as the waves washed sideways up and over her. But still her eyes, her mind, her very soul were fastened on that hand, as Beth gunned the shrieking motor up to the side of it and Robin reached out towards it with all her strength and might.

The clap of those two hands coming together was nothing in the monstrous roaring of the storm and the waterspout, but it was a sound that would echo in her heart for just as long as she lived.

She pulled, and the simple weight of him steadied the boat. His face broke the water beside her with a grin as wide as her own must have been. Their lips met, cold and wet at the water's very surface, as their arms entwined and they squeezed each other with simple, ecstatic joy.

So that it was only Beth, on a far lower plane of life entirely, who noticed the darkness sweeping over them, as Bob eased *Swallow*'s twin keels to either side of them and sat the strength of her great hull above their heads. And held them safely protected, while the waterspout thundered over them, like a twister over a bridge, then turned away northwards, to whirl itself to death along the line which they had followed to this place. The line which ran up and away across the Lakes through Seul Choix and Au Sable Point, to distant Thunder Bay.